DATE DUE

NOV 0 6

GAYLORD

PRINTED IN U.S.A.

BY ALAN DEAN FOSTER

Published by The Random House Publishing Group

The Black Hole
Cachalot
Dark Star
The Metrognome and Other Stories
Midworld
Nor Crystal Tears
Sentenced to Prism
Splinter of the Mind's Eye
Star Trek® Logs One–Ten
Voyage to the City of the Dead
. . . Who Needs Enemies?
With Friends Like These . . .
Mad Amos
The Howling Stones
Parallelities

THE ICERIGGER TRILOGY:
Icerigger
Mission to Moulokin
The Deluge Drivers

THE ADVENTURES OF FLINX OF THE COMMONWEALTH:
For Love of Mother-Not
The Tar-Aiym-Krang
Orphan Star
The End of the Matter
Bloodhype
Flinx in Flux
Mid-Flinx
Flinx's Folly
Sliding Scales
Running from the Diety
Trouble Magnet

THE DAMNED:
Book One: A Call to Arms
Book Two: The False Mirror
Book Three: The Spoils of War

THE FOUNDING OF THE COMMONWEALTH:
Phylogenesis
Dirge
Diuturnity's Dawn

THE TAKEN TRILOGY:
Lost and Found
The Light-years Beneath My Feet
The Candle of Distant Earth

TROUBLE MAGNET

TROUBLE MAGNET

A PIP & FLINX ADVENTURE

ALAN DEAN FOSTER

BALLANTINE BOOKS • NEW YORK

Published in the United States by Del Rey Books, an imprint of The Random House Publishing Group, a division of Random House, Inc., New York.

DEL REY is a registered trademark and the Del Rey colophon is a trademark of Random House, Inc.

Library of Congress Cataloging-in-Publication Data
Foster, Alan Dean.
Trouble magnet : a Pip & Flinx adventure / Alan Dean Foster.
p. cm.
ISBN 0-345-48504-1 (alk. paper)
1. Humanx Commonwealth (Imaginary organization)—Fiction.
2. Pip (Fictitious character : Foster)—Fiction.
3. Flinx (Fictitious character)—Fiction. I. Title.
PS3556.O756T755 2006
813'.54—dc22   2005056949

Printed in the United States of America on acid-free paper

www.delreybooks.com

2 4 6 8 9 7 5 3 1

First Edition

Text design by Niqui Carter

In fond memory of Ron Walotsky.
Friend, artist, raconteur, traveling companion.
I'm sorry I didn't get the picture of the lion because
I was too busy trying to roll up the window.
But you wouldn't get out and fix the flat, either.
I hope you're painting the elephants now.

TROUBLE
MAGNET

CHAPTER

1

A most peculiar thing happened to the battleship as it departed the Repler system: initially daunting in size and form, it proceeded to undergo a kind of reverse metamorphosis, as if a butterfly were turning backward into an ungainly caterpillar. Intimidating weapons blisters collapsed in upon themselves like so many glistening, harmless bubbles. Lethal wave-form projectors shrank and slivered. Vast projecting appurtenances shimmied and vanished like the ominous illusions they were, until the menacing martial shape had imploded completely. In its place gleamed the far smaller fast-moving footprint of an ordinary cargo carrier approaching changeover. Clearly not a craft that was part of the impressive fleet component still orbiting the planet that was rapidly receding behind it, nor one that was likely to attract undue notice.

Visually revamped, externally overhauled, and mechanically facelifted determinedly downscale, the *Teacher* slipped unchallenged into the physically unreasonable but mathematically coherent state known colloquially as space-plus, whereupon it swiftly left the Commonwealth border system known as Repler not only far behind, but far beyond it.

"Changeover complete. Exterior appearance modified as per necessity. Proceeding on general Almaggee vector. Awaiting instructions." A pause, then, "Resume search?"

Resume search. Flinx stared out the command port at the splay of distorted stars forward. Resume search for what? His ship was doubtless referring to the search his friends and mentors Bran Tse-Mallory and the Eint Truzenzuzex had sent him on. The one he had agreed to undertake provided only that they see to and look after his injured love Clarity Held back on New Riviera. A simple enough quest request.

All he was being asked to do was search and scour the vast reaches of the largely uninhabited section of the Sagittarius Arm of the galaxy opposite the Commonwealth, locate and establish contact with an unbelievably ancient planet-sized weapons platform of the long-extinct—except for one recently demised individual—war-like species called the Tar-Aiym, and persuade it to aid in defending all civilization against an immense, undefined menace steadily accelerating in this direction from a region of space near Boötes known as the Great Emptiness. And do this while avoiding the attentions of the increasingly persistent and curious Commonwealth authorities, the crazed suicidal adherents of the Order of Null who badly wanted him dead, certain elements of the AAnn Empire, and perhaps the isolated Qwarm assassin. All in hopes of saving the galaxy and, with luck, of in a few years making it to his thirtieth birthday. And maybe, just maybe, finding out who his father was.

He took a deep breath. From her position sprawled across the center of the command console, the minidrag Pip looked up at him, yawned, and stretched her brilliant pink-and-blue wings without unfurling them. He nodded, though not particularly at her.

Time for tea.

The *Teacher* brewed perfect tea. Many was the time, and more frequently lately than not, he found himself considering perfection tedious. But not when it came to the making of tea. Darjeeling tea from Terra, anar tea from Rhyinpine, unique forest teas from Alaspin; the ship was steeped in those and more. Various chemicals both natural and synthetic for calming the mind and easing the body were available to the *Teacher*. Except on rare occasions he disdained them all in favor of flavor in the form of natural tea.

When it was delivered to him in a pot and cup whose functions, if not the material from which they had been made, would have been recognizable to a tea drinker from a thousand years ago, he stirred in additives, leaned back, and wondered at how many ancient ship captains had similarly sat and sipped their own favored libation while studying the stars. They had done so from a considerably different perspective, of course. They had been sailing along beneath the stars, not among them.

The hot, sweetened, dark gold liquid calmed his body but did little to settle his thoughts. Behind him lay the threat of the alien Vom, extinguished. Ahead lay a search for something to help deal with an infinitely greater threat. A search that might well take years. To what end? Not for the first time he wondered why he ought to bother. What about his own personal priorities? What about the future for himself and Clarity he dared to dream of in quiet moments? If the evil he had perceived within the Great Emptiness was not due to arrive for hundreds or even thousands of years, why should he care about it? Why should *he* have to be the one to sacrifice his life and happiness in a probably futile attempt to forestall the inevitable?

Everything went in cycles. Perhaps the eventual arrival of the Great Evil represented nothing more than the ending of one such cycle and the beginning of another. Neither of which, as he lived out his normal life span, he need be expected to deal with.

Still running away, he told himself as he sipped. The realization burned him more than the hot liquid.

After what he'd seen on Repler, the wild thought occurred to him that maybe he should take drugs to make himself feel better. Perhaps try something stronger than tea. Given his singular abilities, however, there was no telling, no way of predicting, what the cost of such an action might be. While he felt he could deal with any consequences that the sampling of artificial stimulants might pose to himself, there was no telling what kind of harm such an indulgence involving his increasingly unmanageable abilities might visit on those around him. He decided that such experimentation was, at least for now, not a viable option.

All right then, the voice inside himself demanded. If you're going to devote yourself to saving something, maybe what you need to stiffen your resolve is to prove to yourself that that something is worth saving. That it's worth the sacrifice. What he had recently experienced and observed while on Repler was not encouraging. Selfishness, greed, violence. Conscious misuse of intelligence. Willful consumption of sentience-altering drugs. Bloodhype. The noblest creature he had encountered during his sojourn on Repler—the one with whom he had personally empathized the most—had belonged not to one of the existing races whose future he was being asked to help save but to a Tar-Aiym named Peot: the last surviving representative of that long-dead, war-like species.

On the other hand, despite his recent, self-challenging, near-defiant, and very brief dalliance with the United Church officer Kitten Kai-sung, there was Clarity. Not to mention Bran Tse-Mallory, Truzenzuzex, Mother Mastiff, and other exemplary examples of contemporary cognizance and compassion. Even those who hungered first and foremost for wealth, like the old prospector Knigta Yakus, were at heart good folk whose heritable lines were deserving of preservation.

Maybe that was it, he told himself as he sat up straighter in the command chair. In the course of his short but very full life, so many of those he had been in close contact with had been in one way or another exceptional or atypical. Easy enough to rationalize risking all to save such. But what about the great, restless, surging mass of others? Did they deserve salvation? Was the future of those vast, unknown, swarming genetic masses worth the sacrifice of his personal happiness? That was really what was at stake. That was truly what he needed to decide.

He had told the now deceased Peot that he needed to acquire wisdom. Where to go and what to do to find it? In his short life he had seen much. Love, hate, all manner of planetary environments. But not, his recent encounter on Repler with the disreputable drugger and emoman Dominic Rose notwithstanding, the full wickedness and inventive iniquity of which humankind and others were capable. In order to pass judgment on his fellow sentients, and to acquire the fullness of wisdom that he sought, it was only reasonable to believe that he needed to experience that as well. Needed to proceed counter to his natural impulses and immerse himself in the worst that full-blown civilization had to offer.

He mentally and methodically worked his way through the most relevant steller schematics. The source for the kind of learning he desired lay a good way distant but not all that far off his present vector. Determination overrode a hesitancy that as recently as several years ago would have held him back from proceeding. Determination, and a seriously advanced case of what-the-hell.

Sensing his change of mood, Pip spread her wings, rose, and glided over to land on his right shoulder. As her tail end curled affectionately around his neck, he reached up with his free hand to absently stroke the smooth, scaly back of her head.

"Course change," he announced aloud, lowering his cup. "We will remain within the borders of the Commonwealth, but off the Almaggee vector. Set a course for Visaria."

The *Teacher*'s ship-mind was programmed to emulate an extensive and varied assortment of human reactions, but pausing for emphasis was not one of them. Therefore, its skepticism was immediate.

"Permit me to point out that Visaria represents a considerable detour from the most direct route into the Blight, the region you wish to search for signs of the absented Tar-Aiym artifact."

He glanced toward one of the numerous visual pickups that were scattered about the command chamber. "Yep."

Nonexistent applicable programming notwithstanding, the ship-mind momentarily did seem to hesitate. "Visaria is an N Class One, highly industrialized human-dominated colony world. It has no links that I can discover to the alien weapons platform you are engaged in seeking out, and its heavily concentrated and urbanized population is the kind you prefer to avoid whenever possible."

"Yep," muttered Flinx a second time. He took a swallow of tea. Forward of the curving port, stars and nebulae whirled about one another in an eternal crazed tarantella—fused hydrogen partnering with torn particles to produce all the colors of God.

"You are being deliberately unresponsive. Cold statistics and classification aside, my records indicate that Visaria is considered one of the most disreputable, debased, dangerous, and generally unpleasant settled worlds in the entire Commonwealth. It has a reputation for corrupting representatives of even such generally well-thought-of species as the Quillp and the thranx themselves. It is a place whose occupants are primarily preoccupied with building wealth as opposed to character. Since you already have both, I am perplexed as to why you should wish to go there. Particularly now."

"Well," Flinx replied evenly, "it's not for a 'vacation.'"

The ship-mind's response was calculatedly cool. "The acerbic reference to the recent awkward sojourn on Jast is duly noted. My query and concern remain unaddressed."

"I indeed intend to spend an undetermined length of time there," he continued deliberately, "to further my education."

"At the risk of your life?"

"Ah yes," the tall young man in the command chair murmured, "that would be a first, wouldn't it?"

"If sarcasm were gravity and could be channeled, I would be the fastest vessel in the Commonwealth."

"By which comment you indicate that you're not averse to occasionally employing it yourself," he shot back.

The ship-mind collected itself. "My sole concern is for your well-being. Visaria is a patently dangerous place. You are already under threat from various sources. My logic processor fails to see why you would willingly pile one danger upon another, when that other is easily avoided."

"You don't accept a desire to gain knowledge as a valid reason?" He stared in the direction of the nearest visual pickup.

"One must consider the question of demonstrable risk versus theoretical benefit," the *Teacher* insisted.

"I've done all the analysis I need to," Flinx replied irritably, "and it is my intention to proceed."

Another suggestion of circuitous, or perhaps merely circuitry, hesitation. "You are not feeling suicidal again, are you?"

A dull pounding started at the back of Flinx's skull. He willed it away. "If that was the reason for my wanting to visit Visaria, there are quicker and easier means of fulfillment."

"Granted." The ship sounded relieved. "Visaria, then. Do you wish upon arrival to enter into an announced orbit?"

Rising from the chair, he placed his cup in the appropriate receptacle and started back toward the ship's lounge. "If the folks who run the place are as cagey as you suggest, I don't see how we could sneak in unobserved. If it's as crowded as you say, I don't imagine we'll need to. And if it's as shady even on the sunward side, I'm sure we can convince the appropriate authorities to take a pass on any detailed arrival and entry formalities."

As its master left the command chamber, the *Teacher* set about negotiating the necessary alterations to the appropriate dimensional mathematics, with an appropriate kick in the right direction. It worked flawlessly, efficiently, rapidly.

But insofar as it was capable of contemplating the consequences of the impulsive course change, it was not pleased.

Habitable worlds were like tolerable people, Flinx mused as the *Teacher* decelerated through normal space toward Visaria. Viewed from a distance, they all looked similar. Draw closer, and individual features made themselves visible. The lines of a continent on a planet; the lines of character in a person's face. Canyons and crevices, rills and revelations, some carved by wind and water, others by life and experiences. He had encountered both weathered worlds and weathered people. It was no different with sentient nonhumans. One simply had to study the different physical features to learn what they signified.

Move in closer still and fine detail became apparent. With worlds, individual streams. With people, streams of consciousness only he could perceive. Mountains and forests, cities and roads and seaports. Shifty or straightforward eyes, digits or tentacles reaching for handshakes or weapons. To isolate such features, one just had to know how and where to look. Surviving both worlds and individuals was a matter of leavening alertness with knowledge. He had been born with plenty of the former, and through circumstance had been force-fed an abundance of the latter. In this he was not really all that different from his fellow sentients. In one other highly significant way he was.

Worlds whispered to him.

Inhabited worlds, mostly, though his Talent had grown sensitive and sharp enough to allow him to perceive the emotions of less intelligent orders of beings. It did not matter whether the worlds he visited were dominated by his own kind, or by the insectoid thranx, or the aggressive AAnn, or even more outré sentients such as the Vssey. If they possessed an inner emotional life, their feelings encroached on him. Through practice and time, he had gained the ability to shut out some of the emotive shouting of others. But not all of it, and not always. Just as he could not predictably control his ability to perceive the feelings of others, so he could not always completely banish them from his Meliorare-altered mind. That was why he often chose to avoid worlds that were crowded with intelligent life. That was why he was deliberately choosing to immerse himself in one now.

At this distance, the murmuring of millions of minds exerted only the gentlest of pressures on his thoughts. Only millions, because while it was developing rapidly, Visaria was still a colony world. Should he find himself overwhelmed, there would be extensive open spaces where he could rest his mind. Aware that the immersion he was about to willingly subject himself to bordered on the masochistic, he found that he was starting to feel a little nervous. Perhaps this wasn't such a good idea after all. Perhaps he should direct the *Teacher* to halt some distance away from Visaria, in the outer, quieter reaches of its six-world system, while he meditated further on his decision.

No. He had chosen this course with forethought and intention, and would not renegotiate with himself now. Coiled on his lap as he relaxed in the forward command chair, Pip glanced up at him curiously, unable to decide whether her master was unsettled or merely being his usual intensely thoughtful self.

"Are you all right?"

Always watching, the ship-mind. Ever attentive to his needs—even when he didn't voice any.

"I'm fine. Situation?"

"Cutting orbit of outermost moon, of which there are three: one Lunarian, two small and irregular. We have been under non-hailing-system tracking for some time now. Initial demands for identification preparatory to assignment of orbital position have been received. I anticipate shortly follow-up requests demanding proportionately more significant information."

Flinx nodded to himself. "Nothing out of the ordinary. Respond with, oh, description of minor outsystem cargo. Low value, nothing likely to arouse curiosity even here." He rose from the chair. "If the specs on Visaria are accurate, the last thing we want is for local authorities to take an interest in our nonexistent cargo with an eye toward appropriating a share of it."

"Edible plant matter en masse is usually a sufficiently bland manifest to put forward." This time there was no sarcasm in the ship-mind's voice. "A quantity of easily traded but undistinguished varieties unobtainable locally and insufficiently exotic to command elevated prices."

The melancholic master of the *Teacher* smiled. "Yes, that should bore Customs adequately. Speaking as a onetime thief myself, I know that even the most avaricious thieves find it hard to get themselves worked up at the prospect of stealing vegetables."

Ever efficient, the *Teacher*'s resourceful response to the inquiries of the planetary arrival authority elicited a response that was reassuringly insipid. As predicted, naught interest was shown in either the battered, undersized cargo vessel or its outsystem "cargo" of nondescript compacted vegetable product. As adroit as his ship, Flinx took a few moments to study up on the imaginary consignment. He would not take the chance of being caught out should some eager immigration interviewer, be it man or machine, request actual details about the makeup of his shipment.

He dressed appropriately in his usual simple, dun-colored, two-piece work attire and service belt. The garb was utterly unadorned, devoid of so much as a simple insignia or integrated impression. Combined with a pair of worn, comfortable, slip-on flexboots, his outfit clearly stamped him for anyone to see as that ubiquitous traveler known as No One in Particular. From the time he had been old enough to choose his own clothes, it had been his favored identity. By the time he had finished securing the contents of a small travel pack and taking extra time to ensure that his medipak was fully stocked, planetary authority had assigned the *Teacher* orbital coordinates.

Familiar with its owner's preferences as well as his desire never to waste time, the ship's smaller shuttle commenced release procedures even before Flinx and Pip had settled in on board. By the time he had locked himself in braceplace and had secured Pip nearby, the tiny craft was pushing away from its dock in the *Teacher*'s bulbous underbelly. It did not deploy the compacted delta wings at its stern. There was no need until the time came to enter atmosphere.

Following a steady stream of high-speed broadcast directions, it commenced deceleration parallel to the surface of the glowing, cloud-streaked planet below. Flinx's shuttle was only one of several dozen that were either arriving, departing, or awaiting clearance. Settling himself into the compression seat, he declined the opportunity to chat with ground-based orbital control. The cautions that had protected him as a youthful thief had retained their validity as he matured: keep as low a profile as possible, both technologically as well as personally, and avoid attention.

The greeting voice that provided final approach and arrival instructions to the shuttle's sub-branch of the *Teacher*'s ship-mind also chose to address the small landing craft's occupants. The speaker made no effort to mask her boredom with the procedure.

"Attention freehold cargo carrier *Remange:* be sure you follow all vectors and instructions to the letter, or you'll lose your place and be denied a landing slot. You don't want to have to abort and reapply from orbit, and I don't want to have to go over basics with you again."

Flinx kept his voice as even, if not as jaded, as that of the woman on the other end of the surface-to-ship communicator. "Understood." Thrusters angled the shuttle sharply down and to starboard. "Complying."

Wings deployed as the compact craft approached atmosphere.

Diffused light flashed briefly through the narrow foreport. As with a bicycle crossing a rutted road, bumps and jolts rattled ship and passenger as it entered Visaria's outer airspace. Communication and conversation between ship and ground ceased. It was time for electronics to converse, taking control of calculations too complex for mere organics to optimally manipulate.

Bursting through the underside of a heavy cloud layer, the shuttle continued to slow. The view forward was of extensive stretches of undeveloped native forests and desert; the latter familiar, the former startlingly rich in oranges and reds. This was not a world on which the magic of photosynthesis held sway. As the shuttle continued to descend, it passed over a vast valley that looked as if it had been chewed up and spit out by some mud-hungry giant. Possibly a mine, Flinx mused. Records indicated that Visaria was rich in the minerals and metals that formed the basis of its hastily industrialized society.

Though he could have released it, he allowed the compression seat to continue to constrain him: always a sensible decision when coming in for a landing at a previously unvisited port. Equipment whined softly while instrumentation on the console in front of him flickered and winked. Though he could have assumed manual control, crowded urban shuttleports were no place to practice one's touchdown technique. Better to let ship and port control handle the details while he relaxed and took in the scenery.

There wasn't much to see. There usually wasn't in the vicinity of a major shuttleport, whose operators preferred to retain the open space surrounding it for future expansion—and to contain debris from the occasional failed landing attempt. Just before touchdown, he did get a glimpse of Malandere. Visaria's nominal capital and largest city loomed on the northern horizon. Even at a distance, it looked bleak and nasty. But, he told himself, it was only a glimpse.

The shuttle's landing was smooth and error-free. Taking command of the little vessel, port control eased it into an empty parking place among dozens of other similar vehicles. Nearly all were larger and more impressive than his, which was just how he liked it.

It was a very short walk to the lift that took him down to one of several subterranean transport levels. In that brief time when he was walking between shuttle and corridor, he noted that despite being of comparatively recent vintage, Malandere's main port was already showing signs of upkeep neglect and heavy wear. Too much growth too fast, he reflected, where haste took precedence over proper planning.

A tsunami of emotion washed over him as he allowed the moving walkway to carry him toward Arrival and Immigration. It was mostly human, but like a thick pudding blended with bits of nuts and flavor chips, there were also sparks of alien feeling. Thranx for certain, which was to be expected. A surge of anxiety that might have been Quillp. Something sensuous distinctly Tolian, a faint touch of Astuet, and a flurry of no-nonsense Deyzara completed the emotional flood. But as to be expected, the great majority of feelings that ebbed and flowed all around him were those of fellow humans.

Fellows, inasmuch as he was human himself, he thought cynically.

Though occupying an extensive underground chamber, Arrival and Immigration had the air of a section that was never finished, whose layout was a hodgepodge of add-on electronics and hurriedly improvised subrooms. Directed through the maze, he found himself in an alcove occupied by a single public servant who wore a look that matched the jaded tone of the woman who had addressed him prior to atmospheric insertion. The man, who was middle-aged, underweight, and anxious to be anywhere but here doing anything but this, barely glanced up at him. In contrast with his lackluster personality, his shaved skull glowed with an ornate inlaid tattoo of fantastical mythical creatures battling for control of the word ALICE.

An initial quick glance was followed by a longer one. A flicker of interest showed in the man's hitherto dull eyes. "Interesting animal. I don't believe I've ever seen one like it before." A soft hum indicated that a privacy screen had been activated, enclosing the alcove in a bubble of solitude.

Reaching up with his left hand, Flinx ran his fingers along his companion's back and across the pleated pink-and-blue wings that were folded against her flanks. "Pip's an Alaspinian minidrag. An empath."

Ignoring the forms, information spheres, and hovering displays that swarmed his desk, the bureaucrat cocked his head slightly to one side as he studied the flying snake.

"Empath, eh? I'll be sure to think only happy thoughts, then." He grinned humorlessly. Curled around Flinx's neck and left shoulder, Pip stared back at him out of unblinking eyes. The mixture of hostility, envy, and fear she sensed from the man in front of her was no reason for excitement. Fortunately for him, she chose to ignore him.

Turning to one of the several displays projected by his desk and drifting above it, he stroked his fingers through hovering controls. Manicured eyebrows drew together.

"According to this, your pet ranks impressively high on the danger scale." Flinx felt fresh fear bubble up in the man's mind. "*Really* high," he finished, turning back to face the tall young man standing before him.

Flinx did his best to shrug off the other man's concern while simultaneously putting him at ease. "Pip only responds when she senses that I'm being threatened. She's extremely perceptive and has never made a mistake."

The bureaucrat was eyeing the serpentine shape fretfully. "I infer, then, that she has previously acted in defense of your person?" Flinx nodded. "For a shield pet, she's not very big."

"No, she's not," Flinx agreed unperturbedly. "My feeling is that with any weapon, speed and agility are more important than size."

"A sound philosophy." The man smiled. "But you can't bring a lethal, toxic animal onto Visaria. Not even as part of a commercial venture, much less one that's just a personal favorite. Unless you have the appropriate permit, of course."

Though he thought it excessive, Flinx paid the bribe. He haggled over the amount only because it was clearly expected of him. It was all right for the bureaucrat to dismiss him as young and inexperienced. It would not do to have the man think of him as outright ignorant. So he played the game for the several minutes of his life that it wasted, and was rewarded with the requisite "permit" allowing him to maintain Pip on his person for the duration of his stay on Visaria. Under no condition was he being granted consent to sell the minidrag or give it away. That he would as soon give up his own life as that of his lifelong companion was an admission that would have been wasted on the covetous public servant.

From the time Flinx entered the alcove until he left, his interrogator never once bothered to ask him about his ship's "cargo." The bribe was the point of the interview, Flinx realized. If not obtained on account of Pip, he was sure that his questioner would have found another reason to bring up that minor matter. As he made his way in the direction of the port exit, following the hovering indicators that showed the way to public transportation, he felt more confident than ever in his decision to come to this world.

He had only been on its surface for a very short time, had only interacted with one of its residents, and had already encountered the kind of grubby attitude and approach to existence that was likely to convince him he would only be wasting his own short, precious life if he chose to devote it to preventing the future extinction of his fellow so-called civilized beings.

CHAPTER

2

The public transport that was available to take travelers from the shuttleport into the city proper was of similar style, design, and ill-maintained decrepitude as the spontaneous sprawl of urbanization it served. Like much of the shuttleport's infrastructure, it had been constructed with an eye more toward utility than toward standardization. Even Flinx's untrained eye was able to see that the system had been cobbled together from bits and pieces of systems existing elsewhere, rather than being designed and built as a unified whole. It was undoubtedly the cheaper, as well as quicker, option. Get transportation up and running fast, worry about aesthetics and economy of scale later.

Even the transfer elements themselves were antiquated throwbacks, consisting of public modules designed to convey twenty or more people at a time instead of allowing for individual transport to separate destinations. Unlike on Terra or Hivehom, he found himself forced to share space with several fellow travelers. Of course, private transport into the city was also available as an option from the port, but that would have meant providing personal identification, if only in the form of an alias, to the automated vehicle selected. Disdaining luxury in favor of obscurity, he chose anonymity over comfort. Besides, utilizing public transportation over private offered the chance to encounter the denizens of Malandere sooner rather than later.

That potential was about to be realized. His head was already starting to hurt.

There were four of them. The biggest was as tall as Flinx and much heavier. What the others lacked in stature they made up for in swagger. Their attire consisted of cobalt-blue singlepiece slip-ons festooned with symbols stained black. Highly local in origin, the meaning of these was more alien to Flinx than High Thranx. Scalloped, sleeveless uppers allowed ample arm to protrude. Flashing from where they had been surgically embedded in the exposed flesh of arms and shoulders, a multitude of tiny pins, loops, and hooks carried forward and accentuated the motifs inscribed on the dark blue suits. One squat fellow in his midtwenties sported a circlet of chromed hypoallergenic metal that crowned his skull like the rim of a metal cap.

Their emotions were as florid as their appearances. Without even glancing in their direction, Flinx could sense the approach of open hostility, anger, expectation, fury, and exactly the kind of atavistic bloodlust he had anticipated encountering on this world. A few more such encounters would solidify his budding resolution to forget about looking for the Tar-Aiym artifact, return to Clarity Held, and live out the remainder of his life in as much peace and isolation as he could manage. Civilization would have to find another savior. But he was not at that point. Not yet.

Meanwhile, there was the quartet presently confronting him to be dealt with.

"Tall and skinny." The nearest of the four was looking the seated traveler up and down. The noninvolved occupants of the fast-moving vehicle huddled at the far end of the transport, doing their best to ignore the confrontation. They reminded Flinx of so many frightened rabbits trying to hide at the back end of their burrow. He supposed he couldn't blame them. One more small weight to add to his sinking opinion of humankind in general.

"Offworlder." The second speaker was missing his lower lip. Whether the half-finger length of flesh had been lost to violence or fashion Flinx could not tell. "Snap him in half, not half trying."

"Easy, Jolo," declared the first speaker. The man extended an arm ornamented with jiggling, decorative metal implants. "Give us your bag and we'll leave you your eyes."

A small, winged shape slid out from where it had been concealed inside Flinx's shirt and hissed. The expectant fingers drew back quickly.

"Toy pet," rumbled the biggest of the four. He reached out sharply. "Twist its little head off."

Pleated wings unfurled as Pip took to the air. Startled, the four drew back slightly. Two of them started to reach for weapons. The one with the embedded head rim was quickest. Opening her mouth slightly, Pip spat in his direction. A slender stream of venom struck him just above the right eye.

Smoke started to rise from the shaved skull. A drop of toxin dripped downward into the eye, which also began to smoke. Screaming and clawing at his face and head, the man stumbled backward, bouncing off a seat and the inner wall of the transport. The second time, he fell to the floor, kicking and clawing at himself. In less than a minute he lay still, except for a few final twitches of both lower legs. His right eye was gone, melted away. So was part of the flesh and bone had that formed the enclosing socket and part of his forehead. A section of the ornamental metal rim that encircled his skull had been dissolved through.

Hands had paused halfway to weapons. The smell of fear-sweat now permeated the section of the transport vehicle where the offworlder sat. His three remaining antagonists began to back away. Occupying seats halfway down the transport, they formed a little knot of their own: distant from Flinx, separate from the other passengers. No one moved to check the damaged, motionless body lying on the floor.

Her agitation giving way to more moderated alertness, Pip settled herself back down on her master's right shoulder. Her eyes never left those of the three would-be assailants—nor they hers.

Throughout the entire compelling, shockingly brief confrontation, Flinx had not moved or said a word. He did not address his assailants when he finally exited the transport. They, wisely, said nothing to him.

The heart of old Malandere was not all that old, because the city and colony themselves were not that old. It was, however, as rundown and decaying as a metropolitan area of its age could be. Every building, every street screamed neglect. Wealth had been wrung from the rocks of Visaria. Fortunes that had gone elsewhere, leaving the descendants of those who had toiled to extract it and refine it with little but the leftovers. More evidence of humanity's disdain for itself, Flinx decided as he made his way along what passed for a main avenue. If the majority of the species did not and would not care for its brethren, why should he?

Too early to render judgment, he told himself. He'd just arrived. Only one attempt had been made on his person. The decision he needed to make should not be rendered in haste, no matter what he was feeling. Visaria was entitled to time to solidify his opinion one way or the other.

So far its prospects of convincing him that altruism should be an important component of the rest of his life were less than promising.

It started to rain. As a colony world, Visaria could not afford to maintain the infrastructure necessary to manipulate its meteorology. Engulfed by a surfeit of emotional misery ever since he had exited the transport, Flinx saw no need to suffer the added discomfort of being both cold and wet. Ads for a variety of side-street hotels clustered around him, competing for his attention. Settling on one, he followed it around a corner. The place looked quiet, isolated, and the service lobby was halfway clean. The automated concierge accepted his cred without question, not even asking for an identity check. One recommendation for AIs as administrators, he reflected as he took the lift to the floor where his room was located, was that as a general rule they did not ask for bribes.

The room was like the rest of the establishment; semi-clean, compact, utilitarian. The omnipresent tridee offered a varied selection of entertainments. He chose the news. Local content was salacious, sensationalized, and aimed at an audience devoid of higher interests. Irritated and tired, he verbally isolated the surround imagery, ordering it to restrict itself to the far corner of the room. From the street outside and the building enclosing him, emotion was pouring in. His head was beginning to throb.

Choosing from among several drugs contained in a pouch on his service belt, he medicated himself. The embryonic headache diminished but did not disappear entirely. Pip settled herself beside the single oval window, curling up away from the transparency. Rain streaked the exterior. As he lay down on the humming, solicitous bed and let it unwind him, an already discouraged Flinx tried not to dwell on what the morning might bring. He was determined to give this place a chance to prove him wrong about the current state of humaniform sentience. He would be fair.

But based on what he had seen and encountered merely in the course of getting from the shuttleport into the city, humankind and its allies were going to have an uphill struggle convincing him to sacrifice the rest of his life to preserve their distant, unimaginable future.

A plain but nourishing breakfast in an eating establishment on the main avenue served to raise his spirits somewhat. *Homo sapiens* had not evolved to the point where food failed to energize mind as well as body. Feeling a little better about himself if not his species, he set out on a walk to see more of Malandere. Trusting neither pet nor possessions to the questionable safety of his room, he let Pip ride comfortably in the pack on his back.

Opening himself to the swarm of sentients who surrounded him on the pedestrian walkway was the empathetic equivalent of going on a three-day bender. Seething emotion overwhelmed him: joy, misery, delight, sadness. His mind was wave-washed with intimations of murder, accomplishment, seduction, betrayal, hope, despair, and a thousand other sentiments. It rocked him so severely that several passersby glanced uncertainly in his direction. One even paused to inquire as to his condition. The encounter would have raised his opinion of his kind ever so slightly had not the self-proclaimed good Samaritan been busy trying to find a way into Flinx's pant pockets while expressing his seemingly heartfelt concern. Fortunately for the nimble-fingered fellow, he did not get the opportunity to fumble in the tall young visitor's pack, where he would have encountered not valuables, but the scales of justice.

Autonomous transports propelled by a variety of technologies carried people as well as goods through the streets. Skimmers with airspace permits soared above the more plebeian, groundbound traffic. Unregulated noise bombarded his hearing at levels long since banned on more settled, civilized worlds. This was what cities were like prior to the adoption and enforcement of laws designed to protect the health of their inhabitants, he knew. This was what they would revert to in the absence of the controlling civilization of the Commonwealth.

Malandere was a cauldron. People were thrown in, stirred, spiced with ambition, and boiled until only the most successful rose to the top. It was a stew fueled by money. Visaria was still a world where fortunes could be made by those without connections, inheritances, or special knowledge. A place where humankind could revert to the jungle, where laws were still new and their effect tenuous. The only difference between Visaria and someplace like Midworld, he felt as he forced himself down the crowded street, was that here one was more likely to be killed by another human. On Midworld, the descendants of the first settlers had survived by learning how to emfol, or empathize directly with their alien surroundings. On Visaria, survival would be a matter of learning how to socialize with one's own kind.

And just as on Midworld, or Moth, or the deserts of Pyrassis, one learned quickly how to adapt to the immediate environment, or perish. Unfortunately, he had never quite been able to blend in no matter where he was. He was too much the outsider, too conscious of the differences that marked him. And as always, too interested in the welfare of others to look only after himself.

A perfect example of this debilitating condition manifested itself within the hour, when he heard panicky hooting coming from the serviceway off to his right. He was positive several other pedestrians heard it. He could tell by the way they picked up their pace to hurry past, and the sharp stabs of fearfulness they radiated in all directions. He knew he ought to do the same. Blend in, adapt, do as the locals did. But he simply could not. He was not local and, as was so often the case to his detriment, he could not ignore the plight of others.

Turning right, he entered the serviceway.

The encounter was almost a cliché, except that the two men and one woman were assaulting an alien and forced sex was not involved. One protruding from the top of its head and the other from the lower portion of its face, the Deyzara's breathing and speaking trunks were writhing helplessly. Centered on the hairless ovoid of a skull, the large dark eyes bulged even more than usual. The woman easily held its limber arms behind its back. Terror was writ almost as large on its face and in its mind as the garish epidermal makeup favored by its kind. Its clothing was an explosion of bright color. Despite its extreme distress, the alien's emotions lay light and feathery on Flinx's mind, a kind of pastel panic.

Rummaging through the waist pack they had removed from the victim, the two male upwardly mobile thugs were arguing over a small, exquisitely made communications device of Deyzaran manufacture. They paused in their skirmishing only when they noticed a tall, slim figure quietly watching. Flinx sensed confusion, rapidly replaced by confidence.

"Vent, visitor," one of the men growled.

His companion's free hand drew a weapon from his chest belt. "Choose or lose, angulate."

Easily maintaining her grip on the Deyzara's arms, the woman nodded sharply in the newcomer's direction. "He's just a big kid, Vynax. Ignore him." As the alien struggled, she twisted both boneless wrists. The Deyzara whimpered, an awkward gurgling sound.

"Let him go," Flinx said quietly. Save an innocent individual, save the galaxy. Small steps always first, Mother Mastiff had frequently told him. Why was he getting involved? A hundred, a thousand similar little conflicts were doubtless playing themselves out all over this fermenting pustulence of a planet. Why insert himself into this one?

Because he could, he knew, sighing to himself. Because even if illegally and immorally genetically modified, he represented civilization, and the trio eyeing him warily represented—something else.

The man holding the weapon was preparing to shoot. Flinx knew this even though the gun holder had not said a word. His intent was plain in the surge of violent emotion that was rising like magma in his mind. So Flinx countered as he had learned to do over the past several years. Having grown up with the ability read the emotions of others he had gradually acquired, if not mastered, the concomitant ability to project them.

Fear replaced fury in his would-be murderer's mind. Fear, and utter panic. Eyes widening suddenly, the hardened fighter let the gun slip from his fingers as he staggered backward, his gaze fixed on the indifferent figure looming before him. Initially slim and harmless, in the killer's mind the tall young man had abruptly acquired horrific dimensions. Here was something to be feared, to be avoided, to run away from as fast as his feet could propel him. What exactly that was, he could not say. The omission puzzled, but did not dissuade him from backpedaling rapidly. His companions eyed him as if he had suddenly gone mad.

"Vynax, what the . . . ?" Viewing the olive-skinned, red-haired youth standing in the entrance to the serviceway in an entirely new light, the other man started to reach for his own weapon. Dark green eyes shifted to meet his own.

Any careful, cool, collected consideration of the confrontation vanished as an overwhelming terror swept through the man. All he could think of was to get away, to flee, to take himself anywhere away from where he was. Whirling, he scrambled and stumbled in blind horror down the serviceway in the wake of his compatriot. Both men were moaning and chattering as if possessed by ghosts.

That left their female companion by herself. Maintaining her grip on the bewildered Deyzara, she stared at Flinx as if one of the graven monoliths of the Sauun had suddenly entered the serviceway and come thundering toward her. Stare as she might, she could not see anything that should have prompted the panicked flight of her normally assertive colleagues. Which made Flinx's nonchalant approach all the more alarming. Though he towered over her, it was not his height that was intimidating. It was the intimation that he controlled something forceful and unseen; something potent enough to send not one but two murderous individuals like Howlow and Vynax running like scared little children.

Still, she stood her ground until something small, reptilian, and angry looking poked its head out of the pack riding on the redhead's back. One hiss in her direction brought her to the swift conclusion that no matter how potentially valuable his possessions, the disposable property of one ugly alien was not worth wrestling with mysteries that took the form of tall, soul-piercing strangers and small, gimlet-eyed serpents. Letting go of the alien's rubbery wrists, she took off in pursuit of her companions. It was not necessary for Flinx to project any emotions onto her: she was sufficiently frightened already.

The Deyzara stood unsteadily for a moment, then bent to recover his property that lay scattered on the pavement. Moon-like eyes regarded the tall human.

"I am very much extremely grateful to you, stranger sir." As did many of its kind, the Deyzara spoke excellent terranglo. "As one engaged in business on several worlds, I am not one to generalize as to the nature of a species." Two-fingered hands adjusted and repositioned belongings recovered from the ground. "But I must say that until your arrival and intervention, my opinion of your kind was undergoing a most precipitous droppage indeed."

"Glad I was able to balance things out. If it's any consolation, your opinion of my species probably still rates higher than my own." Flinx turned to depart.

Like a pale rope, one alien arm hastily transcribed anxious circles in the air in front of its owner. "Wait, good person! I believe it is customary among your people, as it is among mine, for such a selfless deed to be rewarded." The other two-fingered hand began to fumble with a sealed length of some metallic fabric.

"Some would say so," Flinx murmured by way of reply, "but it's not customary among me."

After seeing the visiting Deyzara safely back out onto the main avenue, his rescuer turned and strode off in the opposite direction, leaving the bemused alien to follow him with its oversized eyes. Flinx would have declined the offer of a reward anyway, but he had another reason for wanting to ditch the other visitor's company.

Surrounded, submerged, and enveloped by so many fuming emotions, the medication he had taken was already beginning to wear off and his head was starting to pound as if the masters of some minor race were attempting to drill their way into the back of his brain. He had to find a way to moderate them, or he was going to have to abandon this world without reaching the conclusions he sought to the questions he had posed to himself. This was not recently visited Arrawd, where he could effortlessly shut out the feelings of the locals. Here, as on nearly every other world, he had little control over the emotional storm that raged all around him.

He finally decided that unless the pain became incapacitating, he would not flee Malandere. Instead, he would try to find a less emotionally turbulent space within it.

One hope he held was that the nights might prove to be less invasive and disturbing than the days. This wish was quickly quashed as he lay in bed in his hotel room after sunset only to be emotively assaulted as forcefully as he had been at noon. Unable to sleep he rose, slipped on belt and pack, made sure Pip was comfortable in the depths of the latter, and wandered outside. He could not compress or shove aside the flood of feelings that surged around him, but physical activity helped minimize the discomfort somewhat. Lying motionless was the worst. At least when he was moving, observing, studying constantly changing surroundings, it forced his thoughts to focus on something other than the throbbing in his head.

Malandere at night was as dynamic as it was during the day, though the thrust of activity was different. Commerce was still the principal order of business, but it tended to take place on a more personal level. Companies might be closed for the day, municipal facilities muted, but everywhere one looked, something was being sold, traded, bartered, offered, or exchanged. And sometimes, someone.

Even more so than during the hours of daylight, the darkened streets of the city lay smothered beneath a blanket of emotion. Feelings boiled and bubbled all around him. Foremost amid the sea of sentiment were desperation and desire, the latter often leading to the former. Like many thriving, wide-open colony worlds, Visaria was a first choice of the hopeful and a last refuge of the hopeless, thousands of its denizens driven by the twin dynamos of triumph and despondency. The need to succeed led individuals who might have worked at legitimate professions on other worlds to resort to doing things they would otherwise never have contemplated. Mugging inoffensive visiting Deyzara, for example.

Letting chance and indifference guide him, he turned a corner only to stumble onto a face-off between a pair of local youth gangs. A commonality to civilizations throughout the course of human history, this particular incipient confrontation differed from its ancient predecessors only in choice of attire, weaponry, and the inclusion of the occasional nonhuman in the ranks. While the words being vigorously tossed around were different, the sentiments they conveyed were no different from identical taunts that had once resounded on the streets of ancient Rome or Thebes, Cuzco or Angkor or Mohenjo Daro. Or earlier still, in caves. As ever, they included remarks concerning the legitimacy of specific individuals' ancestry, demeaning appraisals of the sexual prowess of those opposite, and respective suggestions as to how those on the other side might best go about performing certain physical impossibilities.

Flinx had sensed the rising group animosity before he had turned the corner, of course. Curious, he joined several other passersby in standing and watching. Several among the crowd of onlookers egged the opposing groups on. As long as it didn't spread to include spectators, such nocturnal combat promised free entertainment, with the added benefit of allowing those not participating to depart feeling morally superior.

He turned away before the confrontation escalated to more than verbal sparring. The emotions flooding through the bystanders depressed him far more than the adolescent bloodlust being pumped out by the two groups of young ruffians. The outlook of mature lawbreakers he could understand, if not empathize with. They were professionals who had deliberately settled on an antisocial way of life. And judging from what he had already detected in the course of his first day in Malandere, such individuals were in ample supply on Visaria. Their existence did not disappoint him, because he expected it. The same could be said for the rival gangs of misdirected, unguided youth.

It was only when the citizenry at large of a place reeked of unwholesomeness that he found himself losing hope.

Though he wished for it, the days that followed gave him no reason for optimism. He found himself sinking farther and farther into gloom. Pip tried her best to help, not realizing that those very efforts only contributed to her master's intensifying melancholy. What hope was there for a society when its only emotionally selfless denizen was a nonsentient flying creature who hailed from a world whose native civilization was already long past its prime?

If a majority of sentients no longer cared about one another, why should he forgo his life and happiness to do what they could not? Even the martial AAnn, for whom self-advancement was the greatest good, recognized and respected the need to help one another, if only to advance themselves as individuals. Why should he have to be the one to give up everything? Clarity was waiting for him; he was as certain of that as he was of anything in the universe. Returning to her and living out his natural life span, perhaps on an accommodating world like New Riviera, would disappoint his mentors Tse-Mallory and Truzenzuzex. Their displeasure would hurt, but no more so than the assorted pain and suffering he had already, often futilely, endured. He was not a child anymore. Did he deserve happiness any less than the selfish, egocentric swarms busy exploiting worlds like Visaria?

Everybody wanted him to save them. Who was there, except perhaps Clarity, who was willing to sacrifice even a little to save him? With his recurrent headaches and unpredictable Talent and ineluctable burden of knowledge of what was coming this way out of the Great Emptiness, would he even be doing *her* a favor by returning?

It struck him suddenly that he could lose himself here. If he stayed on Visaria, in Malandere or another of its teeming, festering cities, he might go mad, overwhelmed by the flood of raw emotion surrounding him. Would that be such a bad thing? he found himself wondering. He could simply let things go and succumb to himself. Maybe even the pain in his brain would go away, or he would become so anesthetized to its constancy that he would lose the ability to feel it. It was an alternative to suicide he had never before considered. Life as a condition of perpetual numbness.

He wandered on into the night, oblivious to the strobing lights, howling touts human and alien and mechanical, curious stares, intimate come-ons, garbled offers of assorted contraband, and conflicts both observed and sensed. Most folk got out of his way. Those who persisted found themselves unaccountably starting to sweat, or to see small unpleasantnesses that weren't there, or to otherwise find sudden reason to move on.

The night, the noise, and the inescapable emotional storm that was civilization in its most frenzied form closed in around a troubled, lonely Philip Lynx and swallowed him up.

CHAPTER

3

Subar was not an ethical thief in that he stole not just from the crooked but from anybody, everybody, and whomever he could. Being a true citizen of the Commonwealth, neither did he distinguish among species. If a temptingly gullible intelligence was in possession of something valuable he could safely appropriate for himself, he did not discriminate as to its color, sex, size, shape, number of limbs, language, origin, religion or lack thereof, class, clan, or preferred breathable atmosphere. Robbery-wise, the sixteen-year-old was as egalitarian as they came. Given the opportunity, he would hit an easy target over the head no matter what shape or form that protuberance took. Or if a head was lacking, he was quite happy to bludgeon the appropriate substitute.

Alewev was not the worst district of the huge sprawl that was Malandere City. It was too poor to hold that distinction. Whereas other sections like Gijjmelor and Pandrome had cemented their status as sections of the metropolis that churned out evil as fast as they did credit, Alewev merely sustained a reputation for steady decay.

Only occasionally did some exceptional outrage occur there that proved media-worthy.

That was fine with Subar. He was not one of those middle-aged villains whose future was inevitably cut short by a desperate need for publicity. Much more logical, he reasoned, to operate under the scanner, as far away as possible from the attention of sensation-seeking tridee types and the perpetually harried authorities. He had no interest whatsoever in delivering Olympian pronouncements to the municipal media from the confines of one of the city's overpopulated criminal holding facilities. Getting one's image on the tridee was a poor trade-off for selective mindwipe.

Besides, having to live in close quarters with his generally worthless, misbegotten relatives was punishment enough.

He jumped the last level from the roof to the street and strutted the final couple of blocks to the baroon. Chaloni, Dirran, Zezula, Missi, and Sallow Behdul were already there, lounging on chairs or vilators on the second-floor deck out front. As always, his gaze was immediately drawn to Zezula. How she got her slender yet ripe self into the garment known as a twyne, much less kept all the strips of dark glistening fabric in place, constituted a demonstration of practical physics that far exceeded in interest anything he had encountered in the course of his occasional limited sojourns into academics. Sparkling like specular hematite, the lengths of black shimmer only emphasized the whiteness of her flesh. She looked, he thought deliciously, like a stick of some particularly exotic candy confection.

Grinning, Chaloni welcomed him with a gentle chiding. "Better roll your tongue back into your mouth, Subar, before somebody steps on it." The gang leader and Dirran laughed while Sallow Behdul, who rarely showed anything in the way of emotion, dredged a vapid smile from the depths of his gaunt, progeria-afflicted visage.

Subar's tongue was not protruding in the slightest, much less hanging out, but both young men understood the meaning behind the gang leader's words. For her part Zezula ignored them both, in the way of those females who are young, beautiful, and aware of it.

Taking care to position himself as gracefully as possible (in case Zezula happened to be paying attention), Subar flopped down onto a mist-lounge and as best he was able affected an air of sophisticated indifference. The pose was a complete sham, of course. Despite his best efforts, the teen possessed as much actual sophistication as the stuff one found washing down street drains. Only Chaloni, two years older and the more wizened for it, had spent enough time outside Alewev to claim such knowledge. That he rarely flaunted his experience was what made his nominal leadership of the group tolerable.

"Have something," the older boy offered magnanimously.

Subar didn't hesitate. Having nothing at home, he was not ashamed to succumb to Chaloni's charity. There was a plate of small, locally made pastries; something purplish red, sweet, and offworld; mung drops; and geltubes filled with dizzle. As the latter sang in his mouth, he helped himself to a glassful of pale blue frolic. Twenty percent alcohol by volume from the bottle, it dissipated to less than 2 percent by the time it reached the stomach. One could get high on it, but never drunk.

On the street below, pedestrians worked their way around slow-moving groundbound vehicles. The throughway was off limits to skimmers, which needed more space in any case in order to maneuver at speeds fast enough to render ascension cost-effective. One-way transparencies lined the sides of office and commercial buildings opposite the baroon, while seemingly weightless porches protruded from the apartments situated higher up. Occasionally a semi-legal flad would drift by, flashing its images and blaring its commercial message. These fled whenever an automated plad showed up in pursuit. Stay outside and observe the street scene long enough, and one was sure to see a municipal plad catch up to and destroy one or more of the illegal aerial advertisements. Those who programmed and sent out the flads counted such destruction against the cost of doing business.

Stimulated by the food and drink, Subar soaked up the familiar clamor of the street and the chatter of his friends in equal measure. There was much nattering of inconsequentialities. Though shorter and stockier than Zezula, Missi conceded nothing to the other girl. Dirran talked as much as any of them, while Sallow Behdul simply sat quietly and listened. Subar chipped in when he had something to add. While he was as argumentative as any of them, he was careful never to directly contradict Chaloni. Subar knew he was smarter than the gang's leader, and almost as big, but there were mysteries to which the other boy had been exposed that remained closed to him.

Meanwhile, he bided his time and sucked up Chaloni's largesse. He felt no shame in this. When one has nothing, one takes whatever is offered from whoever offers it. Insurrection is difficult to mount on an empty stomach.

"Who's got cred this week?" The gang leader sat up, his mist-chair hissing softly beneath him. Dirran immediately handed over his card. While both boys held on to the identification square of their respective chits, Chaloni touched the other boy's to his own. A transfer was accomplished. The gang leader repeated the process with Zezula, Missi, and Sallow Behdul. He did not even bother to query the youngest member of the group. If not for Chaloni's munificence, and a rare moment of pity, Subar would not even have a card. In any case, the balance on it rarely read more than zero.

Touching a corner of the card to a receptor on his stimshades, Chaloni scanned his account's new, uplifted balance. Satisfied, he ordered another bottle of dizzle, a different song this time.

As liquid found its way to waiting, self-chilling glasses, Missi dared to voice a mild protest. "That's three weeks straight, Chal. I'm tapped. My mother's gonna have a Morion if she finds out."

Chaloni shrugged, grinned. "Don't you secure your account?"

The heftier girl looked away. "Sure, but sometimes she asks to viz the transfer, just to make sure everything's opto. I can't keep putting her off forever." She looked worried. "One of these days she's gonna ask where the cred fled."

Chaloni nodded, as if he had expected something like this from Missi all along. "I know I've been tapping youls hard lately. And that's going to be fixed. Come morn after morrow, you're all going to see your accounts floating higher than zeal on a holiday shrake."

Dirran was immediately interested. "What you got in mind, Chal? We gonna zlip another quicore?" He was remembering the last time they had boosted a couple of expensive players from a display.

In ancient times, Subar knew, it had been easier. Payment was made with discs of gold and silver metal, or pieces of paper that stood in for cred. Except on the most isolated, backward worlds such mediums of exchange had not existed for hundreds of years. It was hard to be a thief when everything was paid for via a shifting of electrons. Hard, but not impossible. Physical objects still had value. A gun, for example, was always exchangeable for cred.

"I'm ready." Zezula's response was a breathy blend of honey and disdain. Her reply could be taken different ways. Sopping it up, Subar's respiration came a little faster.

"Same here," grunted Sallow Behdul almost inaudibly.

"No quicore napping. Not this time." Chaloni's smile widened, the way it always did when he was preparing to spring some new surprise on them. He was letting the moment linger, savoring the incipient revelation. "Bigger strike. Bigger, and easier." As he leaned toward them, his smile tightened. "We're going to scrim a couple of visitors."

Subar's gaze shifted immediately to the street below. They had scrimmed pedestrians before, sometimes profitably, sometimes incurring the risk for nothing. You had to be fast and careful, and burrow to cover immediately afterward. Swamped with casework, the municipal authorities tended to relegate crimes of property to the bottom of their overworked agendas. Those crimes that involved assaults on persons drew swifter attention. That was because, Subar knew, a boosted and cleaned vehicle could not complain as easily as an injured citizen.

"Who?" Dirran was asking. "Where?"

"Something special this time. I've been scoping it for days. Got it locked down. We're in, we're on them, and we're out. If I've evaled it right, everybody's cred is going to wax max like you haven't coned it in months."

Subar was no less intrigued than the others. They edged closer, their concentration now fully fixed on their leader. Well, almost fully. Always hungry, Subar continued to pick at the food while devoting the rest of his attention to Chaloni.

"The location's perfect," the gang leader was whispering. "Bellora Park, east quad."

Missi frowned. "That's not in Alewev."

Chaloni shook his head impatiently. "Huh-uh—Shangside. Easy transport, lots of connections at the nearest station. Afterward, we can each of us get home six different ways. Safe and sane."

Subar chose that moment to show both his smarts, and that he'd been paying attention. "You said you'd scoped 'them.'"

The gang leader eyed him approvingly. "Uh-huh. There's just two. A senior female and one male attendant who's always with her."

Zezula sounded uncertain. "'Senior female'? What is she, some kind of government administrator?"

The fact that Chaloni was probably zoffing her did not keep him from utilizing the opportunity to display his superior knowledge, tinged with just a hint of disdain. "That's how you refer to a female thranx past egg-laying prime."

The two girls looked at one another. Dirran was startled into the kind of dumbfounded silence usually reserved for Sallow Behdul. It was left to Subar to voice what his companions were feeling.

"We're going to scrim a pair of *thranx*?"

Chaloni's tone had turned chill. He was all business now. "Why not? You got anything against cracking chitin instead of bone?"

Reflexively, Subar shook his head vigorously from side to side. He had seen thranx before. Not just on the tridee but also in person, though only rarely. They had little reason to visit Alewev District. There was nothing for them there. But on a bustling, perfervid world like Visaria, where business was ongoing around the clock and cred was being accumulated by the nanosecond, every sentient species whose culture allowed for the accrual of wealth by an individual, clan, family, or group had an interest in establishing a presence in the capital city. Humankind's closest and most important allies within the Commonwealth, the insectoid thranx had a similar appreciation for affluence.

But to scrim one—or in this case, two—that was something Subar had never even imagined. As he sat pondering, his thoughts whirling, it was Zezula's turn to press Chaloni further.

"Why thranx?" she inquired huskily. "I mean, I don't have anything against it: a boost is a boost. But why bugs instead of bipeds?"

Chaloni nodded patiently, his body language showing that he had clearly anticipated the question. "Well for one thing, nobody'll be expecting it." His grin returned, twisted this time. "Show the media that we here in Alewev don't discriminate. Bugs won't be expecting it, either." He fixed her with a mixture of sloe-eyed lust and testosterone-fueled dominance. "I told you, I *scoped* it. We'll be in and out before anybody can raise an alarm." Leaning back on the mist-chair, he folded his slender, muscular arms across his chest in a posture of youthful bravado.

"Thranx are always loaded with the latest stuff from Evoria and places like that. You know what we take off scrimmed locals. Imagine what we're going to be offered for out of the ordinary offworld gear."

"Weapons?" Missi sounded half thoughtful, half hesitant. She did not want to appear to be challenging Chaloni's competency.

He took no offense. "Scoped the bugs three different mornings. Didn't see anything like that. Doesn't mean they're not carrying. But if they are, the stuff's not patent. It's kind of hard to tell. They both wear the typical everyday bug body pouches across the lower thorax. No heavy gear, since near as I can figure the morning walks they take are just for exercise. Then they call private transport to take them back to their hive-hotel. But the packs look like they're always full."

His eyes glittered as he continued. "One morning, I saw them stop on the trail. The attending male kept pulling gear from his pouch and passing it to the female. Communications, body gloss sprayer, all kinds of stuff. All of it new and the latest. Probably a lot more stuff in each pouch. I hope he *is* carrying a gun. A bug weapon would be worth as much as everything else put together." He took a long draft from his glass. "Just two bugs. Should be easy to take down."

Startling everyone, Sallow Behdul spoke up. His tone was as mournful as his perpetually sorrowful expression. "You ever scrim a thranx, Chaloni?"

It took a moment for the gang leader to recover from his surprise at hearing Behdul voice a question. "Uh, no. So what? As long as we surprise 'em and make sure to cover the exits, it shouldn't be any different from scrimming a human. C'mon, Sallow—you know bugs as well as anybody. They're smaller than us, don't weigh near as much. Grab one by the antennae and they'll do anything you want."

Behdul looked less than completely satisfied, but under Chaloni's even stare elected not to comment further.

"You sure it won't bring extra attention down on us?" Dirran inquired.

Chaloni shrugged. "What if it does? Alewev is where we live, Alewev is where we hide. We're crossing district lines anyway. The police won't know where we're from. It's not like we're scrimming Quillp or some neutrals. These are just *thranx,* people. Our blessed friends. No bug deal." He leaned forward again, obviously pleased with himself.

"And the best part of it is, being from offworld, they're unlikely to hang around to help with identifications or testify in person. Visaria isn't a tourist destination. This female's probably on business here. That means she's likely to have more business elsewhere. They'll probably just take the loss as part of the cost of doing business on a less civilized human world and get on with their lives."

Subar had to admit that Chaloni seemed to have thought of everything. Two thranx or two humans; what was the difference? They would ambush the female and her attendant during their morning walk, scrim what they carried on their person, and vanish into the park and the city streets. By the time their quarry recovered from the shock of the confrontation sufficiently to communicate what had happened, Subar and his friends would have scattered in six different directions.

His only real concern was the possibility of their action being observed, and recorded, by witnesses. But if Chaloni had scoped out prey this thoroughly, surely he would have chosen an appropriately secluded site, one that would conceal their activity from the sight of others who might be in the same area of the park at the same time. That was a leader's job. Subar was good at following orders and taking action, but complex strategy still tended to confuse him. Not for much longer, though. He had no intention of challenging Chaloni directly. Instead, he intended to leapfrog the leader of the gang. Not for Subar the occasional zlip or scrim. His ambition was much greater.

There were criminal organizations whose tentacles reached deep into Alewev. Subar knew of them, had seen some of their representatives going about their business. They were *adults,* engaged in adult enterprises. Already he had initiated a few tentative contacts. Such organizations were always looking for new, eager, energetic recruits. This might well be his last outing with the gang. He had plans, Subar did. Intentions to move on to bigger, better, badder things.

But first, a brief morning excursion in Ballora Park. He needed some cred in order to make an important purchase. His share of the forthcoming boost should provide that. It would impress his prospective new employers considerably if he arrived soliciting employment in possession of his own gun. Chaloni and Dirran had theirs. He was old enough. A child's finger could depress the operating button or trigger of a weapon as easily and effectively as that of an adult.

"*Thaie,* Subar!"

"What?" Blinking, he saw that everyone except Sallow Behdul was looking at him.

"Where you transposing to, kid?" Chaloni asked him.

If there was anything Subar hated worse than seeing Zezula let Chaloni paw her, it was being called kid. He did not show any reaction, of course. "Thinking about tomorrow."

The gang leader sniffed. "Don't hurt yourself. You do as you're told; I'll do the thinking." Chaloni's chest swelled as he peacocked. "That way we'll all get out okay."

"Sure thing, Chal," Subar replied dutifully. "Whatever you say."

They rendezvoused at the Yinstram nexus, where dozens of automated transport pods congregated in the early morning to solicit the business of those denizens of Alewev unfortunate enough to have to commute to their daily work. The subdued but steady chattering of citizens just waking up, devices offering services, and vendors both organic and mechanical made for a continuous hum of multiple consciousnesses doing their best to survive another day in Malandere.

Dawn was suitably dreary. That suited the gang just fine. Fog was ever the friend of the scrim-inclined. Selecting a pod of sufficient size, Chaloni swiped his coded (and aliased) card to pay passage for the six of them. Though some conversation ensued as the pod chose a transportation path and accelerated to its maximum allowable velocity, the gang was unusually subdued. While they had run plenty of successful scrims before, this was the first time they were going to opt one on a pair of nonhumans. It was not necessarily a cause for worry, but it certainly was something to think about.

None of them needed to see a sign marking the moment when they crossed into Shangside. One could tell just by looking around. The landscaping blossomed lush, the buildings became fancier, the public facilities were better kept. Ballora Park, where they exited the transport pod, was a shining example of everything Alewev District was not: clean, modern, accommodating, safe.

At least, it was safe until Subar and his friends arrived.

Having memorized the instructions and directions Chaloni had given them, they split up into pairs, the better to avoid attention. Not that there was anything illegal about half a dozen young youths from Alewev choosing to take in the delights of the park at sunrise, but any large nonfamily group ran the risk of attracting interest. To Subar's expected chagrin, Chaloni went off with Zezula while Dirran and Missi made a second couple. That left Subar with a far less attractive partner in the shape of Sallow Behdul. At least, he muttered to himself as the two of them headed south along a public pathway, it would be peaceful until the moment chosen for the assault. Behdul would not talk unless spoken to.

Even this early, the park was occupied. Runners with slickshoes glided smoothly along paved paths and designated grassy lanes. All were human save for one ambitious Tolian, who compensated for his short legs and stride with boundless energy. Occasionally Subar and Sallow Behdul would break into a jog of their own. It was pure ploy, of course. He and his friends had neither the time nor the interest in running for fun. The whole idea struck Subar as a ludicrous waste of energy. One ran *after* something or *away* from someone. There was no other valid reason for the expenditure of energy. As it had been with the first primitive humans, so it was with him and his companions.

Because of the fog, the morning was humid as well as warm. Another, cooler time of year and no thranx would be outside unprotected, much less engaging in exercise. Summer was about the only season they could tolerate on Visaria. For them the humidity this time of year, Subar supposed as he wiped perspiration from his brow, more than made up for the dry air of fall and winter.

He took a moment to marvel at the beauties of the park. There was nothing like Ballora in the older, lower-working-class district of Alewev. Here, native vegetation was pruned and manicured. They passed a stand of slehwesht, the narrow bright red trunks glowing even in the fog, each woody stalk proudly sporting a maroon-and-green crown like a bouffant hairdo. Wire bushes had been planted in place of railings, and served the same purpose. Spurts of vapor rose from ponds occupied by air-breathing Visarian water-dwellers, while the occasional call of a multiarmed nalamode echoed from the orange trees.

Not all the plants were native. It was strange to see Terran macaques cavorting with native nalamodes, but despite their differences in origin and biology, simple simian and slightly more complex 'lamode had developed mutual respect, rarely coming into conflict. The macaques were experts at cropping leaves and fruit from the highest branches while the nalamodes, with their busy multiple limbs, kept the ground cover stirred up, exposing good things to eat on the park floor.

Not everything that moved through Ballora's woods was real. Every visitor knew that the occasional tiger or gorilla, Hivehomian sesemp or flutine from Mantis, was nothing more than a clever sim. They were generated to give the park some juice, as well as for purposes of education. While visitors from an earlier age would have fled in panic at the sight of any one of the highly realistic sims, they posed no issues for contemporary visitors. Any child above the age of four could automatically tell a sim from a liv.

He was forced to wait impatiently while Sallow Behdul ducked into what appeared to be an ancient Visarian colony mound, but was actually an artfully camouflaged hygienic facility. The bigger youth took his time, leaving his companion to svitz nervously outside.

"Sorry," an apologetic Behdul mumbled as he emerged.

"Sky it." Subar picked up the pace. "Just so long as we're not late."

He was relieved when they found only Chaloni and Zezula waiting at the specified rendezvous point. Chaloni was gazing at the dark shine of the park's biggest lake, watching the zinc-colored hantrans scampering after one another on the large island that occupied its heavily vegetated center. Having removed her day slippers, Zezula was dangling her feet in the water, letting uoas pick at her toes with their darting, acquisitive tongues. Subar and Sal's arrival meant that they were still waiting on Dirran and Missi.

Keeping his distance as he alternated his attention between the water and the sealed walking path behind them, Subar addressed Chaloni without looking in the other youth's direction.

"You don't think Dirran and Miz Mis got spined and vented on us, do you?"

Chaloni's expression was rigid. "Look to your right, fool. Under the big bell tree."

Subar complied, and was mortified to see that Dirran and Missi were already present. They lay entwined in each other's arms underneath the solid, transparent dome of the native growth, pretending to be zoffing. Or maybe they weren't pretending. Regardless, it meant that he and Behdul were, after all, the delays.

"Sal had to void," he mumbled. It was a poor pretext for showing up late, and he knew it. Whether it was enough to excuse them Subar never knew, because Chaloni suddenly tensed. Zezula pulled her feet out of the water without having to be told to do so. The six friends were no longer alone by the little cove.

Emerging from the fog, two idiosyncratic shapes were coming up the pathway toward them. Hundreds of years ago, their size and shape would have spread terror and alarm among any humans who happened to see them. Nowadays their appearance was as familiar to Subar and his companions as that of their own kind.

Though beginning to shade into the lavender, the senior female's chitin was still a bright, if clouded, aquamarine. Both sets of vestigial wings had been removed, indicating that she had mated at some time in the past. Her companion was slightly smaller, an intense male blue, and still flaunted both sets of useless if decorative wings. Traveling at either a fast walk or a slow trot, they advanced on all sixes, utilizing their second set of forward limbs as legs. Both truhands were held out in front and bent sharply at the elbow. Even at a distance and through the mist one could see their four sets of breathing spicules pulsing methodically on their flexible b-thoraxes. Red-banded gold-colored compound eyes gazed forward while occasional flicks of feathery antennae sent accumulated moisture flying. They did not, of course, sweat. Not only did they not possess pores; they did not have skin.

Chaloni was delighted to see that for this morning's jaunt both wore not only thorax pouches but small backpacks as well. The promise of that much more property to boost was to the gang leader's senses like spoiled meat to a homeless dog. Giving Zezula a hand up, he nodded at Subar and Sallow Behdul to take up their assigned stations. Having unlocked themselves, Dirran and Missi were already moving out from beneath the bell tree.

As the young humans split up, the two thranx continued toward them, unaware they were the object of incipient threatening attention. Affecting flippancy, Subar and Behdul wandered into position to the left of the pathway. Hand in hand, Chaloni and Zezula remained by the shore of the lake. As the thranx passed them, Dirran and Missi lengthened their stride as they closed off the route from behind.

Everything was going perfectly, Subar felt as he and Behdul abruptly changed direction. The two of them closed the gap between themselves and Chaloni and Zezula as Dirran and Missi closed in behind the unaware nonhumans. There was no one else in sight. It was quiet, the fog just starting to lift around them.

Confronted by the four young humans, the two thranx halted. While the senior female waited, the male advanced. Lifting his foot-hands off the ground, he held all four forward limbs close in front of him as he raised his upper body. His glistening head now topped out at just over a meter and a half, with the antennae thrusting higher. Fingering the collapsed blade resting in his pant pocket, Subar felt more confident than ever. Even he was taller and heavier than this nascent victim. His nostrils were suffused with the creature's natural perfume. Their body odors stimulated by exercise, both thranx smelled like ambulatory bouquets of expensive flowers.

The male executed a couple of complex hand gestures that meant nothing to the Alewev-wise but galactically unsophisticated youths. It then addressed them in somewhat rough but perfectly comprehensible terranglo.

"You are blocking the path. Should we around go, or is there some difficulty?"

Taking a step forward, Chaloni unlimbered his gun. Short, stubby, and fashioned of molded, hardened fibers that were a dull ivory in hue, it looked no less lethal for the shortness of its barrel.

"You know what this is, bug?"

The male eyed the gun. At least, Subar thought he eyed it. Given their huge compound eyes, it was difficult to tell sometimes just what a thranx was looking at. "A weapon."

"Fires shells that penetrate and then explode." As his companions drew closer and flashed their own weapons, the gang leader made *hand-over* motions with his free hand. "Give us your pouches and packs and nobody loses any lenses. Now!"

The male turned to look at the senior female, who had not spoken. She gestured, he gestured back, she gestured again. Glancing around, Chaloni was not yet nervous—but he was growing impatient.

"Quick-step! And no more hand-talk!" He gestured with the muzzle of the ominous little pistol. "Dirran—maybe if you gave the lady's right antenna a quick trim?"

Nodding, the grim-faced youth stepped forward, brandishing his own blade. It was bigger than Subar's, an unfolded arc of sharpened, fine-edged fiber.

"We will give you our possessions," the male declared hastily. "No violence!"

"That's better. Hurry it up!" Chaloni nodded tersely at Zezula, who flicked off the stunbar she was holding, pocketed it, and stepped forward. His movements visibly jumpy, the male was unfastening the fabricine pack from the female's back. Turning, he dropped it, inclined forward to pick it up, dropped it again. Chaloni grinned at his unease while behind the thranx Dirran nudged Missi and shared a whispered joke. Both enjoyed a laugh at the jittery insectoid's expense. Finally finding a grip on the female's pack with a truhand, the male transferred it to a stronger foothand and gave it to the impatiently waiting Zezula.

Right in the face.

CHAPTER

4

The unknown contents of the female thranx's backpack must have included some sturdy gear, because the impact smashed the startled girl's nose. Blood sprayed. At the same time, the female sprang straight at the startled Chaloni. He got off one shot before his weapon was knocked from his hand. Missing badly, the tiny shell struck the ground right in front of Missi. She let out a scream of pain as shards of shattered pathway pavement were driven through her left shoe and into her foot. Forgetting their purpose, Dirran instinctively went to her aid. A dark stain, not large but unmissable, was spreading along the top and left side of the girl's footgear. As a result of their combined action, the two thranx had instantly taken half of their attackers out of the fight.

With one hand feeling of her broken nose and blood trickling down her face, Zezula spat redness from her mouth as she fumbled to aim her stunner. Meanwhile the male thranx had fingered a device attached to his thorax pouch. To Subar's horror, he saw a tiny but bright yellow light spring to life on the instrument. He would have bet every thousand-bar of the cred he didn't have that the visitor had activated some kind of alarm or communicator. A signal had gone out and it was too late to do anything about it. He and his friends had just been deprived of the luxury of time.

Also of initiative, as the male threw himself at Zezula. She massed more than he did, but the size disparity was a good deal less than that which existed between Chaloni and the female who was clawing at him with all four of her four-fingered hands. As the girl struggled to thumb the stunner she was holding and ward off the thranx with the other, the visitor lashed out in frantic defense. A striking truhand would never have caused Zezula to lose her grip. She might even have been able to hold on to the weapon if hit by a foothand. But four hard-shelled limbs all connecting concurrently with her right forearm stunned nerve and muscle. The backstreet weapon went flying.

Recovering from the surprise of the counterattack, a cursespewing Chaloni had grabbed the female thranx around the neck with both hands, lifted her off the ground, and was squeezing hard. It didn't matter that the rigid chitin did not collapse beneath his strong grip, because the air that passed through her throat was utilized for speaking purposes only. An experienced fighter would have yanked off his shirt and tried to wrap it around her thorax, covering her breathing spicules and smothering her. Never having fought a thranx before, the gang leader instinctively fell back on techniques that had been successful in battling other humans. In contrast with his ferocious but improvised efforts, the female was mature—and experienced.

While Chaloni held her suspended, she kicked out with all four feet, striking the gang leader square in the solar plexus. His eyes bugged—an apt simile under the circumstances—the air whooshed out of him, and he let go of her, clutching at his middle. Gathering herself, she jumped again, landing hard on top of him, this time with six feet. Though he was heavier and stronger, having to contend with eight thrashing, stabbing, kicking limbs while lying on his back and trying to catch his breath found Chaloni in more trouble than he would have believed possible.

All this occurred in barely a minute. By that time, Sallow Behdul and Subar had recovered enough from the initial shock to throw themselves into the fight. Rushing to Chaloni's aid, Behdul wrapped both long arms around the female thranx's abdomen and strained to pull her off. Holding on to the prone, scratched, and battered gang leader with truhands, foothands, and her front pair of feet, the female kicked backward with the rear pair. She wasn't strong enough to dislodge Behdul's grip, but her wild kicks to his middle and more vulnerable lower regions prevented him from concentrating fully on freeing his mentor.

Meanwhile Subar had gone to Zezula's aid. Seeing that Behdul was having little luck pulling Chaloni's attacker off him, the younger boy chose to stand off to one side and throw kicks at Zezula's assailant. He also struck out with his blade. Several slashes that would have opened the ribs of any human, however, only scratched the thranx's chitin before sliding off.

His repeated kicks had more effect. Slamming one foothand into Zezula's already injured face, the male stepped off away from her and turned his full attention onto Subar. Possessing nothing in the way of flexible flesh, the meter-and-a-half high insectoid's face was inherently expressionless. Light flashed from the lenses of his golden, red-banded compound eyes. His four opposing mandibles were spewing forth a steady stream of modulated angry clicks. Unintelligible alien words mixed with whistles of varying pitch and intensity. Doubtless, Subar thought as he crouched and sought an opening for his knife, the visitor was cursing him out in his own language. He would have countered with some colorful phrases of his own, but he was too busy and needed to conserve his wind.

The thranx, on the other hand, seemed to have air to spare. His thorax expanded and contracted as steadily and evenly as a gleaming metallic-blue bellows. Two truhands and two foothands wove patterns in the air in front of him, their combined sixteen digits alternately extending and flexing. Whether these represented words, phrases, or obscene gestures Subar did not know. Four trufeet kept the creature stable and well-balanced. As they confronted each other, it struck Subar that despite being smaller and less muscular, a thranx represented a formidable opponent.

There was something that might help, if only he could recall what it was. As his adversary took a wary step backward, Subar remembered. Charging, he jabbed forward with his knife, aiming for the joint between thorax and b-thorax. All four forward limbs came up to block the deadly thrust.

It was a feint, designed to let Subar slip in beneath the visitor's defenses. But he didn't try to stab a second time. Instead, wrapping both arms tightly around the thranx's lower thorax where it joined to the abdomen, he dug in with his feet and pushed. His knife fell from his fingers as his opponent kicked at it with a hind leg. Subar let it go, having realized that he was not going to penetrate his adversary's gleaming chitin with anything less than a vibrablade anyway.

Locked together, they stumbled off the path and onto the neatly trimmed russet-hued ground cover. Helped by the slope of the land, Subar continued to use his weight to lean into his opponent and force him backward. All four of the thranx's hands were striking at him now, the more delicate truhands jabbing at his eyes (he turned his head), the stronger foothands stabbing stiff, hard-shelled fingers into his midsection (he tightened his stomach muscles).

The repeated blows were having an effect, and it was likely that the thranx would soon have dropped him with more of the same. Except something that lay in the direction they were staggering and stumbling caused the thranx to panic.

The lake.

Having their air intakes located on a part of their body instead of on their faces as humans did made all but the most daring thranx extremely uncomfortable around water. The fact that their respiratory systems did not include disproportionately oversized internal air bladders akin to human lungs caused them tend to sink instead of float. Together, these two physical traits inculcated in nearly every thranx a very rational fear of drowning. If he could just force his adversary into the lake, Subar knew, the thranx would abandon any pretext at self-defense in his frantic need to get free. He had no intention of drowning the visitor. The objective had been to rob the visiting pair, not kill them. Preoccupied and even outright corrupt authorities who might be inclined to ignore a simple, straightforward boost tended to become very involved when a crime escalated to murder. Especially if representatives of another, visiting species were involved.

Energized by fear, the thranx had given up trying to injure his assailant with repeated kicks and was now using all six legs in an attempt to halt its backward motion. Only the smaller truhands still jabbed and poked at Subar's face and body. With six strong feet now clawing at the ground and providing desperate resistance, progress toward the lake slowed. They were very close to the water, Subar saw. Once the thranx felt his rear legs sliding in, his defiance might collapse. A little help, and Subar was sure the fight would come to a rapid and favorable end.

"Zezula!" he shouted without turning his head, needing to keep an eye on his opponent. Despite her broken nose, if she could just lend her weight to the effort, together they would have the thranx half submerged in no time. "Give me a hand! Just—help push! Zezula?"

He decided to risk a look behind him. His jaw dropped.

Zezula was indeed moving fast—in the opposite direction. Blood still streaming from her face, she was hanging on to Chaloni's right arm as the two of them stumbled toward the cover of the thick native brush from which they had originally emerged. The gang leader held tightly to his recovered weapon but made no attempt to use it. Sallow Behdul was loping along behind them, occasionally glancing backward. Only once did he happen to meet Subar's gaze. As he fled, the only visible hurt on the bigger boy was to be found in his expression. Of Dirran and the foot-dragging Missi, there was no sign.

They'd left him, every one of them.

Everything that had so shockingly and unexpectedly gone wrong with Chaloni's carefully planned boost now accelerated. Unable to force the thranx in whose embrace he now found himself into the nearby water, Subar also discovered that he was unable to free himself. Behind him, the female had not only recovered her poise, but had also recovered her strength and was limping determinedly in her companion's direction. Deep inside Subar, fright began to replace fight. Frantic now, he fought to free himself from the grasp of the thranx whom moments ago he had been gripping as tightly as possible. Truhands would not have held Subar, but seeing his companion intact and coming up behind the young human, the male thranx lifted his foothands off the ground and used them to grab the boy around the waist.

Reaching out with one hand, Subar tried to seize one of his opponent's sensitive, feathery antennae. Reacting defensively, the thranx slapped them both flat against the top of his head. Subar's swipe gathered only air. At the same time, a front leg slammed sideways into the boy's right ankle. Had a human executed the blow, it would have been described as a skillful judo move.

Feeling himself going down, Subar forgot everything he had learned about street fighting. Laboriously acquired techniques were useless against adversaries whose vulnerable parts lay elsewhere on and within their bodies, and whose exterior was composed of a natural armor. Then the female arrived. Together, the two thranx began pummeling and kicking him. Their irate whistling and clicking filled his ears.

Swinging and kicking wildly, he landed a lucky blow when one of his closed fists made contact with the male's right eye. That at least was both vulnerable and unarmored. Letting out a shrieking whistle, the thranx momentarily drew back. It was enough to allow Subar to regain his feet. But the female was on his back, clinging to him with all eight limbs, refusing to allow her remaining assailant his freedom. An assaulted human would have been relieved to have escaped. Something in thranx nature, or maybe in just these individuals, demanded greater satisfaction.

Swinging and spinning, he was unable to land a solid blow. Though she massed less than he did, her weight was enough to keep him from breaking into a run. Meanwhile the male was recovering from the blow to his eye and was stumbling forward to rejoin the fight.

"All right, all right!" Subar howled. "That's enough! Let go of me and I'll go, I'll go!"

The female alternately whistled, clicked her mandibles, and chattered in his ear. Some of it was nothing more than noise to him, some of it must have been Low Thranx, and despite his exhaustion and fear he thought he also caught some terranglo. Only one word was short and taut enough for him to make out for certain.

"No!"

The park offered a visual respite from the emotional cacophony in which he was drowning, a sore and weary Flinx reflected, but not a mental one. He had spent the entire previous night in a state of emotional overload, wandering the streets of the city—some mean, some accommodating, none particularly attractive—without any destination other than exhaustion in mind. Having reached that, he had stumbled onward, only to find himself on the outskirts of Ballora just prior to sunrise. The park being much closer than his hotel, and no public transportation being within immediate range of his sight or hearing, he had considered using his communicator to call for a vehicle, only to finally pass on the notion with a mental shrug. From the pedestrian walkway he had followed a designated turnoff into the cool, silent confines of the vast public recreational space. Perhaps within its damp depths, he had mused unenthusiastically, he might encounter an emotion or two that would prove uplifting instead of generally depressing.

What he eventually stumbled upon, both physically and mentally, was a situation as unusual as it was unexpected.

At first his wide-open mind had perceived only more of the same common, depressing emotions, albeit less of them. The same general feelings of despair, of despondency, of anger and envy and paranoia that afflicted the very few late-night and, later, early-morning visitors to the park. What little hope and inspiration was present came from the park's nonhuman inhabitants. The emotions they projected were at once infinitely simpler and more straightforward than those of the wandering simians he was compelled to call his cousins. Some flying creature projected nothing but subtle feelings of great joy at finding a bit of food, while a ground dweller's atavistic delight in finishing the digging of a small tunnel shone like a tiny star amid the cesspool of bitterness and jealousy that radiated from a trio of drunken humans.

Perhaps it would have been better, he thought as he struggled to work through the morass of mental misery that threatened to overwhelm him, to have been born a genetically altered animal instead of a human.

That was when a burst of emotion flooded through him that was more powerful than anything he had felt since leaving the hotel. It was stronger than anything he had encountered on the busy streets, more dynamic and forceful than the loud confrontation between a woman and her lover whom he had stumbled past sometime after midnight. Halting, he strained to locate the source.

At first all was fury and bloodlust jumbled up with fear. Fear, he noted with a mixture of interest and anxiety, that bubbled up from a pair of nonhuman sources. As he altered his route to track them down, the latter changed slowly and methodically from fear to determination. A lull in the emotional brew gave way with stunning swiftness to a flash outpouring of conflicting feelings in which fear, terror, anger, desperation, determination, and a raft of other complex emotions surged upward, crashing into and through one another like storm waves on a rocky coast. By now he had positively identified two of the sources as thranx. As he increased his pace Pip took off, tired of bouncing on his shoulder.

Improvising a shortcut through a hedgeline of carefully maintained decorative undergrowth, he emerged to find himself confronting by far the most singular scene he had set eyes upon since arriving on this miserable world. Directly in front of him a youth was struggling in the grasp of two thranx. Though none of them was armed, a simple blade lay on the ground nearby. One moment the youth appeared to be struggling to reach it, the next he was slumping in the multilimbed grasp of his opponents.

Off to the left, a group of youngsters were disappearing into a wall of dense park vegetation. Signs of a larger struggle were evident in the disturbed surface of the ground cover, a single but deep blast-mark on the winding, paved walkway, and the presence of blood in several places. Only human blood, he noted. If the bodily integrity of one of the thranx had been compromised, a lot more blood would be present; once violated, their open circulatory systems tended to gush profusely.

Though no further confirmation of the confrontation that had taken place was necessary, it was present in the still hyper emotions of both those fleeing and the three still engaged in combat before him.

This was none of his business, he knew, though the involvement of thranx both puzzled and intrigued him. He hesitated, and even retreated a step back into the bushes. What finally persuaded him to do otherwise were the emotions spilling out of the young man sandwiched between the two active thranx. There was fear, yes, and anger, but more significantly, more involvingly, there was a youthful desperation, a hopelessness tinged with a burning desire to succeed, that reminded him of someone else he had once been intimately familiar with. Someone he had known a long time ago.

Himself, at the same age.

Besides, he chided himself as he strode determinedly forward, had he not made a life out of sticking his nose into other people's business? Why change, why act rationally now, just because he found himself on yet another world, confronted by yet another crisis that had nothing to do with him?

If nothing else, he decided sardonically, saving this kid should prove easier than trying to save civilization. And in the end, wasn't it all one and the same thing?

"Hey!" As he approached, he held up both hands, palm outward, to show that he was not armed. Gliding overhead on the warming air of morning, Pip gave the lie to that apparent declaration, but it was unlikely that either the struggling youth or the two thranx noticed her. Even if they should, Flinx doubted they would be familiar with the nature of a visiting Alaspinian minidrag.

His own sudden appearance was surprising enough. All three combatants ceased their struggling as he came toward them. But the thranx did not let go of the younger human. Three sets of eyes focused on the slender approaching figure.

Even in his exhaustion and distress, Subar managed to frown uncertainly at the tall youth coming toward him. Definitely not a cop, he decided. Not even undercover. Older than himself, but still young. Not park maintenance, didn't have the air of officialdom about him. So what the hell was he doing? Stumbling onto an ongoing conflict in their midst, any sensible citizen of Malandere would have given it a wide berth. This stranger was heading straight toward one, waving his arms and—smiling. He did not look drunk or drugged, either. It made no sense. Out of the corner of an eye, Subar noted the presence of an unfamiliar flying creature circling overhead. After taking initial notice, he paid no further attention. The new arrival was now close enough to speak without shouting.

The thranx who had battled their way out of the ambush gone awry were no less wary of him. Wary, but not fearful. For one thing, this new human was noticeably older than those who had attacked them. For another, he was manifestly not armed. And lastly, his mouth-flaps were curved upward at the corners in a sign betokening friendship.

Then he spoke to them, and they both relaxed. Though not to the point of letting go of their remaining assailant, who continued to struggle futilely in their many-limbed grasp.

Drivel, Subar thought. The longsong was speaking drivel. Or so he thought, until first one of his adversaries and then the other responded with matching drivel of their own. His opinion of the newcomer changed drastically. When communicating with thranx, the great majority of humans spoke terranglo, which their chitinous allies could speak well. In contrast, it was an unusual human indeed who could converse with them in their own language. And in the case of this stranger, not merely converse, but do so fluently. Without looking, it was impossible to distinguish the newcomer's drivel from that being clicked and whistled by the two bugs. Subar would have been even more astonished had he known enough to realize that the stranger was speaking High Thranx, utilizing his hands as well as his mouth to communicate.

If Subar was astonished, the thranx were at least surprised.

Having furnished a terse explanation of what had taken place, the female demanded harshly—but respectfully—of Flinx, "Why should we let this thief go? We would not do so with one of our own. He deserves to be turned over to the authorities to face appropriate punishment."

Flinx considered. "I sense mitigating circumstances within him."

The two thranx exchanged a look. The male gestured expansively with both truhands. "You *sense*?"

Flinx hurriedly rephrased his comment. "Better to say that I recognize hope in his essence."

The female bent toward Subar. As he struggled against her, the white tips of her antennae brushed his forehead. "I recognize nothing in this human's face except dirt."

"Grant that I may be more perceptive, *rr!ilkt*. This post-pupa is, after all, of my kind."

"This one's 'kind' transcends species." The antipathy in the male's voice was as unmistakable as it was intentional.

"Nevertheless, I would appreciate it if you could see it in your hearts to grant him the clemency of the Hive. I ask this as one who is an honorary member of the clan Zex."

The thranx exchanged another hard look, accompanied by additional gestures employing both tru- and foothands. Trapped between them, Subar could not tell if they were conferring, arguing, or discussing the weather. Unable to free himself, he watched the stranger watching them. Why did this lanky stranger care what happened to him? Why had he intervened? Most important, what did he want? It did not occur to the youth that the newcomer might not want anything. For Subar, *altruism* was a term as alien to his existence as anything in High Thranx.

Something made the stranger suddenly turn sharply and look to his right, off to the north. Reflexively, Subar strained to see in the same direction. His verbal reaction was automatic.

"What is it, what do you see?"

"Park authorities coming." Flinx spoke without looking back at him. "Local police."

The announcement was enough to cause Subar to resume struggling. Though he had yet to sample the dubious delights of his hometown's juvenile restraining facilities, he had heard all too many tales of what life was like within its superficially sanitized walls. Sallow Behdul, for one, had spent time there. There were worse fates Subar could imagine than ending up like Behdul—but not many.

"I don't see any officials coming this way," the male commented. Both thranx were also staring in the same direction.

"Nor I," added the female uncertainly.

"I have a, uh, different vantage point," Flinx explained. He could hardly tell them that he could sense the approach of determined police long before they came into view, and that his exceptional perception had nothing to do with his height or his eyesight.

"*Prandahs*, let me *go!*" Subar cursed desperately. It was, ultimately, more of a cry than a demand.

A minute later the first municipal police could be seen heading toward the location of the abortive ambush. Traveling on individual transports, the dark dots rapidly resolved themselves into bipedal shapes. Turning her attention from the oncoming officials to the tall human, the female thranx addressed him intently.

"They are coming from well below that far rise. How did you see them approaching?"

Before Flinx could respond with a fresh evasion, he sensed a brief flash of murderous intent. All too familiar, it invariably presaged a more vivid physical response. As he ducked down behind the squirming youth and his pair of insectoid captors, the long-range shot that the quick flicker of emotion had foreshadowed singed the air where he had been standing a moment before.

Startled by the shot, which struck both thranx as auguring a conspicuous recklessness on the part of those humans ostensibly sent to rescue them, the pair momentarily released their grip on the remaining attacker. Not one to waste an opportunity, Subar threw all his remaining strength into a successful effort to break free. Under ordinary circumstances, he might have been expected to bolt immediately for the cover of the thick vegetation that fringed the park. Instead he hesitated, clearly torn between what he knew he should do and what he felt he ought to do. The latter, imperfect feeling was enhanced by a powerful curiosity as to the nature, origin, and motives of the newcomer who had interceded on his behalf.

Concerned that the only remaining potentially dangerous aspect of their present situation involved overzealous human police firing indiscriminately in their direction, both thranx dropped to their tru-legs and began waving all sixteen manipulative digits in the direction of the oncoming officers. Able to vocalize as clearly but not as loudly as humans, their shouted insistence that they were unharmed and okay was not immediately heard by their would-be saviors. Seeing the thranx they had come to assist scampering toward them, how-ever, did cause those officers in the front rank to slow their personal transports to check on the health of the two visitors.

Without the proverbial moment to lose, Subar came to a deci-sion. Reaching out, he grabbed Flinx's left arm and pulled.

"Come on, come on! We've got to sky out of here!"

The bright green eyes that met Subar's own were full of toler-ance. That, and something else. Muffled amusement, perhaps.

"You mean, *you* have to get out of here." As Flinx spoke, he raised a hand. This caused a rapidly descending Alaspinian minidrag to break off the power dive she had begun the instant the younger human had laid hands on her master. She circled nearby, restless and a bit bemused.

"No, no!" What was wrong with this person? Subar wondered frantically. Was it possible he didn't know *anything*?

"The alarm the bugs set off will show that they were attacked by a bunch of young humans. You're a young human."

The amusement in Flinx's eyes vanished. "The thranx will ex-plain to them that I—"

"*After* you've been put down and taken into custody for ques-tioning," Subar interrupted him, still pulling on the visitor's arm. "If they don't shoot you first." He looked anxiously to his left, where the first police to arrive had halted and were now conversing with the two thranx. "The cops here have a tendency to shoot first and ask questions—"

"I've heard it before." It was Flinx's turn to cut the youngster off. He, too, found himself staring in the direction of police and thranx. Maybe the youth was right. Better to let the thranx explain exactly what had happened. Give the local police a chance to calm down and digest the official report. Besides which, the last thing he wanted or needed was to be held in custody while the Visarian authorities ran a background check on him. His current alias might well withstand their probing—but why take the chance? Especially when a city like Malandere offered a plethora of opportunities to avoid such unwanted attention.

Also, he was no less weary than when he had first entered the park. The fleeting surge of adrenaline he had experienced upon interposing himself into the human–thranx confrontation had now faded. As fatigued as he was, from both ongoing mental strain and lack of sleep, he couldn't think straight. And his head was pounding.

As much for the novelty of it as out of a desire to take flight, he decided to allow the boy to take him where he would. He was convinced it could be no more depressing or disillusioning than any other environment he had encountered on Visaria. Might as well go along with this youth as wander aimlessly through town on his own, he decided.

In his rest-deprived, fatigue-addled state, he could not quite rationalize his decision. A reason would come to him soon enough, he was convinced. For now, it would be enough simply to move on, in search of further enlightenment—and sleep.

CHAPTER

5

Gazing down at the slender, slumbering shape, Subar badly wanted to rummage through the contents of the service belt the young man wore. Not only was it fashioned of the latest and most durable material, but its bulging pouches hinted at the presence of all manner of readily salable gear secured within. There was also a medipak of a manufacture he did not recognize. Oddly, the dozing visitor's attire was of a design and material that was purely utilitarian. Its simplicity and lack of interwoven or add-on adornment contrasted markedly with the tantalizing hints of expensive equipment attached to the belt.

It all added up to a puzzling and possibly profitable challenge. Exploring or profiting from it further would have to await the visitor's return to consciousness. In the meantime, Subar had determined to leave him and his goods alone. Not out of a sudden surge of selflessness, not because his morals had undergone an abrupt seismic shift, but because deep-seated instinct told him that if he tried to unfasten so much as a single pouch on that tempting belt, the colorful winged demon coiled on the visitor's chest might raise a violent objection to said course of action. Ignorant of both the creature's taxonomy and its possible potential for wreaking grief, Subar sensibly decided to keep his distance.

Turning away, he moved to a window and brushed his hand across the surface. Reading his DNA, the material recognized him as one of those authorized to give it commands. Atoms within obediently realigned, and the dark rectangle promptly turned transparent.

Outside the makeshift hideaway, the decaying rooftops of Alewev District stretched off into the distance. A pall of chemical fog too persistent to be wholly banished by the city's secondhand atmospheric cleansers turned sunlight to saffron. Since being led to the priv place by Subar, the visitor had barely managed to mumble a dispirited "thanks" before collapsing on one of the bunks. The flying creature had immediately settled itself onto its owner's sternum, a place of resting—and watchfulness—from which it had not stirred since.

It was now late afternoon. If the visitor didn't wake soon, he was liable to sleep on into the evening and wake after sunset only to find his biological clock in need of still another reset. Subar was determined to rouse his guest, not least because he wanted to learn more about him before someone like Dirran or Chaloni showed up, monopolized the conversation—and saw the same possibilities he did.

But how? Every time he drew near, the dozing flying creature would open an eye in his direction. Was it poisonous? Did it have other capabilities he knew nothing about? It was not a matter of wishing he had paid more attention in school. Subar had never gone to school. He'd been too busy working at the business of survival. Occasionally, when time and life and other occupants permitted, he would attempt to access information via the battered terminal at the main house. He dared not spend too much time on a free public terminal lest the activity be noticed by his friends, who would then tease him unmercifully. It wasn't that he didn't *want* to know. He just did not know how to safely go about it.

Though it was unlikely, he reflected as he stood staring at the lanky figure snoozing away on the fraying, salvaged lounge, maybe this visitor had an idea or two about how someone like himself could go about the proper gathering of information. One never knew about strangers.

That was more wishful thinking than realistic assumption, he decided. Though older than himself, the stranger was much too young to have acquired anything noteworthy in the way of knowledge or experience.

Still, Subar was curious about him. That curiosity could not be satisfied while the visitor remained comatose. He considered how best to proceed. He'd already tried waking him gently. The stranger had slept through each of Subar's successively louder entreaties. An actual shout had roused the flying creature to open both eyes and raise its head. Its pointed stare was enough to persuade Subar that additional screaming was not a good idea. And if loud noises were enough to trigger the colorful creature's protective instincts, it did not take a genius to realize that physically shaking the stranger was undoubtedly a worse idea.

How then to rouse his guest? What manner of intercession would the scaly little monster tolerate? At any moment Chaloni or Dirran or even the girls might show up at the makeshift, clandestine meeting room. He had to take a chance.

Turning, he walked over to the crude but functioning illegal water tap Sallow Behdul had punched through the wall and filled one of the half-dirty glasses stacked nearby. Keeping one eye on the glass and the other on the flying creature, he sipped. Both small, slitted eyes remained closed. After a couple of minutes of this, they opened sharply and unexpectedly. It was almost as if the small flying thing knew what Subar intended. If so, it was either too slow or too uncertain as to the youth's motives to intervene in time.

From childhood Subar had displayed a strong arm and excellent aim. The half glass of city water struck the sleeping stranger square in the face. His reptilian guardian unfurled her dampened wings in a blaze of blue and pink. But before she could take to the air, Flinx had sat up and was rubbing water from his eyes. It did not appear to the tense, ready-to-bolt Subar as if the stranger said anything to his pet, but the latter refolded her wings and slithered off his torso without attacking. While she relaxed to one side, licking droplets from herself with her pointed tongue, Flinx sat up and swung his legs off the bed. Still wiping at his face, he eyed his circumspect assailant. His expression was half ire, half grin.

"What did you do that for?"

Taking heart, Subar also took a step forward. "I've been wanting to talk to you, but it looked like you were going to sleep all day." Still wary, he indicated the grooming minidrag. "Your animal wouldn't let me near you."

Flinx nodded knowingly. "Her name's Pip. She's an Alaspinian minidrag, or flying snake. She's very protective of me."

"*Tsha,* that's the truth. I had to try something. Since words wouldn't wake you, a little cold water seemed the next most harmless thing to try." He jabbed a thumb into his chest. "I'm Subar. I saved you from the police."

Dragging an arm across his face to wipe up lingering drops, Flinx blinked at his bedraggled surroundings. "I kind of remember it as being the other way around. Where are we? I remember taking public transport, and I remember stumbling in here, but I didn't pay much attention to much of anything else. I was *tired.*"

"Tired?" Subar made a face. "*Tchai,* you were opting *cataleptic.* Couple of times, I thought you were going to fall asleep on me standing up. I think you were out before you went horizontal." He nodded tersely in the minidrag's direction. "I would've woken you sooner, but I couldn't take chances. Did I guess right? Is she dangerous?"

"Only when she needs to be." Clear-eyed again, Flinx eyed his host.

"And you?" Subar asked boldly.

"Me? No, I'm not dangerous. I'm too mixed up to be dangerous to anybody except myself."

Crossing his arms, Subar leaned back against a battered cabinet. Inside were two guns. He saw no reason to apprise his guest of their presence.

"What do you do?"

"You're a straightforward one." Flinx yawned. "I'm a student."

"*Tsai?* What do you study?"

"Everything," Flinx informed his host without a hint of guile.

Oh *shatet,* Subar thought. A dilettante. A philosoph. Useless. Maybe it would have been better to have left the tall target for the trigger-happy Malandere police.

On the other hand, the stranger *had* saved him from the determined grasp of the two thranx and, by reasonable inference, from the loutish attention of those selfsame municipal enforcers. There was also, Subar reminded himself, the distinct possibility that the visitor was lying. Most people possessed ample lying skills. He did not know nearly enough about the visitor to be able to estimate his capabilities in that discipline. But the longsong was no lifter, no Qwarm, no emoman. And certainly no undercover authority figure. This Flinx radiated an odd mixture of confidence and confusion, wisdom and ignorance. Subar felt a little better about his visitor.

"Why did you sky me from the bugs?"

Flinx spoke without looking at his youthful inquisitor. "You reminded me of someone I knew once. Also, at the time I intervened, you might say I was slumming in despair. Helping you gave me something to do. Call it whatever you will. A desire for momentary focus. A jolt of intravenous altruism. A bad attack of what-the-hell."

Subar did his best to affect an air of studied indifference. "Good luck for me. Though I would have slipped the bugs by myself anyway."

"Uh-huh, sure you would." Flinx nodded and tried not to smile.

"The thranx aren't big, and they're not particularly strong, but chitin is harder to push against than muscle, and to my way of calculating a grip of thirty-two digits beats ten every time."

"Okay, okay, *tshai!*" Unsettled by Flinx's perception, Subar turned away. "So maybe it was a good thing that you came along, with nothing better to do." He looked back. "At first I thought you were drunk. Or elevated."

"I was suffering from lack of sleep," Flinx explained. "And, um, emotional excess."

"Oh." Subar was suddenly sympathetic. "Y chromo trouble, huh?"

This time Flinx had to stifle a grin. "No, not exactly."

"What then? You just an emotional kind of guy?"

The grin vanished. "You have no idea, Subar."

Nodding, the youth moved closer. This time the flying snake did not even look up in his direction. It was as though she could instinctively distinguish between inoffensiveness and a genuine threat. At the moment, he did not take the time to wonder how.

"So, *tsa,* Mr. Flinx—where you from?"

Rising, Flinx moved in the direction of the cabinet. Subar tensed, but his visitor's goal was only the side window and the view it offered of the rooftops beyond.

"Just Flinx. I'm from offworld."

"Well *tsai,* as if I couldn't figure that," Subar sniffed condescendingly.

"My homeworld is a place called Moth." There was a wistfulness in Flinx's voice that even someone Subar's age could not miss.

"Never heard of it. I know Terra and Hivehom and some of the other major worlds, but I never heard of a place called Moth."

Flinx's gaze roved the rooftops. The city was awake, but for some reason the deluge of emotions flaring from its frenetic citizenry hammered less heavily against his sensitive inner self than they had the day before. It wasn't that his system had become acclimated. To the best of his knowledge and experience, such a thing was not possible. But the previous day's reckless, full-out immersion had toughened him somewhat against its effects.

"Moth's a minor world. Pretty place, though. Went back for a quick visit not too long ago. Didn't stay long." Turning, he looked back at Subar, and for a startling instant the youth felt as if his visitor were looking right through him. "I like to move around."

Like to move around—or have to? Subar wondered, fixing his guest with the shrewd gaze of a survivor. Maybe he had been too hasty in his judgment of this longsong. Maybe they had more in common than he'd first suspected. Despite his visitor's reticence, there were ways of drawing such things out.

Unintentionally, Flinx helped. "I've told you about myself. What *do* you do?"

"*Tschu,* for one thing, I'm no student!"

"Yes, I can see that." Flinx's flat tone and neutral expression made it impossible for Subar to tell if this crisp response constituted agreement or insult.

"I make my own way," the youth continued proudly. "Plenty of others can't. Malandere, and especially Alewev District, where we are now, is too much for them. They end up begging on the streets, or dancing the custody revolve, or candidates for selective mindwipe."

"But not you," Flinx murmured appraisingly. "You do whatever you have to do in order to survive."

Subar blinked. It was not the kind of response one expected from an offworlder. Although, he reflected as he regarded his guest in a new light, for all the strange look in his eyes, this Flinx was not all that much older than himself. Could it be, perhaps, that he was also not all that much different? Or did the tall stranger mean to suggest something else?

"You'd better not be making fun of me," he muttered warningly.

Flinx smiled. "I wouldn't dare." He started toward the door. Subar moved quickly to intercept him.

"Wait! I—I'd like to talk some more." He forced a smile of his own. "It isn't every day I'm slipped from the system by an off-worlder."

As Pip hummed over to land on his shoulder, Flinx looked back at his host. "Maybe you do want to talk. But what you really want is to figure out a way to get hold of my service belt and disappear down the nearest alley with it."

The smile stayed on Subar's face, but his insides gave a little jump. "Don't be crazed! You saved me from those thranx, and from the police. Why would I do something like that?"

"To 'make your own way.' Hey, don't look so outraged. When I was your age, I did things to survive that I'm less than proud of today."

For a moment, Subar considered holding fast to his denial. It would do no good, he saw. His guest was far too—too what? Perceptive? Or something more? "What did you do—read my mind?"

The tall offworlder chuckled. "No. Not even your emotions. Your eyes. Every other second, especially when you thought I wasn't looking, they were fastened on my gear. Greed is a tantrum of the face. You'd make a poor gamester. You need to look away from your target, not at it."

Flinx caught himself. What was he doing, giving that kind of advice to a strange youth? For a moment he had reverted to the wily adolescent who had haunted the streets of Drallar, on Moth, always keeping an eye out for an easy dishonest mark or any other advantage that could be turned his way. After everything he had been through over the past ten years, it was something of a shock to find that he could slip so easily back into old ways.

Something of a shock, yes—but not wholly unpleasant.

"I can't stay," he told his bemused but energetic young host.

"Why not? Just for a little while longer. Just to answer some questions," Subar pleaded with him. When his guest shrugged and turned again toward the doorway, the fast-thinking youth raised his voice. "Where do you have to go in such a hurry? You have to save the galaxy, or something?"

Flinx's hand halted halfway to the door's jury-rigged activation panel. Subar's comment was simultaneously stunning in its incongruous perceptiveness and breathtaking in its unknowing innocence. Flinx's spirit, which for an instant had regressed to a childhood dominated by poverty and carefreeness, was roughly wrenched forward to the present, with all the awesome burden of responsibility and knowledge it incorporated.

For the first time since he had sat up on the mattress, pain returned to the back of his head. It was joined by frustration, laced with a soupçon of anger. Though he said nothing, his expression and the look in his eyes were enough to cause Subar to take several hasty steps backward.

What did I say? the youth wondered. It was as if he had somehow touched more than a nerve. His guest had undergone a sudden transformation from amiable longsong to something much deeper and darker. Something haunted those dark green eyes. Meeting the offworlder's gaze without flinching, he tried to see if he could find a clue as to what it might be.

It reached out and touched him.

It was unintentional on Flinx's part. He hadn't meant to project. Certainly not what he was thinking about. Only a sliver of what he had seen and experienced; of his past decade, of things whose existence very few sentients were even aware of, was projected onto the youth standing before him.

Subar was tough, Subar was self-reliant, Subar had been through a great deal in his young life.

Subar screamed.

"It's all right, it's all right!" Reflexively, Flinx moved to comfort the younger man.

Subar had retreated until he was backed up against the old cabinet. One hand clawed blindly for the recog panel that would open at his touch. A gun. He had to get a gun, had to kill this *thing* looming before him.

Something else flowed out of Flinx. Reassurance, a gentling, a calm born of long practice and much meditation undertaken during long passages between the stars. Subar's fingers relaxed, stopped fumbling at the front of the cabinet. His breathing slowed, returned to normal. The bottomless dark that had filled the longsong's eyes had gone away, to be replaced by a caring and understanding that arose from other, less traumatic experiences.

"I'm sorry." Flinx held out both hands to the younger man. "I didn't mean for that to happen, for you to perceive that. I was upset. Not at you: at something within myself. It was something I couldn't prevent. It was an accident."

Swallowing hard, Subar took a wary step away from the cabinet. "What happened? How did you do that? I felt—I felt . . ." He could not put what he had felt into words, and said so.

Flinx turned away slightly. "Don't feel a lack. The most venerable philosophs couldn't put it into words. It's beyond words. It's something that's at once within and outside me."

For the second time that morning Subar saw his guest in a new light. Only this time, it was not as a potential victim, but as someone to feel sorry for. That was quaint. Him, feeling sorry for this well-off, well-traveled offworlder. If he had only been made privy to a tiny bit of what hid inside this pitiable longsong, then . . .

He preferred not to pursue that particular line of speculation any farther.

It was an unfamiliar situation. He was used to dividing up the world into friend and foe. The idea that a total stranger, and a most peculiar offworlder at that, could be something else, something different—not friend, but not enemy, either—was totally new.

Could he be, perhaps, somehow useful? Being in the longsong's company, he decided, was akin to walking around with a large bomb. It gave him something to threaten others with, but at any moment it might also go off in his hand. Was it a chance he dared risk taking? Making his determination a lot more complicated was the fact that the bomb had an agenda of its own.

"I should go." Flinx turned to do so, the minidrag riding on his left shoulder, her tail coiled around the back of his neck.

"Wait, please . . ." Again Subar tried to restrain the visitor, only this time with a different purpose in mind. It was no use. Flinx opened the door. As it swung wide, Pip lifted her head and hissed sharply.

The portal was already occupied.

Visitor and newcomers eyed each other appraisingly. *"Tchoul,"* a surprised Chaloni murmured as he looked the offworlder up and down. "Who, or what, is this?" Flanking him, Dirran and Sallow Behdul let their hands slide in the direction of concealed weapons. Flinx regarded the trio calmly.

Subar crowded close behind him, struggling to make himself seen as well as heard. *"Laze,* Chal! He's pure lucid, he's a friend."

The gang leader ignored the younger boy's hurried assertions. His attention remained fixed on Flinx. "You brought him *here*? To our priv space?"

Still fighting for room in the narrow portal, a deferential Subar pleaded his case. "I told you; he's lucid. He skyed me clear of the bugs—and away from the police." Demonstrating a shrewd knowledge of the intricacies of mature diplomacy, he tactfully refrained from reminding Chaloni and the others that they were the ones who had abandoned him to that potential fate. "How's Zezula—and Missi?"

The gang leader weighed his follower's words, his voice a soft murmur. If he detected anything more in Subar's tone than formal concern for Zezula, he didn't show it. "They're still at Kolindu's clinic, getting patched up. Every time Zez feels her nose, she wants to go out and kill the first bug she sees." His hard gaze rose to meet Flinx's quiet stare. "How about you, longsong? How you feel about killing bugs?"

Unlike with Subar, Flinx perceived that there was nothing am-
bivalent about the one the younger boy had called Chal. Had he been
the one caught in the grasp of the fighting thranx, Flinx would not
have raised a hand to help him. The emotions that flowed forth from
him embodied everything Flinx had come to despise in his own kind:
greed, selfishness, a nasty delight in the discomfiture of others, a raw
craving for power, and more. His two companions were little better,
with the larger of the pair possibly being an exception. The bulky
youth's emotions were as flat and dull as the rest of him.

Subar, now—there might be some hope for Subar. And if there
was hope for him, perhaps also for the rest of civilization, insofar as
Flinx's further involvement with its uncertain future was concerned.

As one hand slipped into a pocket, Chaloni took a step into the
room. "I asked you how you feel about killing bugs, scrawn."

Flinx had to put up a hand to restrain Pip, whose perception of
the gang leader was no less exact than that of her master. "Depends
on where they are."

Chaloni halted, perplexed and trying not to show it. "'Where'?
What do you mean, 'where'?"

"Whether they're in my gut, my bed, my food, or my head."

Dirran laughed. It was more of a sharp expectoration, like spit,
than a sincere chuckle. Chaloni hesitated, then found himself smiling. "True, true. Spoken like someone who's had plenty of experience of both." A glint of light bounced off the cylindrical device he
withdrew from his pocket. Gray and tapered, it was not sharp. It did
not have to be.

"You know what this is, scrawn longsong?" Chaloni was clearly
enjoying himself.

Flinx nodded slowly. "Sonic stiletto."

The gang leader pushed out his lower lip, his expression and tone
approving. "You *have* had some experience. So you know the wave
form it emits will punch through almost anything." He flicked the tip

in the direction of Flinx's shoulder. "Including that wingthing weighing down your neck, if it tries to bite me."

"Pip doesn't bite," Flinx informed him truthfully. "Neither do I."

"That remains to be decided, doesn't it?" Chaloni started forward.

Internally, Subar was a mass of conflicting emotions. If he didn't react to intercede on behalf of the visitor, Chaloni was surely going to cut him—if only to demonstrate that he could. If he *did* try to talk the bigger, older youth out of the hostile, Chaloni would not forget whose side Subar had taken. Unable to decide what to do, he did nothing. Let the visitor get himself out of it, if he could. Chaloni wasn't angry—he just wanted to make a point. He probably wouldn't cut the stranger bad.

Then a strange thing happened. Chaloni stopped. Just stopped, as if he had run into an invisible wall. There was no wall: Subar could tell that much when Sallow Behdul advanced beyond where the gang leader was standing. Then he, too, halted. Both boys started twitching slightly, as if afflicted with sudden chills. They were joined by Dirran a moment later. Mouth agape, Subar leaned forward to glance up at the visitor. Flinx's eyes were half closed but otherwise fixed on his would-be assailants. He, too, looked paralyzed.

No, not paralyzed, Subar corrected himself. Deep in thought. He considered asking his guest what was going on. Realizing that for the moment he, at least, was *not* twitching, the younger boy wisely decided to keep quiet and out of the way.

Normally, the emotions that filled Flinx to bursting stayed caged within him. Everything that had happened to him from an early age to the present—every experience, every disappointment, every confrontation and conflict to which he had been a participant, every iota of misery and unhappiness, of death and destruction, of malevolence and pure evil—remained put down and locked up in one small section of his mind he had reserved for that purpose. Now he let those emotions out. Just a trickle, the tiniest seep of forlorn despair. Let them out and projected them onto the emotional receptors of the three young men standing before him. He was very careful about how wide he opened the emotive tap. He did not want to kill.

Tears began to leach from the corners of Chaloni's eyes. His lips trembled like a little girl's. His fingers went limp and the stiletto fell from his hand. It had not been activated or it would have cut its way through successive floors all the way down to the ground before its built-in safety finally shut it off. Chaloni started to sob. Pressing his clenched fists against his eyes, he began hammering against them as he dropped to his knees. To his right, Dirran was lying on the floor crying, holding himself, and rocking back and forth. On the other side of the gang leader, Sallow Behdul had not made a sound. Instead, he sat down, curled up into a tight fetal ball, and began sucking softly on the knuckles of his huge right hand.

Subar discovered that his throat had gone dry. "What—what did you do to them?"

"Nothing much." Flinx's eyes were once more fully open. "Gave them the tiniest taste of dark water."

Careful to avoid the glaze-eyed, blankly staring Behdul, Subar stepped forward and pivoted to confront his guest. "I didn't see any water."

The thinnest of smiles creased Flinx's face. "I turned it off. Listen, I'm pretty rested. Thanks for showing me your 'place.'" He started to push past the staring youth, heading for the exit.

Subar's thoughts moved as fast as they ever had in his life. Somehow this offworlder, this Flinx, had put down the three toughest members of Subar's acquaintance without laying a finger on any of them. It reminded him of another inexplicable moment; of what the visitor had done to him earlier. Something from within, the stranger had told him. It was, it had to be, some kind of trick. But what kind? And if he was right, could his guest possibly teach it to him? Useful—oh yes, the tall longsong could be useful. If he was going to learn anything, Subar knew he still had to figure out a way to keep Flinx around.

"This isn't my place," he announced hurriedly.

Pausing in the portal, Flinx peered back at him. "It's not?"

"No, no. It's just our priv space, where we get together to, uh, socialize."

And plan muggings, and who knew what else. Flinx had been there before. Other times, other worlds. All of them equally disheartening.

Taking the unknown by the know-nothing, Subar ignored his still-sobbing friends and rushed forward a couple of steps until he was standing in front of Flinx. "C'mon. Let me show you my place. You might find it interesting. It might make some things clearer to you."

Flinx hesitated. "I told you—I can't stay."

Steeling himself in case whatever had touched him previously reached across the gap separating him from his visitor to touch him again, Subar entreated as earnestly as he could.

"I don't know what it is that you want here, but if I can help, I will. Because you saved me from the police," he lied.

Flinx knew the youth was lying. As long as his erratic Talent was functioning, he could always tell when someone was lying. But there was something else there, something more. A hunger that went beyond the simple simian emotions that had boiled blatantly within the minds of Chaloni and his companion hooligans. Was he right about the youth? Was there, after all, some hope for one who reminded him of himself, and by inference for the greater humankind whose final fate he might hold in the balance? If so, it behooved him to find out.

Besides, he could as easily take the measure of the melancholic inhabitants of Visaria in Subar's company as he could by his dejected lonesome. What was calling him away so insistently? His nondescript hotel room? Why not spend a little downtime in the youth's company? If he couldn't please himself, Flinx mused, he could for a little while at least provide some small measure of gratification to this aimless, befuddled adolescent.

"Okay," he heard himself saying. "I'll stick around a little longer. So you can show me your place."

"*Tscheks!*" an obviously pleased Subar exclaimed. "You can save the galaxy, or whatever it is you have to do, later."

"Sure," Flinx replied agreeably and without elaboration. "No hurry."

Subar took a step down the rooftop accessway, then hesitated, looking back at his bawling friends. "What about them?"

Flinx considered. "Do you really care?"

Subar's gaze rose from his mysteriously afflicted companions to his enigmatic new one. Was this a trick question? The offworlder, he was by now convinced, was like a neutron star full of tricks—compressed down and packed tight and ready to explode in his face if he took one wrong step or said one wrong word. He could sense that by trying to think of the "right" reply, he was taking too long to say it.

"Yes," he blurted. It must have been the right response. Or at least, not a wrong one.

"They'll come out of it sometime tonight," Flinx assured him, "and they'll never know what happened to them."

Subar was not the only youth present, he reflected as he followed the boy outside the rooftop hideaway and down the accessway, who could lie a little when it suited his purposes.

CHAPTER

6

It was surreptitious contacts that led to Shyvil Theodakris being given his original appointment, and the clandestine manipulation of bits and bytes of history that had allowed him to rise to his present position. That acknowledged, many of those whose participation in his advancement had been crucial were retired, and some were dead.

Everyone involved, not least Theodakris himself, was gratified by the outcome. Only peace and satisfaction had adhered to the analyst. His work had reflected well on all who had come in contact with him, and his role in advancing stability and progress in Malandere had been recognized by both his immediate superiors and the various city administrations that had come and gone during his successive terms of office. He and his supporters had every reason to be pleased with his contribution.

If Senior Situations Analyst Shyvil Theodakris had a fault, it was a predilection to personal vanity. The long hair that reached to his shoulders was both unnaturally lush and dark for a man of his advanced age—the result of multiple transplants and artificial enhancements. His attractively dyed eyes, one dark blue and the other bright yellow in the current style, were a consequence of astute chemical manipulation rather than an obscure genetic imbalance. Periodic melding of expensive skin appliqués hid naturally blooming liver spots and other signs of age.

For all his efforts, there was no mistaking his inherent maturity, though to the untrained eye and unknowing co-worker it was difficult to tell just by looking at him whether he was sixty or a hundred. The disparity was sufficiently great enough to justify his regular visits to an assortment of cosmetic manipulators who might as well have been on regular retainer.

This morning promised to be a good one. Chaos had reigned less than usual the previous night, resulting in a marked reduction in the number of cases he would be expected to peruse. Unless the details of one struck his fancy, he would give them the usual once-over before passing them on to subordinates for deeper analysis. Underlings would deal with the scutwork of breaking down each antisocial act into its relevant components. Other operatives at Authority Central would take these and employ them in an attempt to locate the perpetrators. Armed with these rapidly compiled individual dossiers, active forces would scan the municipality's various districts in the never-ending search for criminals and other antisocial elements.

The system was inherently organic in nature, Theodakris reflected as he settled into the chair facing the familiar blank wall. His body processed air and food. Authority Central processed clues and crimes. Both generated energy and waste products. At AC, these took the form of safer surroundings for law-abiding citizens and incarceration for society's transgressors.

It was his task, one at which he had grown extremely proficient over the years, to speed through the history of an entire crime and single out suggestive individual elements that subordinates might usefully pursue. Thanks to his early training as a genonaturalist, he had a talent for predicting how collaborators in crime were likely to act subsequent to the perpetration. This was an invaluable aid to police in the field. On more than one occasion, for example, he had been able to envisage how certain lawbreakers would respond in the aftermath of their actions, thus enabling the police to find them almost immediately. His modest privacy-screened cubicle boasted a wall crowded with awards while his personal civic sybfile was full of official commendations as well as heartfelt expressions of gratitude from ordinary citizens who had been the victims of crime, and whose assailants had been caught and successfully prosecuted thanks to Theodakris's efforts.

A few murmured codewords, a quick eyescan, and a pair of tridimensional images formed in front of him. The one on the left would unspool those events of the previous day that were deemed significant enough to justify his attention. The projection on the right would provide supplementary analysis, suggestions, opinions, the official reports of the officers involved in the relevant offense, and anything else department researchers thought might be pertinent to the particular case.

It was not a bad life, he mused as both projections filled the air before him. Leaning back in his lounge, he reflected on his unique good fortune as he absently studied the first images. He was a respected contributor to the success of a rapidly developing culture and an honored pillar of the community. Appreciably different from the fate that had been suffered by the rest of his colleagues, whose brave, youthful enthusiasms had been so violently rejected by an ignorant and immature galactic culture.

Within his department, a few hyperenergetic juniors had been pushing for him to retire. He saw no reason to do so. Ever active, his mind would only vegetate and wither in retirement. As long as he could contribute to the health of the Visarian culture that had accepted him, he would continue to do so.

It would help, though, he reflected as the coordinated projections flickered in front of him and he methodically scrutinized one case after another, if more than one wrongdoing every couple of days was of other than passing interest. So many of them replicated little more than the basest impulses of humankind, and were invariably perpetrated with less imagination and inventiveness than might be exhibited by a coterie of trained apes.

Store break-ins were accomplished with blunt objects and blunter minds. These affronts in search of merchandise invariably left behind cascades of clues, so many that his involvement seemed more a bureaucratic afterthought than an appropriate use of department resources. The solving of crimes of property tended to be as dull and business-like as their execution.

Of more interest were transgressions that involved emotion. A lover's spat turned to battery. Murders that evolved out of passion. Crimes of accident and opportunity rather than careful planning. These were where his knowledge of human cogitation and neural pathways were put to better use. Why did that woman kill her best friend? What prompted a good upstanding family man to suddenly abscond with his employer's cred and throw away his entire life? To what lengths would supposedly sophisticated people go to satisfy an urge as primitive and easily sated as simple lust?

Such musings and meldings as he scrolled patiently through the morning's offerings almost caused him to run matter-of-factly past the mugging incident in Ballora Park. What caused him to devote slightly more attention and interest to it was the involvement of the thranx. Though Visaria was as much a part of the Commonwealth as planets with more extensive histories, the involvement of nonhumans in antisocial confrontations on a human-settled world was still something of a novelty.

He scanned the report. Nothing remarkable about the methodology involved. Typical youth gang ambush, demand for goods (standard), resistance (apparently quite effective) on the part of the intended victims, injuries suffered only by the assailants (good for the thranx, he nodded in silent approval), reasonably prompt arrival by police in area (not his place to criticize or applaud), expedient intervention by a passing citizen (good Samaritans were rare in a challenging urban setting such as Malandere). Combination of Samaritan's intercession and arrival of police causes assailants to flee, hauling their wounded with them (a lesson Theodakris doubted would be taken to heart, given the apparent ages of the attackers). No loss of property, no injury to intended victims beyond loss of dignity and slightly lowered opinion of humankind.

Some question as to intent of Samaritan seen leaving in company of single assailant, though distance and lack of contact could also indicate Samaritan was possibly still chasing younger attacker (perhaps in hopes of catching him and giving him a good hiding, Theodakris mused hopefully).

Certainly there was nothing much here for him to do. Considerable postcontact enhancement had been required to obtain any useful visuals, since the only recording made by the onboard monitor on the first of the responding police transports had been acquired from a distance and while the transport itself had been in motion. Despite the substandard quality, the visual was clear enough to enable him to sex the assailants and make out something of individual characteristics. He ran through a few quick stabilized reruns, ruminated, then verbally filed suggestions as to where he thought the Authority might look for the perpetrators, what action they might take next, and—if cornered—which ones might surrender peacefully and which might resist with force.

He was about to move on to the next case when a few final images caused him to pause. Being secondary to the actual assault, there was really no obvious reason why he should spend any time with them. Murmuring verbal commands, he caused the projection to isolate the last visible assailant. No, not the assailant. There was nothing distinctive about the short, skinny scrawn. It was the young man leaving with him—or chasing him. It was not so much that the good Samaritan was taller than average, or even that he had red hair. And green eyes. There was something else about him. Something about his aspect, about the way he carried himself. There was also his distinctive personal adornment, which took the form of an unusual, brightly colored, lopsided necklace. It looked almost like . . .

A venomous Alaspinian minidrag.

Could the imagery be enhanced any further? Sitting up in his lounge and leaning forward was pure reflex; he could just as easily have directed the projection to move closer to him. The departmental processor did its best, but there were limits to the number and size of blank spaces in reality that its programming could fill in. The image of the good Samaritan sharpened only slightly.

Sitting alone in his office, the picture of vigor for his age, as healthy as departmental facilities and the best city doctors could make him, Shyvil Theodakris nearly had a heart attack.

It could not be. It was manifestly impossible. There were dozens, likely hundreds of documented reasons and verified testimonies why what he was seeing could not be so. Probably more than anyone else in the Commonwealth, he was palpably as well as furtively aware of them. Yet he knew, if he knew nothing else, his own history. And the history of his many lost, forgotten friends. Just as he knew what he was seeing with his own eyes.

So long ago. So many exciting, harsh, fervid, desperate, deliberately locked and filed-away memories. So much potential, thrown away. So many deaths. So much rage and rampant mindwiping on the part of the authorities and the general public. All gone now. All lost to time and fury. A hidden episode of Commonwealth scientific history.

Yet there it was, transparently represented not by edicted records or some scrap of accidentally dredged-up information, but by a real, living person. He knew who it was because despite the danger, he was unable to keep himself from occasionally, just occasionally, using the department's excellent search facilities to scan otherwise restricted references. Using appropriate cover and misdirection while doing so, of course, so that such searches could not be traced back to him. For years there had been hints, suggestions, whispers—and nothing more. Nothing concrete, nothing real.

Until now.

He jerked around sharply, but it was only his imagination. The chamber was still empty. No armed and armored figures were bursting through the door to arrest him. To cart him away for summary justice, pronouncement of sentence, and immediate full and complete mindwipe.

What to do?

Clearly, the next step was to make certain he was neither dreaming nor hallucinating. To positively ascertain the identity and history of the Samaritan. There was, however, one alternative. A sensible alternative.

Move on. Pretend that what he had seen, what he was staring at this very moment, meant nothing in the scheme of things. Go on with his life, continue with his work. Doing otherwise meant risking everything he had labored so long and hard to raise up from a virtually nonexistent foundation.

Old memories came flooding back; memories he thought he had managed to suppress forever. Had they been able to view them, they would have shocked the good citizens of Malandere. Shyvil Theodakris was an esteemed member of their society: one might even say cherished.

He was also, though not one surviving person on the planet knew it, something else. Something more. Something that had flared briefly in the life of the Commonwealth's scientific community only to be ruthlessly quashed and stamped out. All gone, all done with now. Except for a single survivor. One whose real name was not Shyvil Theodakris.

That was his name now, he reflected forcefully. His name, and the life he had made for himself. Until this moment. Until the utterly unexpected appearance of this Samaritan, this shadowed and haunted figure from the past. What a remarkable past it had been, too. He—

it—should not have survived. It should have vanished, gone down, disappeared along with every other iota of evidence of the group's work and existence. He should ignore it. He should pretend that it did not exist, and certainly that it did not exist on Visaria. That was the logical, the reasonable, the sensible thing to do.

Of course, if Shyvil Theodakris had been any of those things, he would not have been involved with the history of the Samaritan in the first place.

Recognizing as he did something of himself in the younger youth, it was not surprising that Flinx should also think Subar an orphan, as he himself had been. Not wanting to offend his young guide, he pondered how best to broach the subject as Subar led him away from the gang's priv space and down into the teeming depths of Malandere.

While the ambience reminded him somewhat of his home city of Drallar, the mood was quite different. Darker and more frenetic, as befitted a larger, more modern city more closely attuned to the pulse of Commonwealth commerce. Even the alleyways and back avenues through which Subar led him seemed wider, the buildings that canyoned them in on both sides higher and more impersonal. Or maybe, he mused, despite recent visits he was still remembering Drallar as the playground of his adolescent self, when everything would have seemed bigger, darker, and more intimidating.

No matter. Malandere had its own perverse charms. Alewev District, however, seemed singularly devoid of them. It was an area of older, already run-down structures, many of them commercial in origin, that had been taken over and cannibalized for living quarters by the lowest rung of the city's inhabitants. Those futurists who had speculated in the distant long-ago that machines would one day take over all the dirty work of humankind had been little more than entertaining dreamers. An automaton could clean floors and empty itself, but at the end of the disposal chain some poor human still had to decide what to do with the final refuse. Machines could wash dishes, but not sort them according to individual taste. And inevitably, invariably, there were always humans or aliens willing to do the work of machinery for less than the applicable machines cost to operate and maintain.

At least there were fewer floating flads in Alewev, he reflected as Subar urged him along. A lack of disposable income among the local populace corresponded to a parallel decline in neighborhood advertising. Damaged machines competed for space on the streets with damaged people. The emotional aether he could not shut out was ripe with treachery, envy, despair, frustration, hatred, desire, and ennui. The fate of all humankind, he wondered—or just of this particular slice of the species? His head throbbed.

He was glad Clarity was not with from him, that she was back on New Riviera and safe in the ministrating hands of Bran Tse-Mallory and Truzenzuzex. Better she recuperate from her wounds there than have to suffer his increasingly despondent company in such disheartening surroundings.

Subar took no notice of his melancholy. Either that, or the youth was indifferent to it. Reaching out with his Talent, Flinx could not tell. It didn't help that his guide was not yet emotionally mature.

Then they turned down a ridiculously small, substandard walkway, mounted a series of winding stairs that had been laboriously laid into an old drainage sluice, and, on the third level, paused outside a doorway that was so primitive it was utterly devoid of watchful electronics.

"Home." Subar's expression as he spoke said far more than did the word itself. A lifetime of experience was encapsulated in that one semi-expletive, Flinx suspected as he studied Subar's face. A lifetime that had not, insofar as he could perceive from the youth's emotions, been filled with delight. Subar used a key—an actual primitive polymorph key, Flinx saw in amazement—to open the portal. The interior was filled with the stink of the unwashed and the shouts of the uncouth.

They proceeded down a hallway that consisted of a single prefabbed molded tube. From the shape and wear evident on the curved interior, Flinx decided, it was a decommissioned commercial component salvaged from a scavenged industrial site. At the far end, another door yielded to Subar's primitive input.

Flinx had visited zoological parks before, on other worlds such as Nur. Without exception, all had been both quieter and cleaner than the landscape spread out before him now.

A small girl was chasing a smaller boy from one chamber to another. Homicidally intent on one another, they ignored him and his guide completely. The girl's hair had been neocharged and was standing straight out in every direction. The boy held tightly to a small device that rendered him immediately suspect. Beyond them and farther into a large room whose omnipresent stink could not be dispersed even by the cheap yet powerful area deodorant whose nose hair–curling scent irreversibly corrupted the local atmosphere, a pair of adolescent females lay slumped atop a torn and frayed sonomound. Their eyes were glassy and the skin of their tattooed skulls vibrated to the pulse that emanated from the mound to pass through their bodies via direct induction. Off to Flinx's right, a woman was screeching.

"Not on my time you don't. If you were half the man you claim to be . . . !"

Sounding vexed and vituperative in equal measure, a male voice cut her off. *"If you were half the woman I cojoined, it would take three houros to keep you quiet!"*

Subar glanced up at Flinx. "Sire and dam. Take your pick. Me, I don't get that choice."

Fuming, a woman appeared in the doorway off to the right. Beneath the garish singlepiece that draped her prematurely aged form, she was skinny and straight. Her face, like her life, had been badly whittled. Her skin was flushed, and not from overexposure to the sun. It supplied the only color to an otherwise pallid expression. She started to shriek anew at the unseen male of the household, caught sight of Subar and Flinx, and stopped herself.

"Oh." Her expression darkened, albeit ritualistically. "Where you been, boy?" Out of reflex more than emotion, she mustered a smile in Flinx's direction. "Brought home a friend, I see?" The rage that had underlined and given force to her screaming was fading within her, Flinx perceived. But though the emotional pot no longer boiled over, it continued to simmer beneath the woman's otherwise cordial façade.

"His name's Flinx," Subar muttered without meeting her gaze.

A man appeared, following behind the woman. At the sight of the tall stranger he frowned, eyed his mate, then his eldest male offspring, and finally stuck out a hand.

"Gorchen's the name. Flinx?" He looked like he wanted to burst out laughing, but did not. He did not have to. Flinx could sense his derision without having to hear it vocalized. "Unusual tag."

"It's a nickname," Flinx told him pleasantly. On his shoulder, Pip raised her head. The woman's eyes widened slightly.

"A pet? Does it bite?"

"Only when provoked."

"That's better than somebody else I know." Beset by his own wit, the man roared. "Come on in, I guess. Can't offer you much. Work to do, too." He glared down at the youth standing alongside the visitor. "Boy, offer your friend something to drink."

But nothing too much, Flinx inferred, *and the cheapest we've got.* The man's emotions were as easy, and sordid, to read as a three-way projection. Somewhere off in the distance the boy and girl continued to scream. With a look of faux apology, the woman went in search of them. Within seconds she was promising her unrestrained charges traditional hellfire and damnation if they didn't shut up.

From the sound of it, her threats had no effect. One of the girls lying in semi-comatose state on the sonomound opened an eye, observed Flinx, and promptly shut it again. Meanwhile the man of the house, if such he could be called, had drawn forth the day's recyclable outer-coat and was departing.

"Leave you two boys to chat." A grin that could only be described as positively ugly in inspiration split the haggard, pulpy face. "Don't do nothing in private you wouldn't do in public." When the door sealed automatically behind him it was difficult to tell whether Flinx or Subar was the more relieved.

Subar was not an orphan, then. Another supposed similarity rescinded. Evaluating what he had seen of the youth's family so far, Flinx found himself wondering which of them had suffered the more grueling upbringing. His young acquaintance, who was "blessed" with a family? Or himself, an orphan adopted by a rough-hewn but caring older woman.

Similar in construction to the hallway tube, yellow prefab ovoids of analogous industrial-strength material had been melded to its sides and top. One such large ovoid formed the main body of the apartment occupied by Subar's family. Smaller ones served as side rooms. From the outside, such buildings resembled stacks of insect eggs laid on twigs. The analogy, Flinx reflected as he followed his young host deeper into the overheated familial complex, went beyond appearances.

Subar's "room" was smaller than the transport that had brought Flinx from the port into the city. The curving walls were lined with flashing, blinking images of genetically modified females, weapons, and sports figures that were remarkable only in their deadening predictability. There were a few cabinets and drawers fastened to walls, a pile of the latter whose permaseals had proven to be anything but, and the ubiquitous communit. An ancient model from the look of it, not even capable of full-dimensional projection. The living area was as ragged and unkempt as its denizen. Remembering his childhood on Moth, Flinx had felt cleaner and more at home on the city streets of Drallar than he ever would have in a claustrophobic urban cocoon like this.

"A real hole, ain't it?" Subar passed a hand across the far curved wall, rendering it transparent. The view outside consisted of another, similar egg-like wall a couple of meters distant. Variety was provided by a leaking water pipe. A second pass of his hand over the print-coded wall and it turned opaque again.

Flinx tried to show some interest. "When I was your age, I spent most of my time on the street."

Subar let out a sardonic chuckle. "You think I do anything here besides sleep?" He nodded belligerently back in the direction they had come. "Sometimes I don't know which is worse: getting yelled at by my dam, smacked around by my sire, or having to listen to the scrawn siblings I didn't get to choose and can't get rid of."

This visit was doing nothing, Flinx realized, to improve his view of humanity. By coming, he had fulfilled his promise to Subar and seen all there was to see in the youth's immediate environment. It was time to move on, if only in search of further disappointment elsewhere.

"I'm going." He had to bend to exit the cubicle. "You wanted to show me your home, I've seen your home." Burrowing beneath his shirt, Pip had hidden most of her body from view.

"Wait!" This was not working out the way he had hoped, Subar saw as he followed his guest back to the main chamber. "There's one more person I'd like you to meet."

Flinx was already at the door. Neither of Subar's older sisters glanced up from the sonomound and their self-imposed music-and-image-fueled stupor. He sighed. "Another member of your confrontational social group?"

"No. She has nothing to do with the pod." He smiled, and it was a different kind of smile. One that was inspired by genuine satisfaction instead of cynicism. "She won't have anything to do with my other friends."

A positive development? Flinx mused. If so, except for the visiting thranx it would be a first for his time on Visaria. He was more than ready to meet a halfway redeemable human being. And the sooner the better. The sounds of Subar's mother pursuing his younger siblings threatened to come closer.

"Where?" he asked briskly.

Relieved, Subar gestured with one hand. "Couple of buildings over. Her family's rich." The sarcasm returned to his voice. "Their thrown-together partition is on *top* of a complex."

CHAPTER

7

Subar was not old enough to know if he was in love with Zezula or simply in lust with her, but he did know that Ashile was his friend. Speaking to him through his communit and with visual off, she agreed to meet him on the roof of her building. Her tone was both eager and wary.

Her feelings on seeing Subar reflected this internal turbulence, as befitted both her circumstances and her age. Her reactions to Flinx, as she stood waiting on the rippling rooftop in the haze-laden sunshine, were equally confused but in different measure. He found her wiry but attractive; not truly beautiful but pleasing. A splash of generic multihued freckles enhanced her pale complexion with cheap cosmetic color. A late developer physically, Flinx decided, but not mentally or emotionally. Holding one hand above her eyes to shield them from the glare, she squinted suspiciously at her boyfriend's companion.

"*Tcoum,* Subar. Who's this?"

Subar stood a little straighter. "A friend. Helped me out of a spine spot this morning."

"Spine spot." Ignoring both Flinx and the curious reptilian head that was now peeping out from the collar of his shirt, she turned on the youth. "What happened? It's that scrug-scrawn Chaloni again, isn't it? What did he opt you into this time?"

Raising both hands defensively, Subar affected sophisticated cool. He did not wear it well. "*Tworaleen*—eval back! I'm here, aren't I? It was no big deal." He cast a quick sideways glance at his new acquaintance who, thankfully, said nothing. "We just came from my place. I introed Flinx to my family." An appealing grin transformed his expression. "As counterbalance, I wanted him to meet you."

This compliment somewhat mitigated her initial annoyance. She studied Flinx more closely. As she was doing so, bright wings appeared from beneath the taller youth's shirt, spread wide to catch the haze-shrouded sun in a dual splash of bright blue and pink, and launched a diamond-backed, emerald-headed shape straight toward her.

A startled Subar started to reach for something concealed in a pocket. Flinx restrained him with a hand and a murmur. "It's okay. If Pip wanted to hurt her, she'd already be down."

To Ashile's considerable credit, she leaned her head to one side but otherwise held her ground as the alien flying beast landed on her. Pip proceeded to collapse her wings and drape herself over the girl's shoulder. Flinx looked on approvingly.

"She likes you," he told the understandably uneasy adolescent.

"I think I'm glad." Ashile guardedly eyed the serpentine shape lying athwart her left shoulder. It did not weigh much, and the iridescent green head and neck lay flat against the upper part of her chest. "Is she dangerous?"

"Only when she senses hostility."

Ashile looked up at him. "Senses?"

"She's an empath."

"Tuorlu!" Subar was as impressed as his girlfriend. Moving closer, he took the opportunity to examine Pip closely for the first time since he had encountered the tall offworlder. "I thought the bond between you two was awfully tight, but I had no idea. First empathic being I ever met."

The second, Flinx thought, without elaborating. "We've been together a long time." As much out of a sense of mischief as out of genuine curiosity he added, "How about you two?"

Subar immediately backed away from the girl. "Known each other for a couple of years, I guess." He shrugged, feigning indifference. But his emotions gave him away. "When you live this close in the same neighborhood, sooner or later everybody gets to know everybody else."

"Tnone," Ashile added. If anything, her emotions were transparent where Subar's were somewhat confused. With his Talent operating at optimum, Flinx was able to read them both like an open book. He felt no shame at doing this and did not regard it as prying. Given a choice, he would have preferred to have been born without the ability. For him not to perceive the emotional states of others would have been the same as requesting the hearing-enabled not to listen or the sighted not to see.

One thing was immediately clear: while Subar's feelings toward the leggy, awkward girl were decidedly mixed, no such ambiguity existed on Ashile's part. Age notwithstanding, she was deeply, profoundly in love with Flinx's boldly confident guide. It was an affection that bordered on adoration, though if confronted Flinx doubted she would confess to it. He sensed no guile in her. In her, the qualities that he so pessimistically sought among Malandere's population could finally be found. She was caring, compassionate, and thoughtful. Perhaps even honest, though that was something he could not sense. Honesty was not an emotion, though there were those who could give hints to its presence. He was not surprised at his discovery. Had she been otherwise, Pip would not have taken to her so quickly.

She was no saint, however. The frenetic, driving, money-hungry culture that dominated life on Visaria did not accommodate saints, who would be better advised to seek hospitality elsewhere. What Flinx had seen of Malandere in particular suggested that the gullible and trusting would survive its voracious streets and nightlife about as long as a naked fat man on Midworld or Fluva.

He could sense that she was still suspicious of him. "So," he ventured, striving to make conversation, "what do you do besides home-study?"

His query caused a sharp swing in her emotional state, suggesting that he had unwittingly struck a key in a personal sybfile better left unopened. The emotive shift affected Pip immediately. The flying snake rose from the girl's shoulder and winged back to her master. The minidrag was not hostile, or panicked. Something had simply upset her.

Ashile replied, her explanation tinged with a bitterness that colored its clarity. "I'm a subvent."

"I don't—" he began.

She continued rapidly, as if wanting to get the confession over with as quickly as possible. Subar looked away, uncomfortable. "Every few nights I go to a certain place downtown. It's kind of a club. I'm not the only one. There are other girls my age, and boys. There's supposed to be an age limit, but . . ." She did not need to fill in the rest of the sentence. "Connections are made. Older—people— hook in. They pay to get inside your head. Your mind. They pay to share what it's like to be young again. Sometimes they mess with your thoughts." She swallowed and turned away, staring in the direction of the smothered sun. "Some of their thoughts aren't very nice. They think about doing things they would never do themselves, to see how your thoughts react. It can get—ugly."

She looked back at him and continued. "I've never had a serious problem. There are sensors and emergency disconnects. But once in a while one of the subvents gets hurt." Reaching up, she tapped the side of her head. "Here. Then the staff take them away fast, so that the screaming and crying doesn't upset the other customers. Maybe I've just been lucky."

"*Tinaw*," Subar broke in, trying to lighten the mood. "You're tough, Ash. That's all."

She didn't want to be tough, though, Flinx sensed. She wanted to run. Away from her work, the description of which represented a new perversion Flinx had not previously encountered. She wanted to run away from her life. Given a preference, he surmised, she wanted to run away with Subar.

If the younger man was aware of those longings, he gave no indication of it, either physically, verbally, or emotionally. Flinx wanted to tell him, but doing so would have constituted an unforgivable invasion of the girl's privacy. It also might not have the intended effect. Flinx could not stay out of people's emotions, but he could stay out of their business. At least, he tried to.

It was one thing to intrude on the feelings of dozens of unnamed, unknown, faceless passersby on the streets of a city; it was something else entirely to find himself involved in the seething and probably hopeless passions of these two young residents. It was time for him to separate himself from them, to return to his own private isolation and deliberations. He said as much.

Aware he had just about run out of options for keeping his noteworthy new friend around, Subar resorted to naked pleading. "I wish you'd stay awhile longer, Flinx. There's more people I know would like to meet you, and a lot more of Malandere that I'd like to show you."

"Sorry. I have work of my own to do, and it's not getting done. Other people are relying on me." He scanned the rapidly warming rooftop. "I'll find my way back to where I'm staying."

"*Tloor,* no need for that." Still reluctant to concede that he was going to have to let the offworlder go, Subar resolved to retain his company until the last possible instant in hopes of wringing, if not valuable personal property, at least every last bit of useful information from him. "I'll help you find your way."

"No need for that," Flinx assured him. A slight smile creased his face. "I have some experience at finding my way around unfamiliar localities."

"It'll be easier and faster if I help you." Having settled the matter and before Flinx could voice any further objection, Subar quickly turned to head back the way they had come. "Besides, it'll give us the chance to talk a little longer."

Ashile immediately started forward. "I'm coming with you."

Flinx did not have to ask why. Her need was writ large all over her feelings.

Subar, however, did not possess his offworld acquaintance's unique perceptiveness. "Why?" he asked her, puzzled. "Think I can't find an address in the city without help?"

"No." Standing close to Flinx, she squinted up at him. Her gaze was open, direct, and unapologetic. "Maybe I'd like to ask your friend a question or two myself."

Subar was clearly unhappy with her decision, but not to the point of contesting it. As a consequence, while two had entered the jumble of a building, three left.

Ashile was like a shield, Flinx found. Well, more like a gauzy veil than a shield. Her intense emotional nature could not completely mask the flood of obnoxious public emotion that ebbed and flowed around him as she and Subar guided him through the maze of public transport, but her apparently indestructible good nature and honest affection for Subar helped to take the edge off the worst of the rage and envy.

It was at once amusing and sad that she felt it necessary to affect an impression of sardonic toughness. Every time she snapped angrily at Subar, what she felt inside gave her true feelings away. These were concealed from everyone except Flinx and Pip. The same awareness allowed him to pay no heed to her challenging stares and sometimes biting comments. She did not particularly like him, he sensed, but neither was she filled with unconcealed hate. As they rode public transport, her feelings toward Subar's offworld friend vacillated between curiosity and caution: a sensible response.

As they crossed through three different districts, Subar spent the bulk of the traveling time ignoring Ashile while trying to convince Flinx to remain longer in Malandere—to no avail. Both youths were visibly uncomfortable on the street that led to Flinx's hotel. Outside their home district they were out of their element and knew it, Subar's bravado notwithstanding.

Since there was no reason for them to come inside, and as Flinx did not extend the offer, Subar was reduced to shaking the offworlder's hand.

"*Tmorn*—thanks again." Having tried everything he could think of, Subar realized clearly that this was the last he was going to see of a potentially powerful and intriguing new friend. While Flinx leaving later would have been better than sooner, he consoled himself with the knowledge that such a departure had been, realistically, only a matter of time.

"Stay out of trouble." Flinx turned toward the entrance. Reading his eyes, the outer security doors parted to admit him. The inner ones would not open until the exterior pair had shut behind the guest. "And stick with her." Smiling, he nodded in the direction of a startled Ashile. Then he disappeared inside.

Acutely aware of how far they were from their home district, socially as well as physically, Subar and Ashile turned and started back toward the transport station.

"What a waste." Subar was shaking his head regretfully. "You should have seen how he handled Chal and the others! If only I could have cogited a way to keep him around!"

Ashile glanced back over her shoulder as a neatly dressed couple changed direction to avoid them. Though the woman smiled at Ashile, it was just as well that Flinx was not present to read her true feelings.

"You're better off without him, Subar. What did you expect? He's an offworlder. Did you think you were going to start a new gang with him as your sidekick and bodyguard? You should be glad he took an interest in you at all." They rounded a corner. "Me, I think you're better off away from him."

Subar edged away from her, deliberately putting emotional as well as actual space between them. Ashile could be such a weight sometimes. "You weren't there when he downed Chal and Dirran and Behdul. You don't know *anything*."

She was not intimidated. "I know that he was strange. Nice maybe, but strange."

Subar sniffed derisively. "Because he was an offworlder."

"No." Almost as if she expected to see something noncorporeal lingering behind her, she looked sharply back the way they had come. "Something else. You know how sometimes you get the feeling from some people that they're looking right through you? With this Flinx, I got the impression he was looking right into me."

Subar deliberately lengthened his stride, forcing her to hurry to keep up. "And you think *he* was strange. Hurry up or we'll have to wait for a pod."

They rode back to Alewev in silence, a disappointed Subar staring out the transparent wall of the transport, Ashile alternating between ignoring him and casting concerned sideways glances in his direction. Back at her building, his parting kiss was perfunctory, fleeting, and, worst of all—polite. He was not being deliberately spiteful: it was just that his thoughts were elsewhere.

Tomorrow, she mused to herself as she watched him leave and head back toward his own building. By tomorrow he would have forgotten all about it. The offworlder would be out of their existence and life would return to normal. She contented herself with that thought as she entered her own complex of cobbled-together, utility-sharing residences.

Things might have returned to normal had Subar managed to make it back to his chamber cubbyhole within his family's makeshift habitation. He did not, because events conspired to stand in his way. Events, and euphemistically named "friends."

"*Tcal,* Subar."

It was Zezula. Emerging from the deepening shadows to confront him, her luminous eyes were full of amusement and challenge. The effect was somewhat offset by the smoldering stimstick that drooped from the left corner of her mouth. Enhancer smoke curled from the hot tip.

"Zezu, I—"

He did not get a chance to say anything more, as Chaloni stepped out from behind her. There was no amusement in his eyes. Subar took a step backward—to stumble right into the hulking, silent mass of Sallow Behdul. Dirran and Missi were there, too. The bandage beneath the slipshod on her injured foot was painfully apparent, though she walked without too much difficulty.

"How's your mind-twisting longsong of a friend?" The annoyance in the gang leader's voice was not concealed.

Subar didn't have to look around. There was nowhere to run, and anyway, they knew where he lived. Brazen it out, he told himself. In the absence of a real weapon, his boldness had always been his best defense.

"He's not my friend. Tried to make him think so, though." When Chaloni didn't reply, an encouraged Subar stood a little straighter. "Strange liv. Something definitely spine with him. But somehow, I don't know how, he can make you 'feel' things."

"Truth there," agreed Dirran readily, recalling the unsettling emotions that had raced through him back in their priv place.

Subar jabbed a thumb at his chest. "I was trying to win him over, that's all. Figured maybe he could be of some use to us."

"But you didn't," Zezula finished for him.

The younger boy gestured unashamedly. "He's offworld. Leaving soon. I tried."

Chaloni appeared to ponder the younger boy's words. Subjected to that stare, Subar did his best to avoid the gang leader's gaze while maintaining his pose of indifference. If it came to a fight, he knew he'd have no chance against Chal, even if Dirran and Behdul stayed out of it. He'd have to take his beating and live with it.

It was Zezula who saved him, though unintentionally. "What *did* happen up there, Chal?"

Her query immediately put Chaloni on the defensive. More concerned with defending his macho, he abruptly lost interest in teaching Subar a lesson. "It wasn't nothing much," he demurred. "The boys and me, we got hit with some kind of attack. This wire-weird longsong, he must have had some kind of wave-form projector in his pocket. It put us down, but we could have fought through it if we'd had to. He ran before we could get at him." He glared fixedly at Subar. "That's what happened, wasn't it?"

Aware he was being handed an out where none could have been foreseen, the younger boy nodded vigorously as he turned to Zezula. "Chal's right. The longsong got away before he and Dir and Sal could get themselves together."

Zezula looked dubious but, in the absence of evidence to the contrary, found nothing to say. Chaloni's expression as he regarded Subar anew was far from brotherly, but neither did the gang leader look anymore like he was going to beat the wheat out of his youthful acolyte, either. Subar kept his relief bottled tightly inside him.

"Just so everybody understands what happened," Chaloni murmured, mollified if not exactly relieved. Putting an arm around Subar, he drew the younger boy to him as the gang turned to head back the way they had come. "Glad you remember how things really were."

By Chaloni's standards, the remark almost qualified as a compliment. "Everybody's gonna have to work together to bring off what I've worked out."

Subar was instantly on guard. Chaloni's previous venture had not gone exactly according to plan. Dirran and Sallow Behdul, he knew, would comply without question with whatever their leader told them to do. Only Missi looked as apprehensive as Subar felt. Of course, she had her injured foot to remind her of Chaloni's imperfection. As for Zezula, she was languorously indifferent. Watching her, there were times when Subar felt that she did not particularly care if she, or anyone else in her company, lived or died. Neither the future nor the past mattered to Zezu: only the moment was important. It made him think.

Was it possible his feverish desire for her was misplaced? Might there be a more worthy subject for his devotion? Try as he might, he couldn't think of anyone. With Zezula standing there right in front of him, it was hard to consider anyone else. For better or worse she dominated his immediate horizon as thoroughly as the light from Visaria's star did its often hazy atmosphere. Still, her lack of interest in the world around her troubled him.

It struck him suddenly that he had never seen or heard Zezula make a decision of her own. She was brave enough, and forthright, and competent at certain things, but it was always Chaloni who decided what needed to be done. Yet she was far from weak, and when she chose to focus it, her personality could be overpowering. How then to explain the apparent contradiction?

Was it just possible, he decided, that the object of his affections was not very smart?

Chaloni's voice rose as he slid his arm away from the younger boy's shoulders. "Sal! Take that stupid bead out of your ear!" He thrust an obscene gesture toward the largest member of the gang. "How can you hear what I'm saying?"

Behdul looked bemused, then nodded once and complied, removing the induction player from his ear. Subar fought not to smile. At least where the much bigger youth was concerned, intelligence was no mystery. Behdul could, however, snap Subar in half without breaking a sweat, so the younger boy was careful to keep on the giant's good side. Sadly, Behdul worshipped the gang leader.

It was Dirran who prompted Chaloni. "What you got in mind, Chal?"

"No more bugs." Putting an arm around her boyfriend's waist, Missi stared half defiantly at their leader.

Chaloni chose to make light of it. "*Tcnaw,* no more bugs, I promise. Look, we only went after the bugs because we need cred, right?" Without allowing time for rebuttal, he raced onward. "So that didn't go quite like we hoped. Afterward I got to thinking. If we're going to boost some cred, why risk ourselves again and again for down decimals? I mean, if we're going to put ourselves in vacuum, what's the point unless we position ourselves to suck up some serious screed?"

Warning bells were going off in Subar's head. Chaloni was leading up to something major. That implied major danger. But there was no way Subar could vent. Aside from the risk of being labeled coward, he had committed too much of himself to this group. Venting prior to peril was not a choice they would appreciate. If nothing else, he had to at least stay and listen.

"You get cred off the street one of two ways." Chaloni kept talking as they walked up the avenue. There was no need to avoid other pedestrians. Seeing the ranked gang coming toward them, mundane citizens did the necessary circumventing. "You boost tech, which none of us here has the skills for, or you steal something worthwhile that you know somebody else will buy."

Clearly in an unusually defiant mode, Missi spoke up again. "We don't have the aptitude to boost resalable real property from actual stores any more than we do to scrim tech from the Visaria Shell."

"Yeah," an emboldened Dirran added. "Suppose we were to actually zlip a shop someplace like the Kilandria Complex, up in Hendren District? If Complex Security didn't get us, we'd move right up to the top of the city police alert." He looked away. "Me, I prefer hanging around the bottom and avoiding notice."

"We've already moved up from the bottom, thanks to the shot we took at those two bugs." Chaloni did not hesitate to point out the uncomfortable fact. "But not that far up. Not dangerously far." Striding along in the middle of his small group, he lowered his voice slightly. "Suppose, though, we could scrim a place crammed with really valuable solids. Stuff that could easily and quickly be sold all over the planet. Scrimzees the buyers wouldn't howl about, and that the original owners wouldn't report to the police as having been boosted?" His tone was exuberant, though others might have called it maniacal.

Without a doubt, he was pleased at the reactions his words elicited in his companions. These ranged from utter bafflement from Sallow Behdul to suspicious expectation on the part of Dirran and Missi. Even Zezula was prodded out of her apathy by his challenge. As for Subar, he did his best to project a dutiful front. Inside, he was churning. What was Chaloni getting them into now?

"I don't see it," Missi finally said. "Any merchant whose goods are scrimmed is going to wail to the police."

Chaloni nodded slowly, in full agreement with her observation if not her conclusion. "Usually—unless the goods are illegal, their sale is illegal, and the whole operation is less legit than tomorrow's weathercast."

Subar wasn't suspicious anymore. He was frightened. So frightened he forgot to keep his mouth closed. "Chal, are you talking about scrimming malware?"

The gang leader smiled at him. "I've been scoping this for months, during the day. Didn't want to spill it unless I was sure we could make it work." His tone grew intense, the way it did when he was outgrabed on stim. "Any of you ever hear of Goalaa Endeavors?" He waited, allowing each of them enough time to confess their ignorance. "Cansure you haven't. It's out in Tethe."

"Where the main shuttleport is," Dirran pointed out unnecessarily.

Chaloni nodded. "Also Tethe Industrial District. Hundreds of warehouses, storage complexes, shipping and transit facilities. One of which is home to Goalaa Endeavors. Heard about it from—well, you don't need to know. Goalaa brings in offworld goods that aren't manufactured here yet. Specialized appliances, some integrated heavy building customization units, that sort of thing." His eyes were bright. "They also bring in offworld furniture. Not unusual for a fast-growing colony world like Visaria that still can't produce everything it needs or wants. Except that mixed in with the usual everyday, run-of-the-mill, mass-manufactured stuff are antiques. *Real* antiques. Including some from Earth itself."

Not being especially conversant with the details of interstellar commerce except as it might relate directly to them personally—in the matter of the latest bead loads, for example—bewilderment continued to dominate the expressions of the other gang members. The mere mention of the human homeworld, however, was enough to intrigue them.

"Export from Earth of anything over five hundred years old is strictly edicted by the Commonwealth," Chaloni finally deigned to explain. "Such objects are considered part of humankind history. Only museums and recognized educational facilities are allowed to take them offEarth, and for that they have to apply for and be granted a special Terran export license."

Now Missi was impressed. "You've been doing some research, Chal."

He snorted. "You think when I'm not looking out for you flies I spend all my time sleeping and stimming? Real Terran antiques can't be faked. The materials used can be traced right back to their tree, ore, or synthesis of origin. Who wouldn't want to own a piece of the homeworld? Boosting and reselling them throughout the Commonwealth is serious business. Me, I was surprised there was an outfit way out here on Visaria with enough tech and testos to bring it off." His energy and enthusiasm were becoming infectious.

"Wait a minute." As Subar had learned very early on in his active, difficult life, anything that sounded too good to be true usually was. "This Goalaa Endeavors that's bringing in Terran antiques: whose place is it? Who's running the operation?"

"*Tfell,* I don't know—and I don't care." Chaloni's bravado was blatant. Or suicidal, Subar was thinking. "Don't you crawlers *see*? It's the perfect scrim! We boost a transport, change the ident. For one night, it's no big tech. I've been scoping the building for a long time. Dirran and I can neut the automatics. If there's a liv inside, we neut him, too. I've been reading up on what slipslides offEarth. We fill the transport with the real history, unload at our place, lose the lift, and then laze awhile. Then we use an intermede to make the necessary contacts for us and we sky our wares out piece by piece." His smile was broad. "More cred at one time than we've had in our whole lives! And the best part of it is that Goalaa can't say spiss to the police or anyone else, or they get their operation scanned and probed."

"Okay," Missi conceded. "So maybe the police aren't alerted. These Goalaa people, whoever they are, aren't going to be real happy about being scrimmed. They're going to want their goods back. They're going to want *us*."

Chaloni shrugged it off. "How active can they be looking for us without drawing attention to themselves? And who knows Malandere better than we do? These people are out at Tethe, not down here in the guts like we are. Missi, you grew up here. Dirran, Sal, Zezu, Subar—all of you did the same. It's not like we're a formal organization. Just a bunch of friendlies who vent together once in a while." He was almost laughing aloud. "They won't be looking for a bunch of *kids*. They'll think it's another seriosity like themselves, or maybe some flipped police, or some group working with port authority. Not only won't they *find* us, they won't even be *looking* for us."

"History from Earth." Dirran was transposing aloud. "I'd almost be worth the spine just to hold a piece of that."

"Yeah," Chaloni quipped. "Hold it for a month or so, and then screed it."

Dirran exchanged a glance with his girlfriend, then looked back at their leader and nodded once. "We're in."

"'Course you are." To Chaloni, clearly, their participation was never in question. "Sal?" The giant likewise nodded. Without bothering to ask the beautiful slackness that was Zezula, Chaloni turned to Subar. "Kid?"

Used to the snub, Subar let it pass. "Sure thing, Chal. Sounds like a stim deal." Privately, he was increasingly nervous. It all sounded too easy, too pat, too straightforward. Too good.

But maybe he was wrong. Maybe he was worrying needlessly. He had never heard Chaloni spell out a boost in such detail. No question but that the older youth had put an enormous amount of thought into the proposed scrim.

The only problem, Subar knew, was that the brain that had done all the thinking belonged to Chaloni Taher-a-zind who, while slick and sharp and clever in his own street-surviving way, was no *summa cum laude* graduate of the wider School of Life.

CHAPTER

8

They could have been ready to go within a day, but to his credit Chaloni was taking no chances. For one thing, certain special appurtenances had to be acquired and prepared. Furthermore, all such acquisitions had to be made in Cormandeer, Visaria's second-largest city. It wouldn't do, Chaloni explained, to buy anything locally because that would make their purchases too easy to trace. Passing themselves off as a married couple, he and Zezula undertook the journey. They made the buys via crypted electronic transfer from independent sources so that there was no face-to-face, and, when they were ready, brought them back.

That was when the real preparations and rehearsal began. Though Chaloni was upbeat throughout, particularizing instructions and assigning individual tasks, the strain eventually began to show. Not because he was having second thoughts as to the nature of the plan or its chances of success, but because with each passing hour the likelihood of someone getting cold feet and backing out grew in proportion to their competence.

Four days later, everything was in place and ready to go. With final preparations complete Chaloni went over each individual's tasks, assuring him of his confidence in them, and reminding them of what was at stake.

"More cred than you've seen in your whole life," he was telling Subar. "More cred, maybe, than you'll need for a long time. Than any of us will need." Reaching out, he put a hand on the younger boy's shoulder and squeezed firmly. "I know you can do your part. You're the youngest, but you're as smart as any of us, and just as tough."

Whether it was a bold-faced tall tale or not, it had the intended effect. Subar was juiced. The adren was flowing in all of them to the point that successful completion of the scheme had become its own reward and making off with the goods almost secondary.

The building that housed Goalaa Endeavors was one among dozens of similar nondescript storage facilities that occupied block after industrial block on the outskirts of Malandere's vast shuttleport. At two in the morning, the locale was devoid of commercial traffic. Diurnal haze had morphed into the nocturnal fog that drifted in nightly off the nearby sea. There were no moons out, both of them having sunk hours ago below the murk-laden horizon. For what Chaloni and his friends had in mind, it was a night made to order.

Alone, Subar approached the west side of the building. He did not mind being alone because he usually was, and according to Chaloni's plan so was nearly everyone else. His situation was no more sanguine than that of Sallow Behdul, or Zezula, or Chaloni himself. That did not mean uneasiness was absent. But there was nothing for it but to head in when his chrono told him it was time to move. The consequences of abandoning his companions now, at this critical juncture, would be as dire as anything that could happen to him inside the building.

Assuming he could get inside.

It was dead quiet on the service street that separated the Goalaa warehouse from the storage facility opposite. There were no transports in the corridors, no skimmers plying the air routes overhead. They had the lateness of the hour to thank for that. Clad in the negsuit Chaloni had purchased for him, Subar hurried across the street to the truck-sized plastic container positioned up against the wall of the building. While all commercial refuse was properly incinerated and compacted on site, the resultant powdery material still had some recyclable value. Whenever it had filled to a certain prespecified level, the storage bin would notify its contracted automated pickup vehicle that the time had come for emptying.

Reaching the bright orange container, he nearly jumped out of his snug-fitting new neg when a pair of xuelms went whirling past. Mottled gray to blend in with the night, the nocturnal carnivores came rolling and bouncing down the street, their several dozen finger-length feelers fully extended, their eyes tightly shut against contact with the pavement. If a feeler contacted something warm and alive, the xuelms would instantly uncoil from their spherical form to envelop and devour it. By trolling parallel to each another, they could cover more of the street than by hunting individually.

Out on the plains of Visaria it was not uncommon to encounter packs of a dozen or more, rolling swiftly onward, sweeping a chosen stretch of veldt in a long, straight line. Keeping mostly to its less developed, less populated outskirts, some had moved into and thrived within the city, tolerated or ignored by its population. Unable to assemble in full packs, which drew serious attention from the authorities, a couple of hunting xuelms were no danger to anyone over the age of ten. Each about a third of a meter in diameter, this pair was no threat to Subar. Though they had startled him, they angled to their left to keep well away from the young human, who was more of a danger to them than they were to him.

Angry for allowing himself to be surprised by lowly xuelms, Subar turned back to the smooth-faced catchment and began to climb, using the activated suction pads attached to his hands and knees. As long as their storage power lasted, he could ascend a wall of vertical glass. The plastic body of the container provided a much firmer purchase. He went right up and over without being observed.

Safely on top, he withdrew the special mask from his small waist pack and slipped it over his nose and mouth. Goggles protected his eyes. Contact with the compacted refuse was unlikely to be harmful, but breathing in fine particles that might contain all manner of powdered toxic metals and other poisonous elements was not advisable. The check port was sealed, but breaking and entering were among the most basic survival techniques that he and his friends had mastered. A few practiced applications of several appropriate tools, and he was in.

He dropped knee-deep into fine, grayish white powder. It puffed up like talc around him, but his mask and goggles prevented it from entering his body. A quick search located the dump chute that fed the refuse container. Switching on his goggles, he entered the pitch-black conduit and started crawling.

It ascended at a steep angle that presented no problem for his suction grips. A check of the chrono showed that he was well ahead of schedule. The chute executed a few gradual twists and turns—nothing he couldn't negotiate—before light became visible at the terminus. The sight was a relief. Though Chaloni had assured him that his prep work had shown that reduction operations at the facility took place only during the day, the thought of being confronted by a suddenly activated incinerator at the end of the crawl was one Subar had not been able to push out of his mind.

He emerged into a well-lit holding area near the rear of the building. Used packaging and other detritus was stacked on all sides of the reducer bed. Climbing out of it, he removed his mask and goggles, took a couple of deep breaths, and headed for the center of the structure. That was where any manual override for the building's various alarm systems would be located.

Sure enough, a short jog carried him through a doorless portal and out into a much larger, three-story chamber. To his immediate left was a small, illuminated room. Inside were lit panels, floating vits, a couple of chairs, and several appliances. The room was unoccupied. That was not good. Keeping a security room lit throughout the night suggested that it was intended to be attended by something other than automatics.

As he turned to check behind him, he found a particularly large nonautomatic frowning down at him.

"Kid, what the borizone are you doing here?" The make of gun the man held pointed right at Subar's chest was unfamiliar to him. Like its owner, it was impressively large.

Subar did not panic. He did not try to flee. Instead, he raised both hands, one holding mask and goggles, and smiled. "What's your name?"

The man's frown turned to one of puzzlement. "My name? What the hell business is that of yours?"

Subar affected a look of honest bemusement. "Don't you want credit?"

"Credit?" Anger and uncertainty fought for dominance within the night guard's thoughts. "Credit for what?"

"For doing your job. For catching me." Subar gestured behind him, toward the open portal that led back to the refuse disposal chamber. "Could have been a few minutes quicker, but still pretty good."

'What's this credit crola? What are you talking about?"

"You'll find out." Subar's grin widened. "Take me to your leader, Mr., uh . . . ?"

The man hesitated, decided he had nothing to lose by replying. "Harani. Quevar Harani."

When the now uncertain guard didn't move, Subar took the initiative, heading for the waiting security room. "Congratulations, Mr. Harani, and thanks for the name. I hate it when people who deserve credit for their work don't receive it. Don't you?"

"Uh, yeah." Thoroughly bemused by now, Harani fell in behind the youthful intruder he had captured. The guard's weapon did not waver and the muzzle of his weapon remained fixed on Subar's spine, but his thoughts as he escorted his catch toward Central were considerably more muddled than usual.

Boujon would sort it out, he decided. Meanwhile, he had tracked the intruder via the external and wall sensors and had taken him into custody. That was all the credit he needed, he felt. Unless . . .

Unless there was something more to be gained. Something he knew nothing about. The youthful, skinny intruder had given him no trouble, and had allowed himself to be effortlessly apprehended. What he *had* managed to do was plant a seed in Harani's mind. Not of doubt but, just perhaps, of expectation.

Zezula entered the building through an upper-level vent whose seal yielded easily to the special reliever she carried, and whose built-in sensor alarm was disarmed in seconds by the burglary tool Chaloni had provided. It was a tight squeeze, but the shiny silver suit she wore was tight fitting enough not only to show off her exemplary figure, but also to allow her to wriggle her way freely downward. Using hands and feet and knees to apply pressure to the sides of the cylindrical tube, she made steady progress.

The drop to the second-floor landing that ran around the interior circumference of the building was less than what she was used to dealing with when fleeing across the rooftops of the city. Landing quietly on padded feet, she stayed low as she searched for a lift or ladder leading to the floor. The interior of the warehouse was equipped with motion detectors designed to sense movement where all should be still, heat sensors to locate heat where none should be radiating, and listening devices to record and analyze sound where silence ought to reign.

Just as appliances were available to cancel out unwanted noise, so Zezula's suit was equipped with activated fabric that was designed to absorb the beams of motion detectors. They did not see her. The suit's special outer coating was fabricated to completely hide her body's heat signature. Continuously monitoring the landing along which she was running, the plethora of advanced instruments noted nothing out of the ordinary. Cushioned, sound-absorbing slippers not only allowed her to move swiftly and easily, but also eliminated even the slightest hint of footfall from her path.

Reaching a ladder well, she checked below. There was no sign of movement. Except for some far-off chatter, all was silent in the vast chamber. In the distance she thought she could make out Subar's high-pitched singsong rising among other voices. Good. That meant the youngest member of the gang had safely made his way inside. She felt sorry for Subar, always gawking at her whenever he thought she couldn't see him. He would have made an interesting kid brother, though his interest in her was transparently anything but filial. Sometimes she had to force herself to keep from laughing at him. His interest would have been pitiable, if she had any pity in her body, which she did not. Though he had no way of knowing it, she was doing him a kindness by ignoring him.

Making made her way down the ladder as quickly and efficiently as she had across the landing, she started for the nearest row of stacked and shelved merchandise. While the nature of some goods remained hidden within opaque packaging, the contents of others were clearly visible through the transparent coatings that had been applied to protect them. She wished she had time to linger over some of the inventory. Much of it was legitimate and familiar even to someone who was not exactly a sophisticated buyer. Some of it was exotic but not particularly exclusive.

Then there were the objects from Earth.

Even a casual visitor could have picked these out. There was the collection of twenty-second-century long arms, for example, with their simple clips of gunpowder-driven projectiles. Less physically impressive but far more ornate was the sealpak containing eighteenth- and nineteenth-century glassware. Nearby stood a translucent container through which life-sized marble carvings boosted from some ancient Terran temple were visible. An entire mounted saber-toothed cat fossil shared spare with an assortment of intact twentieth-century fast-food containers made from, astonishingly enough, not plastic or cellucene but actual treeboard. Even a quick glance at the shelves was enough to show that there was more, much more. The value of the smuggled Terran items she was seeing was beyond her ability to calculate.

Chal was right. This would put them in serious cred not for months but for years. Disposing of it would be no problem, either. Where there was this kind of cred to be totaled, there was always someone willing to take the chance of handling the marketing end of the business.

She turned right and headed for the back of the building. That was where the automatics that governed the internal alarms and power supply would be located. She was halfway to her destination when a voice hissed at her from the shadows.

"Stop. Do not move. Keep your hands high where they can be seen."

The command came from a peculiar voice. Not only the pronunciation of individual words was strained, but the cadence was peculiar as well. Someone from the other side of Visaria, she decided, where accents tended to be thicker. Or else the speaker was an offworlder. No linguist, she couldn't decide.

She could, however, recognize a life-threatening order when she heard one. Extending both arms, she thrust her hands over her head.

The figure that approached her was also wearing a techsuit, one as loose fitting as hers was tight. Oversized boots and a helmet with wraparound reflective face shield completed the speaker's attire. There was nothing unusual about the pistol pointed at her, however. Letting out a tired sigh, she smiled thinly at her captor.

"Very good. You got me."

There was a pause. " 'Very good'? I am confused. That should be my feeling, not yours." The voice was oddly stilted, as if it was being filtered through a miniaturized but effective real-time modulator.

"Not necessarily. You'll understand in a little while."

One hand gestured. Rather elaborately, she thought. "I hope so. My momentary confusion, however, will not prevent me from shooting you if you attempt to flee, or otherwise provoke me."

She nodded. "I'll be sure to be careful, then."

Without lowering the muzzle of the pistol so much as a millimeter, the figure backed off to one side. The slightly bent-over guard walked with an odd, shuffling motion. A relic of back damage incurred in the course of duty, perhaps. While these idiosyncrasies attracted her notice, they were nothing out of the ordinary. Irrespective of pay, she imagined it would be hard to sign the best people for a job like nocturnal guard duty. But a man or woman bent or otherwise disfigured by disease, damage, or individual genetics might jump at the chance to work where they didn't have to interact with other people. She kept her hands over her head and her eyes forward as her captor marched her toward a well-lit chamber located near the center rear of the building.

Having observed Zezula's capture via one of the warehouse's dozens of carefully concealed surveillance vits, Boujon was waiting for them in the security center. Short, experienced, muscular, and proud of his competence, with a deeply lined face and what remained of his white hair standing straight up in a buzz cut severe enough to double as sandpaper, he was a troubled man.

The two young, well-equipped, would-be scrim artists standing before him with their wrists now secured behind their backs had entered the premises whose space and contents he was charged with holding inviolable. Even if they were ignorant of who was behind Goalaa Endeavors and felt the worst that could happen to them was that they would be turned over to municipal authorities, they ought at the very least to be showing signs of apprehension. Instead, the older girl wore an air of indifference as lightly as she did her negsuit, while the younger boy seemed impatient when he should have been nervous. It made no sense. It did not add up. Being a man who was proud of his ability to do sums, this disturbed Boujon no end. It found him concerned. It was beginning to make him mad.

"There's something the matter with you two." His gaze flicked back and forth between them. "Namely, that there's nothing the matter with you two."

"Should there be?" the boy replied. Apparently, the girl's indifference extended to engaging in conversation. That, Boujon reflected grimly, could be easily rectified. For the moment, however, he was content to converse with only the junior of the pair.

"Yes," the building's director of nighttime security assured him. "At the very least both of you should be uneasy, not knowing what might be forthcoming and ignorant of your possible fate. Your future lies in the hands of someone other than yourselves. Me."

"Well, *tnure*," the girl deigned to reply casually.

Boujon glared at her. "Are you mocking me, you little slipslut? How about if I tell Harani to break a couple of your fingers?" Standing immediately behind the two captives and next to the bent-over shuffler in mask and loosesuit, Harani looked as if he would not especially mind carrying out such a directive. While Boujon's threat did not appear to unsettle its subject, it did prompt the bound boy to take a half step forward.

"Everything will be explained real soon," Subar hastily assured the security director. "You've done well so far."

"I've done . . . ?" Boujon's eyebrows, which were as white as the rest of his hair, drew together in a melanin-free frown. "What the stasis are you talking about? What is this—some kind of suicidal school project? Do you expect to be graded on whether or not you've managed to boost the property of another? If you think this is a game of some kind, maybe I should have Harani start with *your* fingers, kid. 'Real soon'?" He half rose out of his chair. "If you've anything else to say before I decide how to deal with the both of you, you'd better say it now." He did not smile. "While you're still in possession of the necessary speaking equipment."

Inside, Subar had begun to panic, just a little. Then a couple of audible alarms went off and he was able to relax again.

Harani looked at his superior, who had turned to stare at a bank of floating control contacts. A pair of cornea-sized telltales had gone bright red. The soft beep of their aural counterparts filled the room. The sound was not overpowering: merely insistent.

"*Now* what?" a thoroughly irritated Boujon demanded of unresponsive listeners.

Harani spoke up helpfully. "Autorive delivery has gone into lockdown."

Boujon growled without turning. "I can see that, idiot. Go and check it out. No," he corrected himself quickly. "Stay here. You and Joh keep an eye on these two. Either of them tries to fiddle their bindings, blinks too much, or raises their voice, acquaint them with the inflexibility of the nearest wall."

Harani stiffened. "Yes sir, Mr. Boujon, sir." Nearby, the masked operative called Joh continued to hold a pistol focused on both captives.

Holstering his own pair of weapons—one an efficient restrainer, the other lethal—Boujon exited the office as soon as the armor door slid aside. He headed for the cargo receiving area that dominated the south end of the warehouse. What a night it was turning out to be! He needed time to determine the intentions of the two youths who had penetrated outer security only to be detained once they had made their way inside. Each had infiltrated wearing professional-grade equipment, apparently believing that would be enough to prevent their detection. Which meant they were either arrogant or just plain stupid. Not being old enough to have acquired much experience in the way of breaking and entering, they were apparently relying on their high-tech but far-from-omnipotent gear to see them safely through to their eventual goal. He assumed that to be theft.

He had considered calling for backup, but had quickly set the notion aside. First, because it would reflect badly on his abilities and second, because there was no evident need for additional help. Harani and Joh had secured their respective detainees with little effort and no resistance. It was a poorly organized supervisor who called for help before he needed it.

Were the youthful intruders aware of the secrets the warehouse contained? How far did their ignorance, or arrogance, extend? These were questions that needed answers. He would have them before the sun started to warm the urban haze. But first, the early-morning delivery that had gone into lockdown had to be attended to.

The transport remained where automatic detectors had secured it: near the entrance, with the main door shut tight in its wake and appropriate weaponry aimed in the vehicle's direction. The autorive had, of course, no driver. This was the preferred method of delivery. Having no live driver meant there was no one on the transport in a position to pilfer its contents or divert the valuable cargo elsewhere. It was essentially an automated sybfile on wheels. Skimmer transport would have been faster, but skimmers required the presence of a live pilot to deal with the frenetic traffic lanes of the city.

Facing the transport, whose power had been shut down by building security, he saw nothing amiss. There was no one in the programming and emergency control cockpit, and the vehicle appeared undamaged except for the usual urban dings and scratches. Pulling his communit, he queried the warehouse's AI.

"One-one-four, access code Blue thirty."

"Code accepted. Please proceed, Mr. Boujon."

"Transport arrival noted. Detail reason for security lockdown."

"Manifest lists thirty-seven containers marked for delivery. Penetration scan shows thirty-eight containers. Resonance follow-up indicates one container of dimensions three by two by two contains an oxygen-breathing life-form of dimensions—"

"Skip it," Boujon told the AI. With a sigh he drew his retainer, leaving the killing gun in its holster. Given the direction this morning had taken so far, he had more than an inkling of what he was going to find. "Direct transport to unseal and open for delivery."

Following commands communicated by the building's AI, the rear of the transport swung down to become a loading ramp. Approaching, the retainer held out in front of him, Boujon ascended halfway before making a casual gesture in the direction of the transport's container-filled interior.

"All right, you can come on out now." When no movement was forthcoming, he added impatiently, "Your container has been scanned and your presence detected. You have sixty seconds to come out or I'll shoot into the container holding you."

The satisfying sound of seals popping echoed softly through the transport's interior. The figure that climbed out of one oblong container was wearing a recycler mask attached to a tiny bottle of compressed atmosphere. It was only when the intruder responded to Boujon's crisp order to remove it that the security director saw that the latest interloper was as young as his two predecessors, albeit much larger.

Backing down the ramp, Boujon pointed with the retainer as he gave the newcomer plenty of room. He was a big kid, but clearly still a kid.

"Let's go, boy."

"Yes sir." Sallow Behdul hesitated. "Uh, you want me to put my hands over my head?"

"Sure." If he hadn't been so annoyed by the night's goings-on, Boujon might have smiled. "Knock yourself out."

After running a hand-scanner over the oversized youth to check for weapons and finding none, Boujon marched his captive back to security central. One more intruder meant at least one more question. He looked around, studying the high walls and ceiling of the warehouse. Was this going to go on all night? He did not worry about what to do with his (so far) trio of captives. Their eventual fate could, conveniently, be left to a higher authority. What he was looking forward to was an explanation.

One thing he had already decided. The would-be thieves were not wholly unintelligent. Plainly, if the first two failed in their attempts to successfully penetrate building security, it would have been left to this last lummox to hide in his sealed shipping container until all was quiet and then emerge to hopefully make off with a valuable or two. Whoever had planned this intrusion apparently thought of their troops as expendable. That, at least, did make some sense. If one was going to send a couple of advance scouts on a suicide mission, nothing was more natural than to sacrifice the young, inexperienced, and ignorant.

If that was the intent, it had failed miserably. Did whoever was behind the break-in attempt think the owners of Goalaa were ignorant of modern theft techniques, and unprepared for such? A little judicious questioning of one or more of the three captives would reveal who was behind the futile, failed effort. Unless, of course, the trio had been thoughtfully mindwiped of that bit of incriminating knowledge before being sent on their way. Given what he had seen thus far, Boujon was not willing to credit the perpetrators with even that much critical foresight.

Still, one never knew unless one asked. Harani and possibly even Joh might be looking forward to the necessary inquisition, but the security director was not. Harsh questioning was ofttimes unpleasant and sometimes messy work, it was nearing the end of his shift, and given the peculiarities of this night he was more than ready to go home and flop into bed.

With all the activity in the building focused on security central, the rear of the cavernous structure was dark and quiet. That suited Chaloni just fine. As he descended the emergency ladder and tiptoed along the floor toward his destination, the night-vision lenses he wore allowed him to see in the dim and shadowy light as clearly as if it were noon. Impressively impregnated and specially woven, the chameleon suit that covered him from head to toe was fabricated not only to blend in with the color of its immediate surroundings but to bend any type of sensing radiation around its wearer.

Like the structures that surrounded it, the warehouse was hooked into the municipal power grid. On this moonless, cloudy night, turning off the electrical supply to the building should plunge it into immediate darkness. That, however, would be both too easy and too obvious. To properly render the structure's watchmen blind and ignorant, the same negation needed to be applied to the inevitable individually powered emergency backups.

Both necessary feats were to be accomplished by the special device he carried in the backpack he wore beneath the chameleon suit. Plugged into the building's power panel, it would not only disrupt the main supply to the structure but also send out enough homing radiation to quietly fry every electrical connection within. That in itself would, of course, alert any guards to the fact that something was amiss, but by the time they localized the trouble, he should be in and out with an armful of goods.

He needed to move fast and choose wisely. Though the distinctive gear and clothing he and his companions were utilizing was only rented, he had still been forced to borrow against earnings in order to pay the fee. As to the others, ways and means of springing them from the clutches of the building's supervisors were already in place. He grinned to himself. Backup, he had learned early on in his life on the streets of Malandere, was always the first part of a job to be worked out, not the last.

He was sure they had, all three of them, already been picked up. That was the intention all along. Send in the troops one at a time, each utilizing a different approach, to keep the building's operators preoccupied both physically and mentally. Now it was his turn. Through the night lenses he could see the power panel directly ahead, attached to the far wall behind a protective metal grid. A sensor built into the lenses indicated that the grid was not charged. Locked, yes, but that would delay him only until he could get at the tools in his backpack.

He had removed the necessary pair of small, efficient devices and set to work when a cool voice called to him from behind.

"All right, that's enough. Lie down on the floor, legs spread, hands out in front of you and over your head." A pause, then, "I can't see you perfectly yet, so I'd just have to spray the whole area to be sure of hitting you, and I don't want to have my pay docked for damage to walls." He started to look behind him. The voice sounded again, more sharply this time. "Don't turn around! I'd as soon shoot you as talk. Maybe rather."

Taking a deep breath, Chaloni did as he had been directed, dropping prone to his belly and spreading his limbs. A hand was on him almost immediately, checking for weapons. Finding none, the strong fingers pulled off his night lenses and tugged back the hood of the chameleon suit to reveal his face.

"Stand up," she told him. He complied. The woman facing him and cradling the stubby, widemouthed weapon in both arms was short and squat. She wore her hair cut short beneath a service cap, and her duty blouse was bedecked with tubes and instrumentation. Her eyes were a fashionable, and startlingly bright, orange. She eyed him up and down.

"Same as the others, maybe a little older. Turn around." Offering no resistance, he stood calmly while she placed wrist restraints on him. He could feel the slight burst of heat as the synthetic protein bonds melted into place. "Okay," she told him, "let's go."

As they marched off in the direction of building security, he couldn't keep from inquiring, "How did you spot me? I should have been completely blanked."

"You were," she assured him. "No tracking echo, no viz, no heat signature, nothing." Though he couldn't see her fiddling with the relevant instrument, he did not need to. "Carbon dioxide emission. Moving fast, you were exhaling enough to fog the sensor screen, even at a distance. D'you think the people who run this place are scrawn-spawn? Even the portable I'm using is sensitive enough to pick up the breath of intruding mice."

Intriguing, he mused. He hadn't thought of that one; nor had the people from whom he had rented all the infiltration gear mentioned the possibility. Life was a series of learned experiences, he told himself.

Taking his calm for resignation, his captor allowed herself to relax slightly. "I don't figure this. None of us do, including Mr. Boujon. I mean, what were you kids thinking, trying to break in here? If you have any idea what's sometimes stored in this facility, didn't you think it would be properly looked after? Do you have an idea who really owns and runs this operation?"

"No," Chaloni told her honestly. "Why don't you tell me?"

"Not my place to opt," she replied brusquely. "How much you get to know is up to Mr. Boujon." He could not see her grin, but he could sense it in her tone. "That, and what happens to you and your friends. Me, I hope he leaves the close-in work up to the hourly help. Nothing to do night after night, it gets real boring around here. Maybe I ought to thank you for the distraction. Harani and I, we get real lethargic sometimes."

"Glad to be of help," Chaloni told her.

Something hard and unyielding jabbed him solidly in the back, causing him to stumble slightly forward. The grin, both physical and verbal, had vanished. "You think this is funny, you little street scrug? You making fun of me? Wait till Harani's let loose on you. The big guy, he's got hands like a doctor. A mad one." The smile returned, more than a little twisted this time. "And I get to play his favorite nurse."

CHAPTER

9

"Tnay, Chal."

Zezula was the first to espy the latest arriving captive. Following her cheery greeting, Subar and then Sallow Behdul added their own. The hood of his suit still pulled down off his head, Chaloni acknowledged each of them in turn.

Closely monitoring the youthful interaction, Boujon was more perplexed than ever. None of what had happened made any sense. If the four young intruders *had* any sense, they should all be cowering and sniveling in fear, terrified of what might lie in store for them. And with good reason, since Boujon had several unpleasant things in mind. His employers granted him considerable leeway in such matters, and he had no intention of simply turning over the unsuccessful thieves to his superiors—or summarily disposing of them. Not without first discovering their hopes, notions, and specific intentions. His curiosity needed to be satisfied.

It had occurred to him that their presence might be a diversion, intended to draw his attention and that of his staff away from some larger, more elaborate and sophisticated assault from outside. But the storage complex had been on full alert all night, as always, and there was no sign of any additional unauthorized movement either inside the main structure or in the buffer zone immediately without.

To look at them, he thought bemusedly, one would think this was nothing more than an evening's entertainment. Not a one, not even the youngest boy, showed the least concern for his or her important body parts, not to mention life. This indifference convinced Boujon he was overlooking something. It upset him. He prided himself not only on maintaining tight security on behalf of the complex's operators, but also on knowing the details of every attempt at penetration. It was a matter of professional pride. Stepping forward, he determined to find out what he was missing. That he would do so, sooner and simply or later and more messily, he had not the slightest doubt.

"You know," he began casually, "I could just have you all shot, right here and now, and the police would sign off on it without even having to be bribed. Breaking and entering repulsed by force. Filling out the relevant form would take less than five minutes." Boujon focused his attention on the youth who appeared to be the leader of the group. "What have you to say to that?"

Chaloni nodded by way of agreement. "That'd be real efficient of you—but unnecessary. Also counterproductive. We can't put together our report if we're dead."

"Report?" Boujon frowned. "What 'report'?"

Harani was tentative as he gestured at Subar. "The small one there, he kept talking to me about some kind of 'credit.'"

Instead of obtaining answers, Boujon was growing more confused. "What is all this?" He glared warningly at Chaloni. "I don't like games. I don't like being played for a fool."

Chaloni raised both hands and chuckled. Forced amusement, or genuine? the security chief found himself wondering. What was he overlooking?

"Take it easy," the strapping youth advised him. "Everything will be made clear." He adjusted his stance, paying no attention to the weapons that were trained on him. "This has all been a test. Of building security. Of your competence and"—he glanced behind him at the trio of skeptical guards—"that of your staff. To see if this complex could be compromised by intruders you wouldn't expect. I'm happy to say that, at least as far as I'm concerned, you've passed with flying colors."

The woman who had brought him in gestured with her free hand as she addressed her boss. "What a load! Give the kid credit for nerve, though."

An unruffled Chaloni looked back at her. "Think about it. What team of scrimmers would try a serious boost like this without a single gun?"

Her reaction showed that she had not considered this obvious fact. It was the same with Harani, though the expression on the face of the guard Joh remained hidden behind his protective face shield.

The security chief's increasing anger gave way, at least temporarily, to indecision. "You found no weapons on any of them? Nothing?"

Harani shook his head. "Not so much as a pulsepopper, Mr. Boujon, sir." He glanced over at his two associates, who indicated agreement.

That was, if nothing else, passing strange, Boujon decided. It was hardly conclusive proof of the smirking youth's outrageous claim, but if true it would go a long way toward explaining his coolness and that of his companions. Such a thing was not unheard of, nor unprecedented, but it still struck him as a desperate attempt to turn a potentially deadly situation upside down. One way to find out the truth was to simply shoot them one at a time until those left alive finally cracked.

Unless he was all wrong about this, and they were telling the truth. Then *he* would be the one left facing Shaeb holding his future in his hands.

Do like the kid recommended, he told himself. Take it easy. No need to rush things. The truth, whatever it was, could be drawn out.

"Why would anyone wanting to run a check on building security send a bunch of kids to test its efficiency?"

Chaloni had anticipated the question. "It was thought it might lower your suspicions if any of us were spotted outside, and that we might be able to get in close more easily for just that reason: because you wouldn't be as threatened by a bunch of 'kids.' Incidentally, we were all specially trained for this job."

Looking on while listening intently and fighting to keep his breathing steady and even, Subar worried that the older youth might be overdoing things. But the security chief didn't challenge him on the claim. Leastwise, not yet.

Rubbing his chin, Boujon eyed the gang leader shrewdly. "Uh-huh. Then tell me this. If you're here to test security—why haven't I heard anything about it?"

Subar tensed, but once again the wily Chaloni had prepared for the query. "Wouldn't be much of a test of security," he murmured with a diffident shrug, "if the system and managers responsible for maintaining it were warned of the forthcoming test in advance."

Boujon said nothing. Then he gestured at the woman and the one called Joh. "You two: I want you to act as if you haven't heard a word this scrug has said. As far as you're concerned, they're all low-grade thieves. If they move funny, look funny, talk funny, take their legs out." He then nodded at Harani, who followed his supervisor to a far corner of the office.

"What do you think about this, Quevar?" Boujon whispered. "Bunch of crola?"

"With froth on top," the big man agreed. "But what if it's true? Could be a bonus in it for all of us."

"Bonus or a bullet." The security chief let out a snort. "Only one way to know for sure. Check with Mr. Shaeb."

"Sure." Harani nodded eagerly. "Why didn't we think of that before?"

Boujon made a face. "I thought of it as soon as the kid with the sly mouth made his preposterous claim. There's only one problem." He indicated his wrist communit. "It's still three hours to sunrise. You know Mr. Shaeb. If I wake him out of a sound sleep now, it won't matter whether these kids are thieves *or* testers. He'll have all of us mindwiped or worse just to make a point."

Mention of their superior's sometimes toxic habits was enough to make Harani swallow hard. "Then what do we do, Mr. Boujon, sir?"

The security chief grunted. "We wait. Until sunup. If nothing else, Noritski's day crew will be coming on and we can turn the watch over to them while we proceed." He glanced in the direction of the four captives. None betrayed the least indication of unease as they waited for the two men to conclude their private conversation. "Meanwhile, I'll keep questioning them. Maybe they'll slip up and let something out. They're secured, so they can't hurt anything or get away." He smiled softly at his subordinate. "Better to be safe than sorry—especially where Shaeb is concerned."

The two men rejoined the rest of the assemblage. Hirani resumed his watchful stance behind the youthful quartet while Boujon once more confronted them. "My associate and I have decided to let you live."

"Good call," the unfazed Chaloni replied approvingly.

"For a little while," Boujon finished. "Until I can check out your story you'll stay here." A thin, humorless smile creased his broad visage. "Bound and determined, I suppose."

"Really, you've got nothing to worry about." Despite his age, Chaloni sounded very reassuring. "You've all done a great job, and it's going to reflect well on you."

"We'll see," Chaloni responded. "We'll know everything we need to know within a few hours. If you're telling the truth, I'll be first in line to apologize. If you're full of . . ." He broke off, blinking and swaying slightly. "That's funny." Leaning forward slightly, he tried to focus on his subordinates. "You don't look so good, Harani."

The burly guard was swallowing repeatedly, as if he had just ingested something that didn't agree with him. "Don't feel so good, either, Mr. Boujon, sir."

"In fact," the security chief went on, "none of you looks right." Feeling suddenly unsteady himself, he turned sharply to confront the leader of the young pack of infiltrators. "You'd better tell me, right now, if anything is . . ." He failed to finish the sentence. Hands secured behind his back, Chaloni was equally shaky on his feet. He looked distant as well as dazed.

"Don't . . . don't know what you're talking about, *tvan*. Does feel kind of hot in here, though."

"Hey," Zezula piped up, "I think I can smell my own blood." She looked around at her companions. "Anybody else got something wiro or viro up their nose?" With that, she promptly sat down where she had been standing. Ignoring the muffled orders of the guard Joh, she closed her eyes, rolled over onto her side, and was almost instantly asleep. Next to her, Subar gave up trying to keep his eyes open and his attention focused, and he joined her in sprawling out on the floor.

"Get up!" Simultaneously angry and afraid, Harani gestured with his gun. When neither threat had any effect, he kicked the now dozing Chaloni in the ribs. Not hard enough to break anything, but forcefully enough so that the blow could not be ignored by anyone attempting to feign unconsciousness. The hitherto talkative youth didn't respond.

Thoroughly disoriented now, Boujon stumbled toward the one interloper who had not said a word since being hauled into the room. Though misting over, the security chief's gaze was still focused enough to repeatedly take the measure of the biggest youth. Approaching Sallow Behdul, he scowled.

"Say, weren't you . . . weren't you taller when I brought you in?"

Frowning, Boujon's gaze dropped again, this time to the boy's feet. No, not to his feet. To his shoes. The soles, the thick soles—they were almost gone as they seemed to be evaporating before the security chief's eyes. These shut before they could widen, and Boujon toppled over onto the floor.

Only the guard Joh realized what was happening. Seeing coworkers and captives alike collapsing to the ground, he turned and staggered in the direction of a rear cabinet. Wrenching the doors open, he reached in and began fumbling for one of the transparent masks that lay on a top shelf. His other hand he kept pressed to the center of his face, which almost seemed to collapse under the pressure. Realization had come too late, however, even for the most resistant of the security team. Instead of sitting down, the guard settled onto his haunches. Only then did his head fall forward, indicating that he had gone as insensible as his companions.

Sallow Behdul lay not far away, similarly unconscious. The thick soles of his shoes had completely disintegrated. Or rather dissipated, the artfully shaped and solidified chemicals of which they had been fashioned having by now completely filled the security room and much of the storage complex with a narcoleptic gas that was odorless, colorless, undetectable by the sensors that continued to sit silently in their respective holders, and very effective. Focused on the edgy Subar, the beauteous Zezula, and the garrulous Chaloni, Boujon and his subordinates had made the mistake of paying little attention to the silent and complaisant Sallow Behdul. Big mistake.

Behdul was soft-spoken. Not stupid.

Several minutes passed. Within the security room and the complex at large nothing moved. Then a portal opened at the east end of the main building. A small stolen transport vehicle entered as the door closed behind it. Several alarms went off and were ignored. No one notified the nearest police facility of the unauthorized intrusion because the last thing the owners and operators of the complex wanted was representatives of local law enforcement poking through their diverse inventory of highly illegal imports. The complex had been tailored to be guarded and protected from within.

Not this morning.

The transport whined to a halt halfway into the complex and pivoted neatly on its axis so that it was pointed back in the direction of the doorway. Two figures emerged, one from each side of the vehicle. Over their faces they wore recycling masks to protect them from the persistent, long-acting gas. Walking quickly but without panic toward the security center, they found captives and captors alike collapsed on the floor. A nearby console was alive with warning lights, which were ignored.

Working swiftly and efficiently, just as they had practiced, Dirran and Missi slipped masks over the faces of their four anesthetized friends. Once this was done, injectors packed with revival antidote were slapped onto arms or legs. Coughing and swallowing repeatedly, Chaloni, Subar, Zezula, and Sallow Behdul rapidly regained consciousness. Small sidearms matching those the two newcomers carried were provided to the revived, though if everything went according to Chaloni's plan these would not have to be used.

So far, Subar decided as he wiped at his eyes and struggled to his feet, everything had gone exactly as rehearsed.

The alchem broker who had sculpted the shoe-sole-shaped gas solids had assured Chal that in the absence of the antidote, anyone inhaling a good, stiff lungful of the stuff would remain asleep for hours. That should give them more than enough time, Subar knew, to pick and choose the choicest items from among the storage complex's inventory. Rising, he brushed himself off. So subtle had been effects of the gas that he could barely remember passing out.

His opinion of Chaloni, which had always been a mix of respect, admiration, and wariness, rose considerably. It had all gone just as he had enthusiastically described it. The security staff lay sprawled all around them, maskless and insensible. The whole point of their elaborate individual attempts to penetrate the building's security had

been to distract and preoccupy the guards—mentally as well as physically—and to get them off station and gathered together in one
place. He smiled. They had been so busy bringing in him and his
friends that once that had been accomplished, they had relaxed. It
was critical that they do so, because as tough as he and his friends
thought themselves, Chaloni knew they could never have outmaneu-
vered or overpowered trained adult professionals.

Gathered together in one place, however, they could then be
brought down by the solidified gas that formed the soles of Sallow
Behdul's shoes. Of course, for the subterfuge to work, it would
hardly do for Subar and his friends to be found with antidotes, much
less face masks, on their person. They had to subject themselves to
the knockout effects of the same gas as their targets.

Now that Dirran and Missi had entered and revived them, they
could get down to business. Subar let his gaze take in the impressive
contents of the storage complex. Chal was right. They were going to
be rewarded with cred beyond their wildest dreams. And the best part
of it was that the illegal importers, whoever they were, couldn't report the boost to the police. Making sure his mask was sealed tightly
to his face, he started for the doorway. A voice made him halt and
whirl.

"*Tlali!*" It was Dirran, calling out from the back of the security
room. "One of these scrugs is still kicking!"

Literally, Subar saw as he and the others hurried to respond to
Dirran's cry of distress. Lying on his right side on the floor, the guard
called Joh kept kicking out with his left leg, like a dreaming dog.
Chaloni looked disgusted.

"Is that all he's doing? If it bothers you, make him stop." He hesitated a moment before adding, "Don't kill him. So far we haven't
had to kill anybody. Let's try to keep it that way. Not that it makes
any difference to me," he added smarmily, "but a 'radication might
force whoever runs this operation to bring in the authorities even if

they don't want to." Turning, he and the others left to begin rifling through the building's inventory.

That left Subar and Dirran alone with the semi-conscious guard. Subar eyed the body uncertainly. "He's breathing funny, too."

"Sure he's breathing funny." In Chaloni's absence, Dirran readily assumed the mantle of leader. "His respiratory system is full of the gas. Here, I'll show you how it's done." Looking around, the older boy chose a chair, raised it above his head, and brought it down on the side of the prone guard's head with just the right degree of emphasis. The reflexive leg-kicking stopped immediately.

Pleased with himself, Dirran set the chair aside. "See? If you don't want to kill somebody, it's better to hit 'em lighter but more often, until you've achieved the desired effect."

Leaning toward the body, Subar frowned uncertainly. "Looks like you might've smashed in part of his skull. I see a definite depression where you hit him."

"Yeah, well." Dirran sounded less assured. "Can't be too bad. I didn't hit him that hard." Resolutely adopting a more cheerful note, he added, "Let's go join the others. Don't want to be left out of the looting." He turned and headed for the entrance.

Subar lingered just a moment longer. There was something peculiar about the now entirely inert guard. He couldn't quite put a finger on it. Something about the way that leg had kept kicking out, about bulges of muscle where there shouldn't be any and a lack of muscle where it ought to be prominent. About how the right side of the head had been partially caved in by the swing of Dirran's chair, but without the expected echo of cracking bone. His natural curiosity drove him to want to examine the body further.

But Dirran was right. If he stayed here, poking and prodding the unconscious guard, he'd miss out on the chance to pocket a few small souvenirs of his own. *That* interested in the guard he was not. Turning, he broke into a run as he hurried in Dirran's wake. Like his companions, where Subar was concerned, cred triumphed curiosity every time.

Having thought better of Subar, Flinx would have found the younger boy's blanket identification with his friends simultaneously enlightening and depressing.

Deprived of its watchful sentries, the warehouse was a giant candy store. An ordinary group of youths would have found it interesting but would have been overwhelmed and confused by the surfeit of merchandise on offer. Not Chaloni and his gang. Having been apprised of the nature of its most valuable stock prior to planning the raid, he had a pretty good idea what to ignore and what to pull for loading onto the transport Dirran and Missi had brought.

Larger Terran objects such as the Roman-era statue were ignored. While immensely valuable, they were too conspicuous to be hauled around Malandere. "Take nothing bigger than you can carry by yourself" was Chaloni's directive.

Into the transport went a Sung dynasty plate, all blue-and-white earthly ceramic and bonded against the elements in its transparent protective cocoon. Even to Subar's uneducated eyes it was a thing of beauty. Chaloni had to explain to a curious Sallow Behdul that the encasement was necessary to preserve the plate because it could easily be broken. Behdul absorbed this information in disbelief. Poor as his family was, he had never encountered or even heard of a serving dish that was neither biodegradable nor impervious to shattering.

Missi found a small, vacuum-sealed bottle full of flower seeds. Flowers from Earth! As an organic, it was a doubly illegal import. That would not matter to the wealthy collector who would pay whatever was asked to acquire such a prize. The bottle had the additional virtue of being small, nondescript, and easily concealed. Other venerable antiques existed only as fragments of what had once been: half a Russian gold coin, a manual bottle opener with the insignia of the long-vanished Terran brewery still visible on the handle, a printed two-dimensional poster of an unknown actress from the distant past, half a dozen garishly imprinted drink cups made of the early and rare artificial material known as Styrofoam, a real book composed of pages fashioned of tree paper written by a long-forgotten author named Aram Fotep, and much, much more.

As they worked, electronic sensors tracked their movements. Relayed to security central, these set off alarm after alarm. The visual ones the laughing, frolicking young intruders could not see. The audible alarms they ignored. Their rampage was frenetic but controlled; a frenzy of unzipped cartons, debonded containers, and shredded shipping packets.

Though the original plan called for all plunder to be gathered in one place and the proceeds to be shared equally, youthful venality rapidly triumphed over collective purpose. A fair number of smaller objects found their way into shoes and pockets. Subar managed to secrete on his person a battered spoon fashioned of some cheap metal whose head flaunted a depiction of something called THE GATEWAY ARCH and a small, square package of pepper on which was printed the name of a restaurant. Astonishingly, and adding greatly to the value, it still contained its minute quantity of venerable if no longer viable Terran spice. He had no idea what these things might be worth, only that they were worth something.

Coincidental with the arrival of the first hint of morning sunshine, they shut the rear and side doors of the transport, piled in, and abandoned the building to its still-unconscious security staff and its surfeit of winking, wailing alarms. No one challenged them as they drove off. As they made their way out into the maze of the commercial district, going neither too fast nor too slow, other similar vehicles could be seen taken on cargo or delivering goods. Their vehicle, stolen especially for the early morning's work, drew no attention. Once out of the commercial district, they kept clear of the main transportation arteries, sticking to lesser surface accessways, sacrificing speed and automated navigation for control and continued anonymity.

At last convinced that they had pulled it off and were safely clear, the whoops and hollers of the excited perpetrators resounded inside the goods-filled transport. Even the normally jaded and indifferent Zezula joined in the joyful celebration. The kiss she bestowed on a startled Subar was as shocking and unexpected as anything that had happened to him that morning, and as valued as anything he had managed to conceal on his person. It left him feeling at once confused, agitated, and energized in ways he could not describe as he began to peel away his facial sprayon.

Around him, his companions were doing likewise. Chaloni, who had chosen the appearance of an older, pudgier youth of Oriental mien, was flinging shards of collated collagen in all directions. Missi was carefully peeling away her albino visage to reveal the much darker natural complexion beneath. Sallow Behdul exposed his naked and tattooed pate by dispensing with the long black wig he had worn. Nearby, Zezula had slipped out of the shoes that had added six centimeters to her height and was busily divesting herself of the false stomach that had given her the look of a woman in the middle stages of pregnancy.

The warehouse's automated monitoring devices, both prominent and concealed, that would undoubtedly have recorded their activities would reveal to anyone reviewing the numerous recordings a group of six active youths in the process of pillaging the warehouse—not one of whom bore any readily distinguishable relationship to Subar and his friends. The cosmetic sprayons they now gleefully discarded had been created by Missi, the most artistically inclined of the group. They had then been rendered in Shell, purchased anonymously, and applied in secret. There was no trail for any active pursuer to track. Let the outraged owners of the storage complex put out huge rewards for all of them. They would be attached to idents that bore no visible relation to the half a dozen buoyant youths who were presently celebrating their good fortune in the interior of the shrouded transport.

They had only one bad moment, when a police skimmer appeared directly in front of them. It did not slow as it approached them, however, and thrummed past overhead without slowing or pausing to challenge the vehicle with the hastily altered ident code. No further interruptions ensued as they reached the inner-city rental storage facility, identified themselves to the automated security system, entered, and backed the transport into the secure holding compartment Chaloni had rented.

Working silently and in tandem, it took barely an hour to unload, catalog, and stack the spoils. More time was expended piling used household goods of little value on top and around the booty. Leaving their pickings suitably camouflaged, they drove out the transport and sealed the storage locker behind them. So that none of them would feel the least bit apprehensive or slighted, Chaloni magnanimously allowed each of them to enter their signature retinal and bioelectrical impulses into the facility's security system. Now any one of them could access the rented unit.

"We don't want to go putting anything up for sale right away," he counseled his companions as the abandoned stolen transport exited the area and drove itself off. "We need to let the boosted nap, need to let the noise subside a little." His face was flushed with the excitement and triumph of what they had just pulled off. "Then we'll start selling. A few items at a time, to different fences. The cred will flow!"

Following Chaloni's final programming, the stolen transport headed for Inatuku, a city on the far side of Visaria. The likelihood of it being traced back to him, or to any of them, was remote. They then split up, traveling separately by public transport and on foot, until they rendezvoused later that afternoon at the priv place on the roof of the old building in Alewev District.

The brief, earlier celebration inside the transport notwithstanding, it was only then that they all really cut loose. Even Sallow Behdul was smiling and laughing, though he said as little as ever. Chaloni surprised them all by breaking out a packet of mojolo stim-sticks. Very high quality, imported from Fluva, and a varietal they had heard of but had not previously been able to try out. Everyone promptly lit up. Within minutes, the interior of the meeting room was awash in the fragrant airborne stimulus. Colors intensified, the sour stink of their immediate surroundings was banished, and all the troubles and tribulations of their otherwise barely tolerable, wretched existences were wafted away on a haze of aromatic smoke.

After a while, Subar was aware someone was in his arms. At first he took her to be Missi, but soon realized it was Zezula. Her eyes were glassy, her expression beatific. Sprawled across an old couch on the other side of the room with less than a third of a stimstick remaining clamped in his slash of a mouth, Chaloni was grinning across at him. Subar had always been by turns respectful, chary, and envious of the gang leader. But at that moment, he would have died for him.

Though it did not seem so at that especially mind-blowing moment on that particularly jubilant afternoon, it was a possibility that was not as far from reality as he might have wished.

CHAPTER

10

They should have waited several months before trying to market the first of their spoils. Being of a youthful and impatient age, they waited several days. Not even the usually reflective Chaloni was immune to the insistent lure of instant cred. They were each and every one of them dead broke, having spent everything they had been able to accumulate or borrow to finance the raid. In the end, the temptation proved too great.

Chaloni chose the fence carefully. First he vetted the woman via contacts throughout Alewev. Then he paid a visit in person to sell a comparatively inconsequential packet of activated medicines Missi had picked up off the street. Finally satisfied with the choice, he selected a couple of small but extremely valuable items from the hidden stockpile and set off across Malandere with Subar in tow. Pretending to be his "slow" younger brother, Subar would serve as a second pair of eyes and as armed backup.

"I've never used a gun before," he argued when the older boy explained his intentions. "Knives, a stunner—but never a gun."

Chaloni pressed the compact pistol into Subar's reluctant hand.

"Since everything is going to go according to plan, you won't have to use it this time, either. But there are times, y'know, when it's enough to let someone else *know* that you have a gun."

Subar indicated his understanding, conflicted between secret pleasure at having been chosen by Chaloni to accompany him in place of the older Dirran or Sallow Behdul, and concern at having to tote a high-powered weapon.

He relaxed a little when they entered the shop.

It looked a lot like a miniature version of the storage facility they had raided, only with all the goods crammed together, out on display, and none concealed by packaging. The assortment struck him as highly eclectic: a lot of junk interspersed with a few objects of real value. The presence of so much of the former might be intended to draw attention to the latter, he decided.

The middle-aged woman seated behind the long counter flashed maternal as they entered. "Wellup, wellin, boys." She had a permanent squint, a relic of imperfect ocular surgery, and wagged a finger at Chaloni. "You sold me those pop-pills, as I recalling." Her gaze flicked to Subar. "Who's this sprightly youngster?" Subar bristled at the "youngster." She might tag him differently if she could see the pistol presently residing in his right front pant pocket.

"My younger brother, Vione. Thought he'd like to see your place." Chaloni winked. "Thought it would be educational for him to sit on a transaction."

The proprietor nodded, smiling pleasantly. "Would you like some thirps to munch on while your big brother and I are attending to business? I have cinnamon and luret."

"Sure," Subar responded with falsified eagerness. In reality, he hated thirps. For all their imbued flavor, they had the consistency of desiccated packing material. Going along with the suggestion, though, earned him an approving glance from Chaloni.

Munch on the snack food he might, but that did not keep him

from playing close attention to the business at hand. Settling herself in the chair behind the waist-high counter, the woman looked on expectantly as Chaloni set down the innocuous-seeming package he had carried in tucked under one arm. She might affect a motherly countenance, Subar decided, but the gleam in her eye was pure distilled avarice.

Carefully, Chaloni unwrapped his precious payload. Revealed in the beam of the ceiling-mounted spotlight was a booklet of real paper. Beside it, he laid out a trio of short red stubs of similar material. Not having studied these particular items in any detail before, Subar leaned closer for a better look. The booklet advertised some kind of ancient sporting contest involving men in uniform. The accompanying triplet of smaller, darker material was devoid of imagery either flat, multidimensional, or projective. Antique indeed, he thought.

The shop owner's reaction was instructive. Normally steady as robotic digits, her fingers actually trembled as she picked up the booklet. Hesitating, she looked over at the grinning Chaloni. "May I?"

"Buyer has the right to examine the goods," he replied generously.

Page by precious page, she leafed through the fragile booklet. Setting it down as reverently as if it were the original copy of the books of the United Church, she delicately fingered one of the three red bits of paperboard that accompanied it.

"The dates all match," she whispered, as if unable to believe her own words. "Same dates, and the location of the sporting contest is mentioned prominently on all four items."

"Yeah, I noticed that," Chaloni agreed importantly. "I thought that might matter."

"You thought . . . ?" She broke off and waved a hand over the counter. A cylindrical tridee unit sprang to life, its glow highlighting her weathered face in soft green. "I'll make an offer."

Subar nearly choked on a half-chewed thirp when he saw the number that appeared in the relevant portion of the projection. Chaloni was game, but even he was clearly taken aback. He had arrived prepared to bargain. It was expected that he do so. A more experienced seller would have recovered in time to do so.

"That's okay. I mean, we accept." Having failed to keep his expression neutral, he compensated somewhat by maintaining an even tone. But just barely.

"Good. I don't mind haggling, but unlike some shop folk I don't particularly like it." She extended a hand.

Reaching into a jacket pocket, Chaloni pulled out his card and passed it over. As she ran it through the glow of the cylinder, it beeped twice, softly, before she returned it to him. A quick check showed that his pseudonymous account had been credited with a sum never encountered since he had originally stolen the device. He rose.

"We ought to be getting home. Pleasure doing business with you, Ms. Benawhoni."

"And you, Puol." She smiled at Subar. "You too, Mr. Vione. If you don't mind my inquiring," she asked hurriedly as the two youths headed for the doorway, "where did you obtain these very special relics?"

While not prepared for the size of the opening offer, this was a query Chaloni had anticipated, and he was ready with a response. "Third-party sources. Can't say more than that," he finished, having said nothing at all.

"Of course. I'm sorry. Unforgivable breach of etiquette." The proprietor looked properly apologetic. "Can you—do you have access to more material like this?"

Chaloni halted at the doorway. "I might be able to come up with a few pieces. You're saying that you're interested?"

She nodded once, deliberately. "Yes. I am interested. How soon can you bring me more?"

Chaloni shrugged, as if the matter was of no consequence. "Give me a couple of days to talk to my suppliers. Tueswen morning okay?" She indicated agreement. "Maybe something bigger next time?"

"Whatever you can get your hands on, child." Turning slightly, she gestured behind her. "Sometimes the smallest items are the most sought after. In this business it's all a matter of matching merchandise to a market."

Chaloni nodded as he stepped out through the invisible, momentarily deactivated security barrier. It was not until he and Subar stepped off their second public transport of the morning that the two of them finally felt safe enough to free their feelings. Their shouts of ecstasy and excitement drew looks of disapproval from commuters chained to the joylessness of actual jobs. Neither youngster paid the least attention to the judgmental stares their youthful expressions of delight attracted.

"Tvan," Chaloni exclaimed, "did you see how much? Did you *see,* Subar?" The older boy was fondling his credcard with a caress hitherto reserved solely for Zezula.

"I saw, I saw." Unable to restrain himself, Subar was prancing all around the gang leader like a Quillp at the ritual nest pole. "What now, Chal? What do we do next?"

"Do next?" Grinning hugely, Chaloni waved the credcard teasingly back and forth in front of the younger boy's eyes. "We spend, friend. Spend like we're briated, because there's flare more where this came from!"

Despite Chaloni's exultant exclamation they did not spend quite like they were intoxicated. That they were clearly under the influence of something, however, was on display for all to see. Handed *real* cred for the first time in their young lives, all the members of the group felt free to indulge their own individual desires, sometimes in previously unsuspected ways. Who would have thought, for example, that that silent sentinel Sallow Behdul would have wanted to take out a subscription to Benews, buying the headset that allowed one to listen to direct-induction media twenty-six hours a day? Or that

Missi, apparently forever content to hover in the shadow of the alluring Zezula, would spring for a phototropic hair weave that caused her coiffure to change color as well as pattern with every light shift?

They spent and they played and they went their separate ways, keeping their newfound wealth secret from relatives of every stripe. Heeding Chaloni's admonition, they were also careful not to overdo it. Able to purchase personal transportation up to and including a private, enclosed skimmer, the gang leader opted instead for an open street glider. He could customize it to fit his taste without drawing the attention of the authorities. Private skimmers could maybe come later, he explained to his exuberant acolytes, when they had sold more of the goods and accumulated greater cred.

Ashile was stunned when they met on the rooftop of her building and Subar presented her with the necklace. He insisted on fastening it around her throat himself. Mouth open, she found herself breathing deeply as she held the bottom curve of the band up to the light. Befitting the bastard glow of evening, the absorptive faceted gems trapped the city smog and promptly twinkled orange.

"Subar, I—I don't know what to . . ." Her tone darkened and she turned to face him. "Where, how, did you get this?"

He grinned broadly, enjoying himself. "Same way everybody gets things. By buying and selling." He nodded in the direction of the ribbon of refracted light that encircled her neck. "The bigger stones are Burley firestorm. Like it?"

"Like it? I never in my life, Subar . . ."

She ought to have questioned him further, she knew. She ought to have challenged him straight up. But every time she started to do so, a shaft of orange flame distracted both her eye and her attention. So she was left with only one thing to do.

She put her arms around him and kissed him.

His eyes got almost as big as the necklace's central stone. Pulling back, he was still smiling, but wary now. Not only because of the abruptness of the embrace, but because it made him feel unexpectedly funny.

"*Tloat,* Ashile. Take it easy. I'm going to assume that means that you do like it."

Having decided to keep it, she was examining the necklace more closely now. "It's the most beautiful thing I've ever seen. It must have cost you—I can't imagine how much it cost!"

He feigned indifference. "It wasn't so bad. Buying two of them, I got a great deal."

She looked up from the necklace and blinked. "Buying two . . . ?"

"Well, sure," he told her innocently. "This one for you and the other for Zezula."

"Zez . . ." A wealth of emotion distorted her expression in a matter of seconds. "You gave one just like this to Zezula?"

He nodded, in the manner of those males of the species who have paused to smell a flower unaware that the sheer cliff directly behind them has just been shivered by tectonic forces beyond their imagination and is about to collapse on top of them.

"Uh-huh. She liked hers, too. Not as much as you, I think."

Reaching behind her neck, she touched a forefinger to the coded clasp. Reading its new owner's body charge, the necklace released. She caught it as it fell from her throat and tossed it back to him. He caught it reflexively.

"Ashile, what . . . ?"

Her tone had passed beyond frosty into the realm of the arctic. "I've just decided I don't *like* Burley firestorm. But thank you for the thought." Turning, she strode away from him and toward the building's lift, walking fast but not hurriedly, the sinewy shape of her a sine curve counterpart to the stiff rooftop profusion of aerials and vents. Utterly bewildered, Subar stared down at the very expensive piece of rejected jewelry.

He knew how to break into buildings, and how to fool respectable citizens, and how to simulate beggary when times grew truly difficult. He even knew how to deal with offworlders and one or two nonhuman Commonwealth races. But for the life of him, he was sure that he would never come to an understanding of the opposite gender of his own species.

Reflecting his newly won wealth, Chaloni's custom-cut outfit was flashy and fashionable enough to draw the looks of the ladies but sufficiently subdued so that he would not stand out aggressively in a crowd. He had chosen it to attract attention but not a mob. It gave a lift to his gait. Literally, if one factored in the handcrafted glide shoes that added centimeters to his height while simultaneously easing his stride.

Parking his personal scoot several blocks away from his destination, he checked to make sure the autolarm was activated before turning and heading up the street. He was feeling very good about life, and about himself. As well he should, given the several days of splurge he and his friends had enjoyed. It was astonishing how fast, he reflected, a significant amount of cred could be spread once it was split six ways, even if he had kept the largest share for himself.

Well, no matter. He would have preferred to wait awhile longer before making another sale, but he had agreed on a date and it was not wise to keep an important connection waiting. The old woman would be glad to see him, he knew. He still remembered the look in her eyes when he had laid the ancient paper sporting booklet and its accessories out on her counter. He shifted the weight of the pack against his back, anticipating her reaction when he unburdened himself of its contents. Given her response to his first tender, he could only hope she did not go into cardiac arrest when she saw what he had brought for her this time. He did not quite lick his lips in expectation. The cred from the initial sale of goods taken from the scrimmed storage facility was nothing compared with what he and his friends were going to obtain today.

The shop was unchanged and exactly as he remembered it from the previous week. There was nothing to indicate the true nature of its core business: fencing stolen property.

Its owner was also as he remembered her: pleasant, matronly, and welcoming. She was perusing a holovit when he entered. As soon as she recognized him, she smiled and waved the projection into oblivion.

"Wellup and wellfound, young Mr. Puol." Eyeing him up and down, she barely repressed a smile. "You did not have to dress so flare just to come and see me."

He sat down opposite the counter, this time without waiting to be asked. As soon as he removed the backpack, his chair morphed to conform to his back, buttocks, and thighs. "I picked up a few things since I saw you last week. Fine clothes unworn aren't fine; they're just rags."

"A philosoph as well as a sagacious seller." Heavily made-up eyes glittered both literally and figuratively as they fixed on the backpack on his lap. "What nicey-niceties have you brought me this time?"

He worked slowly to unfasten the pack, marking time with the special seals, taking pleasure in making her wait. Watching intently, she offered a casual query.

"Where's your little brother?"

So intent was Chaloni on enjoying the moment that he was nearly caught off guard. "My bro . . . ?" He recovered in time. "Oh, Vione couldn't make it. Life studies class."

She nodded, apparently satisfied. And caught her breath as he removed several objects from the pack and set them on the counter.

One related tangentially to what he had sold her the previous week. It was a small, white ball used in the precursor to a modern game. Though the sphere, fashioned of organic materials, was well-worn, several signatures were still visible on its curves. Alongside this Chaloni placed a couple of garishly decorated plastic cups that at first glance featured the unlikely commingling of heroic figures and cheap food, a ring made of silver and turquoise whose provenance as genuine Terran would have to be established by proper cesium dating, a handmade woman's blouse featuring florid threadwork and sewn-in inserts of small mirrors, and to top it off half a dozen bottles of simple sand glass that not only remarkably still held a portion of flavored sugar syrup, but were contained in the original paperboard carrier.

Chaloni relished the look on her face. An expression like that was not the best one to adopt when preparing to enter into bargaining. It made him feel like he could name his price.

"Well?" he finally asked.

It broke the spell. She looked up at him, back down at the goods arrayed on the counter, and then pushed back in her chair. "Wonderful. Marvelous. That such objects should turn up for sale on a newishly settled world like Visaria is something of an inspiration. It speaks well for what others think of our future prosperity." She took a deep breath. "Unfortunately, childman, I cannot buy them from you."

Despite his preparations, Chaloni did no better at hiding his shock at this response than she had her desire when looking upon the merchandise. "You can't . . . ," he sputtered, concluding with a helpless, "Why not?"

"Because they aren't yours to sell, poor, poor, laddieyouth."

Two figures emerged from the shadows behind her. One of them would have made two of Chaloni. Or maybe three. Aside from unmissable massiveness, the man was toothy and blond and unsmiling. His companion was—his companion was just plain scary.

And alien. Very, very alien, representative of a species unknown to Chaloni. More than two meters tall and exceedingly slim, the creature's short, dense fur was a dark gray streaked with several shades of brown. The eyes were small, dark, intense, and covered with at least one, maybe two, nictitating membranes. Flexible pointy ears thrust out to either side of the head before angling upward to terminate in small furry tufts. Decorative strips of inscribed and burnished metal dangled from both of the extended hearing organs. Not only did one expansive cheek sac bulge impressively, but a frightened Chaloni had the impression something snake-like was moving within it. As the being came nearer, he could see that it was chewing methodically on something unseen. He caught a faint whiff of something offworld and unfamiliar.

Its garb was a clashing couture of multiple flexible bands and gear straps to which were attached hitech instruments that alternated with idiosyncratic primitive carvings and alien embroidery. It was as if the wearer, like his attire, was caught between the primitive world of his origin and the recklessly forward-thrusting society of Visaria and the greater Commonwealth.

Backing toward the doorway, Chaloni struggled to divide his attention between the pair of menacing newcomers and the fence he had been assured was independent and clean.

"What is this, Ms. Belawhoni? Who are these *tskoms*?" No matter how much he waved his hands over the activation panel, the door behind him remained resolutely shut.

Coming around the counter, the man put a hand behind Chaloni's lower back and urged him gently, but implacably, back into the room. Unable to flee the shop but with no weapon pointed in his direction, Chaloni let himself be guided. Not that he had much choice. The hand in the middle of his back that was compelling him forward was as relentless as a metal piston.

"Watch your language, scrim. And take it easy. We just want to talk to you." Once all three of them were behind the counter, the man removed his hand from Chaloni's lumbar and stepped back. That was a good sign, Chaloni decided. The fact that Ms. Belawhoni had vanished into the depths of the shop was not. As he was contemplating the possible ramifications of her disappearance, the heavy hand returned to shove him down into her chair.

"You can call me Corsk." Removing his fingers, the man moved around in front of Chaloni and leaned back against the display counter. It creaked beneath his weight. "This is Aradamu-seh. Arad is a Sakuntala, from Fluva."

On his guard and trying to shrink back into the chair, Chaloni shook his head. "Never heard of it. No offense," he added, with a hasty glance in the alien's direction. Those tight, fiery eyes were focused unblinkingly on him.

Corsk laughed. "Hear that, Arad? Little scrim's never heard of your world."

"That is your people's name for it, not ours," the alien remarked calmly.

"Never been there myself," Corsk commented conversationally. "Hear it rains there all the time. *All* the time." Leaning forward, he whispered conspiratorially to Chaloni, "Arad doesn't like humans."

"You interfere in our lives," the alien declared. "Your presence distorts our culture. You favor the unmentionable Deyzara. Those of us who want no part of your Commonwealth have no choice in the matter. We must participate, or wither."

Corsk was nodding knowingly to himself. "Pretty tough folk, these Sakuntala. Still have a thing or two to learn about cred-based economies. A few of the smart ones have realized they can make more hiring themselves out to perform certain services than they ever could stuck on their soggy, backward homeworld." He smiled at his partner. "No offense."

Aradamu-seh's nonhuman expression was unreadable. "Accumulate cred," he murmured. "Also *mula*."

They were playing with him, Chaloni realized. Well, if they were trying to crack the veneer of innocence he'd worn to the shop, they were going to have to do better than that. "I still don't understand what this is about. What kind of questions do you want me to answer?"

"Oh, we don't need the answers." Corsk leaned closer. "It's our employer who wants answers."

As best he could, Chaloni held his ground. "Who's your employer?"

The big man gestured casually behind him, toward the precious antiques Chaloni had carefully laid out on the countertop. "The owner of those wares. He wants them back." Corsk's voice dropped ominously. "He wants all of them back."

Chaloni shrugged diffidently. "I don't know what you're talking about. My brother brought home a whole crate of that stuff. Crate was all banged up, like it had fallen off a skimmer or something. Said he found it in a serviceway. Being younger than me, he asked if I'd try to find out if it was worth anything. So I asked around, it was recommended I try here, and sure enough, I sold a few pieces last week." Turning slightly, he looked back into the silent shadows that cloaked the rear of the shop. "Ms. Belawhoni paid a lot for them. If I'd known they were that valuable before I sold them, I might have tried to find the original owner." He mustered a smile. "You know— for a reward, maybe. But there were no markings on the crate, and you put out the word, pretty quick there are fifty *tshonds* claiming ownership rights."

Corsk had been nodding patiently while listening to the youth in the chair. Now his head stopped bobbing. "Nice story. The lady who runs this establishment would have been a good choice—except that she values her relationship with our employer more than she does the opportunity to market his stolen property. There's a reward for its return, all right, but she's the one in line to get it, not you, you miserable little lying *yibones*."

Taking offense, Chaloni started to rise from the chair. "*Thoy*, why you calling me that? I be linear with you . . . !"

A massive hand slammed him back into the seat so hard it nearly overloaded and broke the chair's spinal adapter. Corsk didn't care. He was certified to damage property.

"Sure you are, *yibones*." From a breast pocket of his slicksuit, he withdrew a security sensor tridee freeze. Unfolding, it showed several figures inside a nondescript warehouse loading a variety of antique items into a transport. "Recognize any of these cheerful scrawn?"

Heart thumping, Chaloni made a show of examining the freeze. "Never saw any of them, don't know any of them."

Corsk nodded, still patient. "Of course you don't. How about these?"

One by one, several additional freezes were presented to the youth in the chair. His reaction was unchanged. None of them looked like him. He was secretly thankful. The costly disguises had proven their worth.

"Sorry. Can't help you." His expression turned guileless. "Are these the scrims who originally stole this stuff?"

Corsk's tone was mollifying. "Indeed they are. Recognize any of them now?" Running his thumb across the back of one freeze, he enlarged a portion of it until the three-dimensional figure he had isolated filled the entire framing square. It was Chaloni. As he stared at the image, he gave thanks to the invisible powers in charge of Malandere Utilities that it was cool in the front of the shop. Otherwise, he might have started to sweat.

"Don't know the scrim, I told you. I could tell that before you bumped it."

Corsk nodded understandingly. His thumb moved again. "Please. Try just one more time."

Floating in the space between them, constrained by the freeze borders, was a close-up of a portion of the isolated figure. It showed only the side of the individual's head. An utterly nondescript image, except perhaps for the simple triangular earring that punched one earlobe. Held in place by a permanent charge in the exact center of the triangle was a very small synthetic red diamond. Chaloni had worn an earring like that for years. Had worn it day in and night out while zlipping and shopping, while showering, and while making love. Had worn it for so long that it had become a part of him.

A part of him he had forgotten to remove when donning his disguise prior to infiltrating the ransacked storage facility.

Smiling, he reached out to take the freeze, the better to have a closer look at it. Corsk let him take it. As soon as it was in his hand Chaloni brought it closer to his face, frowned—and shoved it straight at the big man's right eye. Letting out a yelp, Corsk stumbled backward, grabbing at his face with one hand while striking out blindly with the other. Fast and agile, Chaloni exploded out of the chair in an instant. He didn't try for the front door, which he already knew had been locked against any possible flight. Instead, he flung himself toward the back of the shop. There had to be a rear entrance. The two scrims had used it to enter without him seeing them, the double-crossing Ms. Belawhoni almost certainly used it to bring in merchandise, and with any luck it would be unlocked and he could use it, too.

He went down, hard, before he could get out of the front portion of the shop. Twisting wildly, he saw that something black and rope-like had wrapped like a whip around his ankles. Even in his rising terror he wondered how either of his inquisitors had managed to unlimber, aim, and loose a rope or wire fast enough to bring him down. Then his gaze rose and the explanation was self-evident. The bulge in the Sakuntala's right cheek was gone. The alien's mouth was open wide.

It had brought him down with its tongue.

Strong as it was, he might still have escaped from the organ's sticky grasp. He could not, however, escape the blows that an angry Corsk rained down on him. The eye the youth had poked with the freeze continued to water slightly as the big man and the Sakuntala slammed the bloodied, battered visitor back down in the proprietor's chair. The ocular irritation served as an ongoing reminder to Corsk as he and his alien associate renewed the questioning. Not that the big man needed any inspiration to continue with his work.

In the rear of the shop where she kept the bulk of her stock, Melyu Belawhoni was using the downtime to peruse a catalog. As had been the case since the advent of commerce, dealers often bought from one another as a way of freshening their inventory and occasionally putting one over on a competitor. In the darkened alcove, articles of value spun and twisted and changed depth and color in front of her, their descriptions playing out beneath them. As the screams from the front of the shop grew louder and more agonized, she switched to audio mode so that the descriptions of the items being displayed were spoken in a pleasantly neutral male voice via the catalog's adjunct virtual speaker. Wincing slightly, she directed the catalog to increase the volume. Though she made it quite loud, the occasional high-pitched shriek still rose above the steady stream of descriptive information.

Feeble, sprightly boy, she mused sadly. He and his brother (if the younger thief had indeed been a blood relative) had seemed nice enough. Personable and pleasant, if a touch arrogant. She had known as soon as she had set eyes on the fragile Terran memorabilia that it had been sourced from someone important. A quick check of the appropriate links had revealed both the extent and the value of an especially brazen recent robbery. Also the name of the stolen property's bona fide owner, who was known to her.

She could have passed along what she knew to the city authorities, of course. But doing so would have made her an accessory to the crime in the eyes of the violated. Property illegally obtained and imported from anywhere outside Visaria, much less from Earth, would be returned to the original possessors and, if those could not be traced or contacted, would end up being confiscated by the planetary government. Such a resolution would not be kindly looked upon by the violated individual with whom she had previously done business.

Much more profitable and much more healthy to inform he who had been ripped off of what she had learned. As expected, that worthy had been properly grateful. That the rest of his property would soon be returned to him she had no doubt. According to what Corsk had told her, there had been at least half a dozen of the shameless and stupid little scrimmers. She had seen the security freezes. Neither of the two youths who had paid her a visit the previous week resembled any of the individuals portrayed in the freezes, but the smiling Corsk had been confident. It was not just a matter of looking at such tableaux, he had assured her, but of knowing how to look, and with the right tools.

Still, she wished he had brought along another human associate to assist him instead of the creature. Intelligent it certainly was, albeit in a primitive way, but its steady stare and hostile attitude gave her the creeps. Well, they would all be gone from her shop soon enough. Another desperate scream infiltrated the expressive monotone emanating from the virtual speaker. She hoped her visitors would finish their work soon.

She would need time to clean up the mess before lunch.

CHAPTER

11

His new Adheres made Subar feel as if he were flying. From microsecond to microsecond, the sensors built into the soles scanned and analyzed the surface underfoot, adjusting the malleable material to the appropriate consistency. If the ground was smooth, the soles morphed to provide additional gripping power. If rough, they comported themselves to follow the terrain. If he so wished, on command they would turn virtually frictionless, allowing him to skate-slide at high speed across paved city surfaces. Through the shoes, walking was transformed into a wondrous, exciting experience that was as easy on the feet and legs as it was on the mind. Also an expensive one.

His share of the first sale of the warehouse loot had more than covered the cost of the Adheres, which had to be custom-fitted to his feet. He had enjoyed having the much older shop staff kowtow to his requests almost as much as he delighted in the shoes themselves. Nor were they his only purchase. His pockets and backpack held an assortment of electronic fripperies designed to do little more than entertain. Shoes and gear, of course, had to be kept hidden from his erstwhile family lest they rapidly become "lost."

The pod's clandestine rooftop meeting room provided adequate storage space for such needs, though at the rate he and his friends were buying things they were soon going to need to build an annex just to store their purchases. He grinned as he worked his way up the narrow pedestrian access. Having too much stuff was a problem he had never before in his life had to contemplate, and one he was more than ready to deal with.

The bottle stopped him. A casual visitor wouldn't even have noticed it. The lightweight, self-chilling metal cylinder lay on the side of the winding walkway where it had been discarded. Frowning, he picked it up and examined the label. As with most such beverages, the temperature differential between the liquid contents and the container's composition also powered the lambent advertising. Now that the bottle was empty, the label had been reduced to unilluminated, flat print.

He knew the brand. A mildly alcoholic brew containing at least two synthetic narcotics imported from offworld. None of his friends drank it. For one thing, it was way too expensive compared with similar-tasting domestic options. Also, it was tart and dry. He and his friends were of an age where tart and dry as yet had no chance when competing against sharp and sweet.

Certainly, given their new-won cred, one of them might have decided to feign sophistication by trying the brew. He could see Chaloni doing so. Alternatively, envisioning the mouth of the bottle sliding between Zezula's parted lips brought to mind another possibility. But there was no ego boost to be gained by trying it out of sight of everyone else. He would have been less surprised had he found the exotic metal container lying on the floor of the priv place. And he doubted anyone else in this neighborhood could afford to indulge in such a pricey libation.

It just didn't feel right.

Tilting back his head, he peered up the walkway. The usual cacophony of squabbling and shouting, of infants bawling and pets disputing, filled the air of the crowded residences. What was he so worried about? It was only an empty bottle.

Standing alone in the walkway, hemmed in by battered, quick-poured walls on both sides, he was sure of only one thing: lack of action never brought enlightenment. Feeling at least half a fool, he turned and descended, retracing his steps until he came to a certain half-hidden marginal accessway. Jogging up to its terminus brought him to a rooftop. Climbing higher, he resumed his ascent. Only this time he abjured any designated walkway, alternately shinnying and climbing over walls, windows, porches, and roofs.

Slow and difficult, the climb eventually put him on a roof opposite the building that was crowned by his pod's improvised hideaway. From there it was a short jump across a twenty-meter drop to the top of the conjoined air recycling and composting ventilation system that served the sprawling apartment complex below. The smell from the latter was a principal reason he and his friends had been able to construct their secret rooftop shelter without interference: nobody and no organization felt inclined to make use of a space that was simultaneously small and stinky, or to object when someone else did.

Keeping low and concealing himself within the forest of moaning vents and massive, concealed blowers, he advanced on the priv place from the rear. Almost immediately, he saw that he had been right to proceed with caution, and was thankful for his new shoes that allowed him to move in near silence. A pair of strangers were standing in front of the entrance. Identical twins, both women were massive, the product of genetic selection and the application of certain hormonal supplements and chemicals. Their faces were as pale and as rough as the raised patterns of bumps that adorned their bare forearms. As he looked on, one of them took a small inhaler from a pocket and sucked out a smile.

Heart pounding, his breath coming at shorter and shorter intervals, he worked his way around toward the back of the hideaway.

High up in the crude, jury-rigged lavatory there was a small window that served as a vent in the absence of proper plumbing. It was usually kept open. Anyone engaged in business within could look out at a patch of sky unmarred by grungy construction or the fetid exhalations of surrounding structures. From the rooftop one could peer down inside and, if the inner door was ajar, into the single room that constituted the priv place itself.

The screaming and crying he heard as he approached should have made him turn and run. The sounds were truly bone chilling, both because of their timbre and because he could identify who was uttering them. But he could no more flee from the vicinity of that former place of refuge without trying to steal a look inside than he could have closed his eyes in the presence of Zezula's nakedness.

She was there, too, though fully dressed. Peering cautiously through the open slot of the vent window, he could see her seated on one of the battered old lounges on the far side of the main room. Her hands were behind her. When after a minute or so she failed to show them, he assumed they were bound. It was the same with Missi, who was seated next to her.

A large, thickset man was confronting them. He was talking, though Subar couldn't make out what he was saying over the loud throbb music that was being played—to blanket the area with sound, not to provide atmosphere—and the constant sobbing and bawling of the two girls. That in itself was unsettling. Though Missi was known to lose it at the mere sight of an abandoned puper, Subar had never seen Zezula cry. Having always thought of her as having a compassionate heart sheltered behind a wall of duralloy, it was traumatic to see her weeping and shuddering as violently as her far more demonstrative friend.

Moving closer and leaning to one side changed the angle of view into the room. That was when he saw the alien. Tall and absurdly slim, with ridiculously long arms and hands that ended in half a dozen fingers apiece, it stood between the lounge and the talking stranger and the doorway. Subar found himself fascinated by the high tapering ears that shifted slowly to point in different directions like furry scanning antennae.

The alien's appearance was almost as mesmerizing as the body draped across one of its shoulders. As Subar looked on, it proceeded to dump this burden on the floor of the priv place at the girls' feet. They looked down at it, recognized it immediately, and resumed screaming all over again. Zezula did not move, but in spite of her bound wrists Missi kept trying to kick her way backward over the lounge. Or dig into its depths—Subar couldn't be sure which. What he could be certain of was the identity of the corpse. He had to look hard at it, though, because it had been—altered. Unlike the girls, he didn't scream, but he did stop breathing for a moment.

It was Chaloni. Or rather, something that had once been Chaloni.

Death was no stranger to Subar, or to anyone who had grown up in Alewev. But there were all kinds and ways of death, from the accidental to the natural, from the premature to the premeditated. Among the later, amateurishness of execution usually dominated. What had been done to Chaloni was different. It showed every indication of having been carried out in a manner that was slow, professional, and merciless. It not incidentally explained how his killers had found their way to the secret meeting place. Before he had expired, Chaloni had told them. Chaloni had probably told them everything they wanted to know, and more besides.

The gang leader's body was naked. It was also missing more than clothes. The work had been carried out slowly and with care. Even to Subar's young eyes, which were inexperienced in such matters, it was clear that a certain amount of time had been expended. Too mesmerized to run and too horrified to turn away, as he examined the crumpled corpse from the vantage point of the high bathroom window he found himself surprised that so much of a person could be removed while still leaving the basic shape intact. There was also a lot less blood than might have been expected, no doubt because the bulk of it had been drained off earlier. He could not recall where he had heard the hoary old expression *dying by inches*. He did not know what an inch was, but the pithy phrase had stuck with him nevertheless.

As he looked on, the tall, slender alien disappeared from view. The creature reappeared a moment later wrestling a naked, bound figure in front of him. Or her. Knowing nothing of the furry, high-eared species, Subar was unable to sex it. Despite his lack of clothing the new prisoner, however, was immediately familiar. Dirran struggled futilely against his bindings. They were causing him considerable discomfort, as were the neat, even strips of skin that were hanging from his face and other parts of his body. His appearance was shocking enough to stop the girls' screaming.

Leaning forward, the large muscular man began yelling first into Zezula's face, then Missi's. Subar reconsidered. Maybe Chaloni hadn't told his captors everything. Or despite his captors' ghoulish professionalism, maybe the gang leader had been inconsiderate enough to expire before babbling everything he knew. Otherwise, why were Dirran, Zezula, Missi, and Sallow Behdul still alive? Why hadn't they already been skyed screaming down the road Chaloni had taken?

A moment later, the subjects of his wondering were reduced by one as the alien placed a huge hand over each side of Dirran's head, lifted him off the floor, and gave a single sharp, athletic twist. Subar did not hear the *snap*. He didn't have to, because Dirran was now looking directly back at the alien while the rest of his body continued to face forward. Exhibiting an air of complete indifference, the creature tossed the now lifeless body onto the couch. It landed between Zezula and Missi, who despite their bonds did their frantic, panicky best to edge away from it.

This time the big man yelled first at Missi before switching to Zezula. A hard, open hand began to rise and descend, rise and descend. A helpless Subar could only watch and grind his teeth. Hair flying, Zezula's head snapped back and forth until the man stopped; then it dropped forward onto her chest. Every muscle, every ligament and tendon in Subar's body felt stretched tight enough to snap. There wasn't a damn thing he could do.

He needed a weapon. But even if he had one, he realized, using it would mean going up against four professionals and trying to take them out without getting any of his friends hurt in the process. He was neither that good nor that experienced a shot.

More than at any previous time in his young life, he felt completely helpless.

Picking up the unconscious Zezula, the alien effortlessly tossed her onto the shoulder that had previously been occupied by Chaloni. The man who had conducted the interrogation gripped the sobbing Missi by one arm. Ungently yanking her off the couch, he shoved her toward the doorway. Turning back, he vanished briefly from view before returning with a more thoroughly bound Sallow Behdul. The big youth's expression was blank as he stumbled after Missi. He looked like someone already dead who was only continuing with the motions of living because he had been ordered to do so.

It was at that moment, making a last check of the priv place, that the interrogator happened to glance up as well as back. His eyes met Subar's. Both sets of opposing oculars widened simultaneously.

The big man shouted as Subar bolted. Absolute terror lent extra energy to his legs and feet. Behind him he could hear more shouts and the sounds of heavy feet pounding on rooftop. A glance backward showed the Amazonian twins in hot pursuit. One was aiming a device in his direction.

As he made the leap across to the next building, something seared his right arm as if it had come in contact with a heated metal bar. Looking down, he saw wisps of smoke rising from his skin. The smell of his own burning flesh would have made him gag, if he'd had the time to squander on such things. The voices behind him commanded him to stop. Remembering the sight of Chaloni and what had been done to Dirran, he knew that his chances for survival would be better if he simply threw himself off the nearest roof.

He was small but quick. In the teeming, festering warren that was Alewev, those were advantages. Down a chute he went, barely bothering to thrust out hands and feet to slow his descent. Then up a serviceway, across a bridge of parallel power conduits, down yet another gap between two buildings, and out onto a side street. No one there even bothered to look in his direction. Like poverty and powerlessness, flight and pursuit were part and partial of everyday life in the district.

The rooftop meeting room wasn't the only covert location known to the members of the rapidly disintegrating pod. In addition to their collective hidey-holes, each of them had his or her own special, private places. Out of breath, strength, and adrenaline, Subar finally threw himself into one of several service bins that were bolted to the back of a large refuse recycler. Inside the bin, the nonstop hum and rattle of the city service unit onto which it backed was deafening. But no one could hear him here, or pick up his heat signature, or smell him out. Huddled back against the bin's interior wall, face pressed between his knees and arms around both, he waited for a massive hand, be it human or alien, to wrench the door aside and fish him out.

Time passed. An hour, then another. He dared to think that he might have shaken his pursuers. He couldn't go home, he knew. Chaloni might have spilled that information along with everything else. With his home and family possibly under surveillance and the priv place violated, he had nowhere to go.

Alone in the gloom, safe for now and having nothing else to do, he finally allowed himself to cry.

He awoke with a start in the dark, the hidden hulk of the recycling machinery rumbling smoothly behind him. Wanting to scream, he knew enough not to. Once he'd rubbed his already sore eyes as clear as he could manage, he slowly opened the bin door a crack and peered out.

The serviceway was empty, the ground damp. It had rained while he had been asleep. There was no sign of the grim-faced twin giant-esses, the muscular interrogator, or the frighteningly silent alien. Pushing open the bin door, he climbed out. It was still dim in the ar-tificial canyon formed by the surrounding structures, but an irregular smear of orange-brown sky showed overhead. A glance at his unduly expensive and absurdly fashionable new communit indicated that it was a few minutes before eight in the morning. Exhausted and terri-fied, he had slept through the remainder of the previous day and on through the night.

He stood there, alone, rubbing his eyes. He could not go home. Depending on how much Chaloni had told his captors before he died—and he had probably told them a great deal, Subar surmised—they might be waiting for him in its vicinity. Secreted in a hallway, perhaps, waiting to snatch him as he wandered in, disappearing him before anyone noticed. Knowing his parents as he did, Subar doubted they would spending much time grieving over his disappearance. Nor could he try to obtain supplies from the priv place: that was cer-tain to be under surveillance.

They would be after him, he knew. People like that didn't let in-sults pass. They would be relentless in their pursuit, not stopping until they had accounted for every one of those who had boosted the warehouse. He had nowhere to go and no one on whom he could un-load his misery. Except, maybe one . . .

The last time he could remember being as relieved when Ashile responded to a communication of his was when that peculiar tall off-worlder had saved him from the thranx and the police. He met her in the usual place on the roof of her building, though not before watch-ing her from hiding as she stood alone and searched for him. There was no reason to suppose that Chaloni or any of the other pod members knew about the place, or even the casual friendship, but he was taking no chances because he knew he wouldn't get any.

When he finally stepped out of hiding, she caught sight of him with a mixture of bewilderment and irritation.

"There you are! What kind of game are you playing today, Subar? I don't think I like . . . hey, take it easy!"

He half guided, half dragged her back into the cluster of service conduits where he had concealed himself. Her attitude changed the moment she got a good look at his face.

"You said it was an emergency, Subar, but I didn't realize—"

He cut her off, everything that had happened to him the previous week spilling out in a torrent of words. She listened closely to all of it, not even nodding, just letting him gush until he concluded with a description of the dreadful events of the preceding day. When he finally finished, she reached out and tentatively put a comforting hand on his shoulder.

"What are you going to do?" she asked as compassionately as she could.

"I don't know." His eyes were haunted with the memory of the horrors he had witnessed yesterday morning. "I can't go home; they're liable to be watching the whole building. The bin-hide I used last night is safe, I think, but there's nothing there. It's just an empty box. I have nowhere else to go."

She hesitated. She had never seen him like this. Typically cocky and fearless, respectful of that awful *shatet* Chaloni but not afraid of him, suddenly Subar looked . . . he looked . . .

He looked his age.

She heard herself replying before her thoughts were fully formed, and she was almost as shocked at them as he was.

"You could stay with me."

He gaped at her. "I mean," she continued hastily, "I could hide you in my building. There are storage places, rarely visited and not at all full, that are climate-controlled. I could bring you food, and you

have your communit for information and 'tainment." Growing enthusiasm replaced her initial uncertainty. "You could hide here for as
long as necessary."

The look he gave her was one she had not seen before; its most
prominent component was confusion. "That might work," he finally
commented, not bothering to thank her. "For a while, anyway." He
nodded, as much to himself as to her. "At least it would give me a
base of operations."

Now it was her turn to show uncertainty. "Operations? Operations for what? Staying alive?"

Gradually he was starting to look and sound a little more like his
old self. "I can't just crawl into a hole and aestivate like some dumb
squinad," he told her, referring to a local species of vermin that
plagued every housing structure in the district. "They took Zezula and
Missi and Behdul away alive. For sure to ask them more questions,
if only for corroboration of what Chaloni told them. Maybe"—he
swallowed hard—"for other things as well. I can't just forget about
them."

"Yes you can," she snapped. But his thoughts were already
streaking ahead.

"Sallow Behdul's big, but he's useless in a situation like this. I
wouldn't be surprised if the *sahongs* kill him out of hand. The girls—
they'll at least talk to the girls. For a while."

"They're not your problem, Subar." She did not like the turn
their conversation had taken.

He met her gaze. "They're my *friends,* Ash. I have to do something. I have to at least try. With Chal and Dirran dead, I'm the only
hope they've got." His voice dropped. "I don't know what the people
who have them are going to do to them, but one thing I know for
sure: they're not going to let them go. I've got to try."

She stepped back in exasperation. " 'Try'? Try what? This isn't
an entertainment vit, Subar, and the people you've described to me

aren't acting. They killed Chaloni and Dirran, they'll kill you, too. What are you going to do? Tell the police?"

He shook his head violently. "Worst thing I could do. People like this, if they get word the authorities are looking into it, they'll just sky Zez and Missi and Behdul out to the Torogon Straits and dump them into the outgoing current."

"Then what are you going to do?" She softened her tone. "You're a great guy, Subar. I—I like you. But you're just a kid. A seriously tough kid," she added quickly, seeing the expression on his face, "but there's just one of you. I'll help you as much as I can, but that doesn't include walking into the house of some semi-legal trading family, or whoever's behind this, with guns flaring. I know my limits, and you should, too." Moving forward, she once again rested her hand on his shoulder. "The more you talk like this, the more I keep seeing you dead, and I—I'd rather not."

He looked up at her, then nodded slowly. "You're right. If I'm going to do anything for Zez and the others I need help. Serious help."

"You don't know any serious help," she told him. "You never went illegal enough to make friends with those kinds of people. You don't know anyone anymore. Except me."

"No." He stood up so suddenly that it took her aback. "I do know somebody. I don't know if he'll help, but all he can do is refuse. That is, if he's even still on Visaria."

She frowned doubtfully. "Subar, who are you talking about? You don't know any . . ." She broke off, remembering. "Are you talking about that strange offworlder you introduced me to? The one we escorted back to his hotel?"

He nodded, a glint of excitement in his eyes. "Flinx, his name was. Yes."

Ashile eyed her friend as if he had lost not only his companions, but his mind, too. "He's just one offworlder. Not all that much older than you and me, either. He didn't strike me as the soldier type, and he doesn't dress like a Qwarm."

"You don't know him," Subar insisted, conveniently avoiding the fact that he didn't know Flinx, either. "I saw him do—certain things. To Chal, and Dirran, and Behdul. I don't know exactly what he did or how he did it." He struggled to remember. "He said something about letting them taste dark water, whatever that means. If he can do something like that to the people who are holding Zez and the others, they might have a chance. If we can just break them free, they can go into hiding, too. And," he finished, "the offworlder said that his pet was poisonous, remember?"

"*Tchai,* I remember." She was more than a little exasperated. "You're going to go up against the people who slaughtered Chaloni and Dirran and are still after you with the aid of one skinny long-song? And his 'pet'?"

Subar was adamant now. "If he's still on Visaria, yes. And if he agrees to help. Which," he was compelled to add disconsolately, "he very well might refuse to do."

"That'll determine if he has any sense," she shot back, "or if, like you, he's lost it all."

Looking as helpless as he felt, Subar spread his hands imploringly. "I have to at least make an attempt, Ash. These scrawn, they've taken my *friends*." He eyed her intently. "Will you come with me? This Flinx, I got the feeling he liked you."

"*Tnai,*" she muttered sulkily, "I'll come with you. I don't know why, but I will. Maybe because I've always had a soft spot for dumb, abandoned animals."

Coming toward her, he gripped her upper arms. His grasp was firm and confident, his expression grateful, his tone gentle. "I knew I could count on you, Ash. You're a good friend." Leaning forward, he kissed her—on the forehead. It was a thankful, respectful, chaste kiss. She wanted to hit him.

While he waited below, concealed near the main entrance to her building, she mumbled an excuse to her parents about leaving to visit friends for a couple of days. Her mother barely looked up from her in-home work to acknowledge her daughter's declaration. Stuffing a few essentials into a backpack, she made her way downstairs. As the lift descended past other overcrowded floors, she found herself pondering.

What in the world was she doing? She could get herself killed. Or Subar could. She told herself that she was doing it for a good friend. A seriously good friend. Who was planning to risk himself for *his* friends.

A series of foul words she would never have used in public slalomed through her mind, tainting her thoughts. "His friends." She knew on whose behalf he was risking himself. That apathetic slut Zezula. He was always talking about her, always going on about how she looked, how she moved, how she talked, how she dressed, how she . . .

What a very great pity, Ashile thought as she exited the building and rejoined Subar, that the brutal unknown assailants had chosen to take out their anger on Chaloni instead of his worthless girlfriend.

CHAPTER

12

Even among the emotive roar and howl of the city, even while lying and relaxing on the bed in his room, Flinx's casually roaming Talent was able to pick out the pair of desperately focused feelings coming toward him. He was able to do so for precisely that reason: because they were coming toward *him*. Years of running, of living in a state of constant wariness, had sensitized him to feelings that were aimed in his direction. Furthermore, he recognized both of them. They belonged, unless he was very wrong, to the two youths he had once conversed with on the roof of a run-down apartment complex in another part of the city.

He was not pleased. He had told the youth—what was his name?—Subar—that work beckoned, and had made his good-byes. Now the boy, and his more estimable female friend, were entering the lobby of the hotel where Flinx had taken a small suite. Their emotional states were—unsettled.

He could simply ignore them, he knew. Refuse to respond to their request for access to his floor, pretend he was not in the room. Check out and move to another residence, another city even, to avoid them. Only one thing stopped him. As it so often did, his damnable curiosity got in the way, just as it had on that morning days ago when he had intervened to rescue the youth from the attention of the authorities.

Might as well see what had the two of them so churned up inside, he told himself resignedly. It wasn't as if his already too-long sojourn on Visaria was otherwise inundating him with admirable examples of his own species. Dealing with whatever was firing the emotions of his unexpected visitors would no doubt only take up a few minutes of his time, and he had planned to leave Malandere and return to the *Teacher* in another day or two anyway.

He could not see the expression on Subar's face when he acknowledged the youth's arrival, nor hear him breathe "He's still here!" to Ashile. But he could sense the relief in the boy's feelings.

That the situation was serious and not simply a ploy intended to let Subar gain access to him again was made plain by the haste with which the youth and his lady friend practically dashed into the outer room of Flinx's suite.

"Thank you." Subar collapsed into the nearest chair, which was hard-pressed to orthopedically accommodate so swift a collapse. "Thank you, thank you, many *tvarin* times over." A more self-controlled Ashile lowered herself decorously onto the arm of the single chair. She let her right arm slip around behind Subar but, Flinx noted, made no contact with him.

Someone else did, however. Spreading her vibrantly colored wings, Pip rose from her resting place on the other side of the room and hummed over to land on the girl's lap. She started slightly, but held her seat. Timidly, she reached down with her left hand and began stroking the flying snake behind the scaly head. Sensing his pet's complete ease with the girl, Flinx permitted himself to relax a little more.

Subar was not relaxed, however. His emotions were a roiling, conflicted storm. Anxiety, fear, expectation, hope, desperation, panic:

all were present, tumbling and folding over and through one another like batter in a bowl.

His tone bordering on irritation, Flinx wasted no time on casual banter. "I told you I had work to do. This better be important."

"I . . ." Now that he actually found himself in the older youth's presence, it struck Subar with sudden force that he had made no preparations for this moment. He had been completely consumed with just finding Flinx again. Now that he had done so he was unsure how to begin. One thing he felt he needed to do if he was going to secure the offworlder's aid was to minimize as much as possible his own responsibility for the current difficult circumstances.

Ashile, on the other hand, had no such qualms. While Subar was deciding what to say and how best to say it, she jumped right in.

"Subar's gotten himself in a right *tconic* mess. He and his 'friends' scrimmed a storage facility run by local illegals. They got founded out. Two of them got deaded." She eyed Subar. "With extreme invention, apparently."

"Chaloni," he mumbled, "and Dirran. You met them."

Flinx remembered. "Go on," he responded guardedly. There was no duplicity in Subar's confession.

Ashile continued when Subar could not. "Three of his other friends were taken. Two *girls* and one other guy." She looked down at the young man slumped in the chair. "Subar insists on trying to rescue them. Why, I don't know. They've never done anything for him that I can see. But I can't talk him out of it. Being his real friend, I agreed to accompany him this far. At least." She looked up at Flinx. "He seems to think you might be able to do something. I don't see why he should involve you—"

A shocked Subar looked up at her. "Ash!"

"—since you're just a visitor here. But you helped him once before, and he believes you might help him again. All I can tell you is that if I were you, I wouldn't get involved." She looked down at the youth in the chair. "He told me in too much detail what these people did to Chaloni and Dirran. I don't know what your profession is, Mr. Flinx, but I'm sure you've never been involved in anything like this."

Flinx nearly choked on the acrid laugh he managed to suppress. "Uh, no, I'm sure you're right, Ashile. Like I told Subar, I'm only a student, and this—this kind of conflict is all pretty new to me."

She eyed him evenly, without embarrassment. "You're one of those professional students who just keeps studying and never graduates as anything, right?" she said accusingly.

He had to look away lest she see his expression. "Something like that. Actually, I am working toward graduating in the near future. It's a goal I hope I can achieve. Unlike some, failure is not an option for me."

Her initial scorn turned to sympathy. "Can't disappoint your parents, huh?" In her lap, Pip squirmed uncomfortably.

Flinx carefully pondered a response before finally replying, "Actually, the entire Commonwealth is depending on me, though its inhabitants don't know it."

She stared at him for a moment, then made a face. "I was just asking. You don't have to get sarcastic about it."

"Will you help?" Subar had had enough of this courteous byplay. They were wasting time. He thought of what her captors might be doing to Zezula. And to Missi and Sallow Behdul, too, of course. "I can't take this to the authorities."

"Because you and your friends invited this reprisal by committing an illicit act yourselves," Flinx commented.

"It's not only that," Subar told him. "This is Malandere. This is Visaria. It's not Earth, it's not Hivehom. The line between those who enforce the law and those who break it isn't so clear-cut here. I could turn myself in to the authorities for protection and wind up in the same sludge pit as if I'd been carried off by the people who've taken Zezula and Missi and Sallow Behdul."

Flinx leaned back into the lounge that cradled him, sighed, and crossed his arms over his chest. "Aside from the question of whether

I'd help you or not, what makes you think that I could do anything if I did?"

On firmer ground now, Subar sat up straight and leaned forward. "You rescued me from the two thranx and the police. I saw what you did to Chaloni and the others when we were up in our priv place. You can do—things. I don't know how, but I know that you can. The more I'm around you, the more I get the feeling that you're not just an ordinary visitor. You might be a 'student' like you say—but a student of what I'd sure like to know." He repeated what he had said before, with as much emphasis as he could muster. "*Will* you help?"

Boredom. Boredom and curiosity. Separately they had sometimes gotten him in trouble. Together, they invariably did.

"All right," he told the youth. "I'll see if I can do anything. Though exactly what, I have no idea."

"Thank you," Subar replied simply. His voice was even, controlled. But the feelings he was holding in still threatened to overwhelm him.

What he did not know, and what the tall offworlder seated opposite refrained from telling him, was that Flinx had agreed to lend his assistance not to aid Subar, but because Ashile's love for him was as transparent and pure and unqualified as it was unspoken, and was exactly the kind of empathetic humanity Flinx had despaired of finding in a place like Malandere.

One thing that escapes the attention of law-abiding citizens on any human-settled planet is that gossip infects the underworld as thoroughly as it does their own. The criminal substructure has its own Shell, through which rumor, innuendo, and news is filtered separate and apart from the tridee media that informs society at large. For those who wish to do so, accessing this flow of illicit information is no more difficult that wading into a river of sewage. The quandary is that the consequences are often the same.

Though Subar's street contacts tended to be younger than the average professional lawbreaker, they were in many ways no less competent. It took him only a couple of days to find out who was holding his friends. This because the word had been disseminated that the unpleasant people in question were still looking for one more thief—him. Anyone with knowledge of his whereabouts was offered a Shell connection to contact, with a substantial reward promised for information leading to his eventual capture. Knowing who held his friends, however, did not automatically suggest a means of liberating them.

"We need guns," Subar was muttering as he and Ashile strode down the busy street alongside Flinx. "And maybe explosives. Blow the entrance and sneak Zez and the others out the back." He coughed. Combined with the thick, particulate-laden air of the city, tension was causing his breathing to come in short, anxious puffs.

"No," Flinx told him quietly. "No guns. No explosives." He did not explain that the one thing he personally had to avoid at all costs was the drawing of attention to himself and to his presence on Visaria. The liberation of Subar's friends had to be done quietly, or not at all. He already knew what he intended to do. Otherwise, he would not now be walking in their company.

Ignorant of his new friend's need to maintain complete anonymity, a baffled Subar piped up, "Then how are we going to get inside?" Ashile's expression, as well as her feelings, showed that she shared his confusion.

Looking down at them, Flinx smiled reassuringly. "We'll knock." He proceeded to detail the approach he had worked out. As he did so, Ashile wondered yet again why she hadn't possessed enough sense to stay out of this completely.

"That's the most *sethet* thing I've ever heard." She was staring at him. "Who do you think you are? *What* do you think you are? Besides insane, I mean."

"He's not." Unlike his friend, Subar was grinning broadly. Flinx's strategy made sense. All it demanded was boldness, daring, and a willingness to place his life completely in the taller youth's hands. "Wait, and you'll see." The near worshipful expression on his face as he looked back up at the offworlder, she noted, was exactly the same as the one he used to bestow on the deceased Chaloni. To her, it was not a good sign.

Flinx went over the final details of the tactics he had concocted as they rode public transport to the address specified by Subar's contact. Perhaps not surprisingly, it was located in the same industrial zone as the storage facility Subar and his friends had boosted, though in another building some distance away. While still confident in the capabilities of his offworld friend, it was Subar's nature to have second thoughts.

"What if the information I got is outdated, and Zezula and the others are no longer being held in the same place where you're supposed to sell me?"

Ashile glared at him. "Now's a fine time to think of that!"

Having anticipated the possibility, Flinx was not put off by the question. "Then we'll just have to leave, and try to find another way to locate them. But I think the odds are pretty good. They've already viewed your 'captured' image via their own link. Knowing nothing about me, they've no reason to suspect I intend anything other than delivering you, as per agreement."

Ashile refused to let the concern go. "If they don't know you, why should they trust you?"

Flinx smiled at her. "It's been my experience that people of this type believe that money trumps every other concern. Once we're there and they 'have' Subar, it's a possibility that they might decide to renege on their part of the deal and not pay me, to save the cred if they think they can get away with it. That's the only kind of fight they'll be prepared for. It doesn't matter, because I'm not looking for pay and we're all going to leave together." He turned to Subar. "With your friends, if they're there. That much I'll be able to tell as soon as we're near the building, before we even have to announce ourselves, much less go in."

Genuine puzzlement fueled her response. "How are you going to do that?"

"Just trust me. I'll be able to tell." Given how frightened Subar's friends must be, if they were still inside he shouldn't have any trouble picking up their fear from outside the structure, no matter what kind of security it had in place.

Ashile was looking at him strangely now. Flinx did not have to read her emotions to know what she was thinking. She was wondering just what his undeclared capabilities might be. He offered what he hoped was a reassuring smile, and said nothing.

After disembarking from the transport, it was half an hour's walk to the address they had been given. From outside the featureless, windowless structure, Flinx quickly perceived that Subar's friends were indeed being held within. He did not have to strain his abilities to verify their presence. The interior of the building reeked with adolescent fear. He then proceeded to remind his younger companions one last time that whatever ensued once they were inside, they needed to stick to the scenario he had laid out for them. Working carefully, he secured their wrists behind their backs. When that was done they made their way to the entrance. It was located off a wide serviceway fronting the rear of the structure, away from the main street.

Having agreed previously upon a delivery time, those inside and in charge were expecting him. Security at the building was tight and seemed to impress Subar and Ashile. To Flinx, who had at times successfully penetrated the security surrounding powerful companies as well as the Terran Shell itself, the measures in place were proficient but hardly awe inspiring. Insofar as he could tell, they were each and every one of them designed to prevent unauthorized personnel from entering the building. Nothing he saw suggested that any measures were in place to prevent someone inside from getting out.

He felt confident, ready to gamble that everything he had carefully worked out with Subar and Ashile would go exactly according to plan.

Detecting their approach, an inner door at the end of a dirty, undistinguished hallway opened to admit them. A very large blond man stood there. Coupled with the physical description of the individuals he had glimpsed inside the pod's priv place that he had supplied earlier, Subar's emotional response was all that was necessary for Flinx to identify the man. Broad and muscular, he was the one who had been in charge of the team responsible for the death of the youth's friends and the abduction of the survivors.

For his part, the blond's attention shifted speedily from Flinx to the downcast bound youngster standing in front of him. The big man did not smile. "Yeal, that's him, the one we put out the word on. The last one. The slippery little feeker who gave us the slip on the rooftop." His tone suggested that Subar was already dead. The man's awareness then shifted curiously to the equally tightly bound Ashile standing dejectedly nearby. "Who's the prebreed?"

"Friend of his." Having spent time in the company of cold-blooded killers, merchants, emomen, and aliens, Flinx could mimic their posture and tone with little effort. "Was with the scrug when I picked him up. Got hysterical, so I thought I might as well twofold the package." He looked away, eyeing a nude image crawling up a nearby wall, indicating that Ashile's fate mattered not a whit to him one way or the other. "Won't charge you for two. Could have done her there and been done with it, but thought maybe you could use her. You know, to help convince him to yammer." He shrugged indifferently. "Or whatever. I like to leave a scene clean."

"Good forethink." Corsk grinned unpleasantly as he took a step back. "Hall scanners opt you clean. Not even a knife. Young, but smart."

Flinx acknowledged the compliment with a slight nod and gave the arm-bound Subar a shove, sending him stumbling forward. Eyes on the floor, Ashile followed meekly. She did not have to feign the fear she was feeling. What if the offworld "friend" to whom Subar was trusting their lives had simply been playing a game with them and had all along intended to sell them to these terrible people? If so, it was far, far too late to do anything about it.

"I ain't stupid," Flinx growled. "Know you wouldn't let me inside armed. Counting on you common-sensing that it's better for your long-term rep to straight me the reward you verted via the Shell than it would be for you to cheap it out."

"Still something of a gamble on your part," Corsk relished pointing out, "coming here alone like this, with the goods in tow." He clapped a friendly hand on Flinx's back. Beneath the younger man's shirt, something stirred in response to the impact. Corsk noticed it, of course, but since security had declared the tall visitor free of any weaponry, he merely filed the observation for future query.

This deep into the building, the emotive stink of pain and fear was ubiquitous. Subar's friends must be very near, Flinx knew. Perhaps as close as the back room into which the big man was now leading them.

Flinx jerked a thumb in Subar's direction. "You said something about this piece of crola being 'the last one.' I heard about the break-in. So you got the others, then? Too bad if so. Means no more opportunity for me to garner some more cred."

"Sorry." Corsk grinned at him, senior pro to the younger. "Yeal, we've got them all. Now. A couple already demised, a few still alive. They'll stay so, along with this new one, until the master is satisfied he has the answers to all his questions." The big man's gaze met Flinx's hard. "Nothing you need to concern yourself about."

"Neal," Flinx replied understandingly. "All I want is the cred boost due me."

Corsk nodded, glanced back over his shoulder, and raised his voice. "Arad, ladies—all's *stret*. You can come in."

Opposing sections of wall slid silently aside. One alcove released a pair of hulking yet well-dressed women. Each held a sonic rifle nearly as tall as Subar. The other—the other revealed an alien with whom Flinx was unfamiliar. Tall, long-armed, high-eared, it stepped out of its recess and in one easy, continuous, flowing motion lowered the pistol it had been brandishing. Flinx had detected them all even before he had entered the room, but the surprise on Subar's and Ashile's faces was palpable. He was pleased that he had been able to perceive the alien's feelings, confusing and jumbled as they were. With a nonhuman, he could never be sure. Had the creature's emotions been closed to him, it would have thrown the entire plan into disarray.

Moving to a cabinet, one of the giantesses unsealed a drawer and took out a credmitter whose guts had been selectively and illegally modified. Corsk nodded at Flinx.

"You've delivered. Now it's our turn. Gail?"

The giantess came forward. Holding the credmitter in one hand, she extended the other expectantly. She was waiting for Flinx's credcard of choice, he knew, so she could first security-clear it and then transfer the verted reward to his specified account. Subar looked over at him, his face reflecting an expectation of a different kind. Next to him Ashile's expression mimicked her feelings. Reflecting her earlier doubts, they were now clashing violently.

There was no time for stalling. It was time for Flinx to do something. Now that the moment of crisis had arrived, what, the increasingly anxious girl wondered, did the offworlder intend to do, confronted as he was by a seemingly impossible situation?

What Flinx did was close his eyes halfway. Corsk frowned uncertainly as his visitor failed to produce the necessary credcard. The Amazonian Gail tensed. So did her twin. The alien's expression was unreadable. Significantly, however, he slid a liquid step backward while a six-fingered hand shifted slowly in the direction of a bandolier replete with a diversity of small weapons.

As he had done a number of times in the past several years, Flinx readied himself to emotionally project onto those surrounding him. Just as he had taken down Chaloni and his companions in the rooftop priv place, he prepared to flood selected minds around him with a wave of focused fright and vulnerability intended to reduce them to helpless, quivering lumps of terrified id. Practice had taught him how to focus his newfound ability so that, for example, he could spare Subar and Ashile from its effects. Beneath his baggy shirt, Pip stirred in expectation.

Frowning, Corsk gestured toward the movement. "You've got something alive in there. Not that it's any of my business, but what—?"

Flinx pushed outward.

"—is it?" the big man finished.

Flinx opened his eyes all the way. Corsk was eyeing him expectantly. The Amazonian twins were staring at him. Off to the left, the alien's limber fingers had coiled around one of several weapons attached to a diagonal chest strap, though the gun had not yet been removed.

Flinx blinked. Ignoring Corsk's query, he strained anew. More forcefully this time. Once again, nothing happened. Subar's expression now perfectly duplicated the growing look of alarm on Ashile's face. And with good reason.

To his horror Flinx realized that his Talent, always intermittent, had chosen that moment to diminish on him. Practice and experience counted for nothing when his unique ability decided to go on vacation. It had chosen a particularly volatile moment to do so.

Remembering Corsk's question, he tried to formulate a reply as he fumbled for the credcard he carried inside a secure pocket. "It's a minidrag from Alaspin. Reptilian in appearance, but not cold-blooded. Opto example of xenoconvergent evolution." Working at the seal on his pant pocket, his fingers were trembling. He could not recall the last time his fingers had trembled.

As he did so, he could not avoid feeling, if not projecting, emotions. With his thoughts racing several different ways at once, he momentarily forgot that there was another present who could also read, if not project, feelings.

Sensing her master's distress, Pip stuck her head out of the neckline of his shirt, surveyed the physical situation as well as the rising emotional squalls that threatened to fill up the room, and decided to take action of her own. Her reaction instantly drew Flinx's attention away from his own internal conflict.

"Pip, no!"

Launching into the air, wings spread, Pip darted toward the ceiling. Analyzing the potential dangers milling below, she instinctively began ranking them according to the degree of threat to her master that each presented. Whereas a human evaluating potential dangers would have looked to the presence and type of weapons, she read emotions in search of differing degrees of friendliness or hostility.

Taking another stride backward, tall ears thrust in the direction of the unexpected flying creature, the alien drew his weapon of choice. At almost the same time, the giantesses retreated and Corsk pulled a pulsepopper of his own. Ducking away from the sonorous hum being generated by the minidrag's membranous pink-and-blue wings, the big man was simultaneously angry and uncomfortable.

"Call it off," he growled warningly. "Get it back inside your shirt *now,* or I'll fry it!"

Flinx raised both hands. The gesture was both entreaty and warning. "Don't shoot! I'll get her down, just don't think hostile at her!" Looking ceilingward, he implored his companion. "Pip! Come down here—now!"

But Corsk wasn't watching the flying snake anymore. His gaze had fallen and turned, to refocus on Flinx. For the first time, he seemed to see his tall young visitor in an entirely new light.

"Don't 'think hostile at her'? Why would that . . . ?" In his business, analysis was something best left to the contemplative. He was paid not to analyze, but to react. Now he did so, bringing the muzzle of the pulsepopper up sharply.

His attention still concentrated on where Pip was hovering just beneath the ceiling, Flinx saw the man's hand come up out of the corner of one eye. He knew what a pulsepopper could do. The tiny globe of plasma it discharged would incinerate whatever it came in contact with. He started to open his mouth to say something at the same time as Corsk's finger slid forward on the trigger.

There was a brilliant flash of light, pure white and intense as a sun. He was not conscious when the sound of the concussion rolled through the room.

Time passed.

Flinx was relieved, but not especially surprised, when he came around. It meant that he was not dead, and that something besides the pistol's plasma ejecta had rendered him insensible. Though still shaken and far from thinking entirely coherently, he had some idea of what might have happened. Because it had happened to him several times before.

On each occasion he had been on the verge of being killed, the difference between life and death a matter of seconds or less. Each time something, some unknown part of him, had risen intuitively to his defense. That it had to do with his still-blossoming abilities there was no doubt, but as to its exact nature, he had no idea. It was different from the kind of collective surge he and the Tar-Aiym Guardian Peot had used recently to defeat the Vom at Repler.

Whatever its true nature, it was evident that it involved generating energy, displacing matter, or both. Most recently, it had flared forth unbidden to save him from an assassination attempt on the primitive world of Arrawd. Being rendered comatose each time it happened prevented him from examining or analyzing it in any way. He never knew exactly what took place, or how. He was privy only to the consequences.

In this instance, as he picked himself up off the floor of the room, these involved the unexpected protrusion from the ceiling of three pairs of feet—three female, one male. The remainder of the bodies that were attached to the dangling feet were embedded somewhere within the ceiling and the lower layer of the upper floor. The trio of individuals to whom the feet belonged had been thrust straight upward from where they had been standing by whatever it was that leaped to Flinx's defense whenever he was in imminent danger of extinction. Shattered and powdered fragments of ceiling material sifted downward from the holes in the ceiling, forming little piles of debris directly below the dangling feet.

A moan came from the far side of the room. The collateral force of Flinx's unbidden defensive response had thrown Subar and Ashile across the floor and into the opposite wall. Thankfully, and unlike those who had absorbed the full force of his involuntary, reflexive, and still-inexplicable reaction, they were not embedded, only bruised. He hurried to them. They were both sore, but unbroken.

"What—what happened?" A dazed Ashile struggled to stand as Flinx worked to unseal her wrist bonds.

Before he could reply, a still-secured Subar shook his head, blinked up at his tight-lipped offworld friend, and muttered, "*He* happened. That was it, isn't it?" Looking around the room, he needed a moment to spot the legs dangling from the ceiling like so many fleshy stalactites. "*Tnuw!* What did you do to them? I remember," he squinched up his face, "I remember a flash, and being lifted up and thrown. Then pain, and then nothing."

"I thought I heard a noise." Rubbing her wrists, the suddenly concerned girl looked around anxiously. "Where's your pet? They were going to shoot her!"

Having released Subar, Flinx straightened and called out. "Pip!"

The flying snake appeared immediately, hovering unharmed in the hole that had been punched in the wall opposite the main doorway. The hole had been made by the body of the tall alien and more or less conformed to his shape. Standing apart and opposite from

Corsk and the two giantesses, who were now decorating the ceiling, the force of whatever had erupted from Flinx had blown him sideways through the wall instead of upward toward the roof.

Pip fluttered back through the new opening. Following her and stepping through the gap, Flinx and his younger companions discovered not only another room but also the abducted individuals they had come for. As they came into view, Subar's lower jaw dropped. Considering herself at least as hardened by life as he was, Ashile promptly covered her mouth with one hand. Her eyes widened. As Pip landed gently on his left shoulder and coiled her back half around his neck, an expectant Flinx took in the full measure of what was displayed before them. In contrast with his younger companions he was disturbed but not shocked. He had seen and experienced far more than them not only of the galaxy, but also of the disturbing inventiveness that his own species was capable of.

Spread-eagled, piercing eyes now permanently shut, the willowy alien stood embedded upright in the far wall. No emotions flowed from it. Flinx did not need his Talent to tell him that the tormenting visitor from an unknown world would trouble him and his friends no longer. He shifted his attention back to those they had come to liberate. Zezula was there, and Missi, and Sallow Behdul. All three were alive.

But they were not well.

They hung in stasis, not between earth and sky but between ceiling and floor. Or—more properly—between the grids that generated a powerful magnetic field. The field was not strong enough to magnetize and levitate the iron in their bodies. It was, however, more than powerful enough to act forcefully on the hundreds of tiny metal squares that covered the three suspended bodies. Some of the metal squares were pierced with holes, allowing the compressed flesh beneath to bulge through them and form tiny pale bumps. Others were studded with pins, or pyramidal points.

From above, below, and on both sides, the magnetic field pushed or pulled on the hundreds of metal shards, driving them into the naked flesh of the three captives and holding them suspended in midair. If the strength of the field was reduced, the trio would crash to the floor in a shower of harmless metal fragments. The more it was strengthened—the more it was strengthened, the deeper the metal squares would dig into the bodies of the three prisoners. If sufficient power was applied to the field, Flinx determined as he searched for the controls, it could conceivably pull the pieces of metal not only into the flesh of anyone unfortunate enough to be so trapped, but in fact through them. Apply enough power, and every magnetized square of metal would eventually meet its opposite being driven from the opposing direction. The ultimate result would be—untidy.

It was a jail "cell" from which a prisoner could not escape, in which the bars had been broken up into hundreds of pieces that pinned captives between them. Reach down, pull one away from your body, and attempt to fling it, and it would only snap painfully back into place. Exhaustion would give way quickly to resignation. And to more pain.

Despite the metal squares pressing against her lower jaw, chin, and skull, a battered Missi raised her head enough to recognize those who had just entered the room. She was trying to say something, Flinx saw. Tears dripped from her eyes, too nonferrous to attract a metal square. Then she passed out.

Locating the instrument panel, he deactivated the brutal machine as quickly as he could. The jolt that the captives would experience as the field was disengaged and they were dropped to the floor would be nothing compared with what they had undergone. Having recovered from their initial shock at the sight of Subar's friends, he and Ashile hurried to assist them.

Though most of the metal squares simply clattered to the floor as soon as the magnetic field was turned off, some had to be pulled from the bodies of the former captives, so deeply had they embedded themselves in exposed flesh. While the two youngsters worked on the newly liberated trio, Flinx scoured the cabinets and storage bins in the room until he found their clothes. A refreshment silo mounted in one corner supplied water that the prisoners had doubtless been denied. One by one, care and fluids brought them around. First Sallow Behdul, who could only mumble a few pained words of gratefulness. Then Missi, sobbing. And lastly Zezula, screaming until a comforting Subar held her and rocked some of the terror out of her. Ministering to Missi, Ashile occasionally glanced in their direction. Since she said nothing, only Flinx knew that one other individual in the room besides the former captives was suffering pain.

Which meant that his Talent, now that it was not especially needed, had returned as abruptly and inexplicably as it had previously taken its leave.

With Subar and Ashile's help, the three hurting but grateful sufferers managed to get dressed. From time to time Flinx approached the crumbling edges of the gap in the wall to look across the outer room in the direction of the main doorway. It remained shut, and he could perceive no immediate threat outside the walls of the building they were in—only staff and employees in other, adjacent structures. These ordinary folk went on about their daily business utterly unaware of the horrors that had been perpetrated in the innocuous structure nearby.

As he turned back to the inner prison, he found Subar confronting him.

"We have to take everybody back to your hotel." The younger man spoke with a new, self-assured authority that belied his age.

"Now, wait a minute." Raising his gaze, Flinx indicated the surviving youths he had just risked his own life to rescue. "I said I would help free your friends. Nothing was said about providing accommodation for them."

Some of Subar's determination threatened to slip away. His voice turned pleading. "*Tlack,* Flinx. For that, I thank you from the base of my cer'bell. But right now they have nowhere else to go. *I* have nowhere else to go." Turning, he gestured with one hand. "Ash can probably go home safely, but once they find out everybody's been sprung, whoever picked up Zez and Missi and Behdul and put a price on me will want us back." He tried not to smile. "Not to mention that they'll be looking for whoever did this. You didn't only scrim somebody's revenge, Flinx. You cost them some cred."

Flinx tried to shrug it off. "Wouldn't be the first time." Bending forward, he put his face close to that of the younger man and lowered his voice. "This may surprise you, Subar, but I already have one or two organizations of some small consequence looking for me. So I'm not worried if some minor Visarian crime syndicate, or whatever, decides to join the pack." He straightened. "I'm leaving. Leaving Malandere, leaving this world. And based on what I've seen and experienced, I don't see any reason why I should be back."

Unable to refute the offworlder's assertions, Subar opted for the simple expedient of ignoring them. "It'd only be for a little while," he insisted. "Just until we can make arrangements to get ourselves out of the city. I've got an older cousin on my mother's side. He has a good business outside Caralinda. Legitimate agriculture. Caralinda's a smaller city a respectable distance from Malandere. He could help us make a new start. We could all get new identities, head for Bondescu on the other side of the planet."

Lifting his gaze, Flinx studied the still-quivering former captives. "What about your parents?"

Subar articulated an unpleasantry. "Zezula doesn't have any parents. Missi's are useless. Sallow Behdul's been on his own for years. And you met mine. I have to contact my cousin, arrangements need to be made, and we have to plan how to slip out of Malandere without being seen. Among other technicalities. But first we need some recoup time, in a safe place."

From across the room a communit built into a tech panel barked unexpectedly to life. Flinx had no idea who might be on the other end. Only that he had no intention of replying.

"Let's go." He raised his voice. "Everybody out of here, now!" Battered and bruised figures began to shamble toward the gap in the wall as long-paralyzed muscles were forced to move again.

"Your hotel?" Subar was gazing up at him, unblinking.

Flinx muttered something under his breath. Curving her neck around so that she could look into his eyes, Pip regarded him questioningly.

"Yes, my hotel." He hardened his tone deliberately. "But only for a day or two. Only until you can make the necessary arrangements with your cousin. Then I'm away from here, off this miserable world. I've got work to do. *Important* work. As soon as you've all recovered enough to slip out of the city on your own I'm done with you, Subar, and also with your intemperate, foolish friends."

As they exited carefully out onto the serviceway and then headed for the nearest transport terminal, it occurred to Flinx that in making what he intended to be his final statement on the matter he was only repeating something he himself had heard once before, a long time ago. It was not until they were safely in a transport pod and accelerating out of the industrial district that he recalled the circumstances under which he had heard it.

Mother Mastiff had said it to him, in Drallar on Moth, when he and two childhood acquaintances had been caught in the main market stealing from a merchant infamous for his predatory pricing. "I'm done with you!" she had sputtered. "And with your careless, hotheaded friends as well!" Though her tone had been harsh, he had known at the time that she hadn't really meant what she was saying.

Well, he assured himself, *he* had meant what he had just told Subar.

What a pity, he thought as the pod zipped smoothly through the teeming, congested cityscape, that the only emotions he could not accurately read were his own.

CHAPTER

13

Aboneh saw that Piegal Shaeb was not happy. Two meters tall, a hundred and a half kilos wide, and hat in hand, he approached the small, narrow desk behind which his master was working. The arc of dun-colored fabric nearly vanished beneath the massive, nervously twisting fingers.

"Mr. Shaeb, sir. I, uh, I have a report."

The master and controller of the Underhouse of Shaeb looked up. Though his vision was preternaturally enhanced, the result of several sophisticated and highly expensive surgeries, his eyes remained small and unimpressive. Just like the rest of him. It was what he represented that was intimidating, not the man himself.

Stretching on tiptoes, Piegal Shaeb would barely have come up to Aboneh's sternum. He could have had his legs artificially lengthened, but the process was painful and anyway, he preferred the anonymity conferred by standing slightly below average height. He was slender but not skinny, and the average dog import on the street was more muscular. His brown hair was of medium length, flyaway, and thinning. Taken together, face and body were a combination no one would look at twice. This lack of physical attractiveness and distinction troubled Shaeb only occasionally, and was more than compensated for by access to cred, power, and the knowledge that he could have almost anyone on Visaria killed for a price.

Looks aren't everything.

The true nature of the master of the Underhouse was reflected in the subservient tone and posture of the much larger Aboneh, who could have snapped the other man like a twig had he been so inclined and irretrievably stupid. Aboneh was neither. Along with fear, there was mutual respect between master and servant. That did not relieve Aboneh from the burden of being the bearer of bad news.

Half a dozen constantly changing vits hovered above the desk, shaping a small, glowing, ghostly crescent between Shaeb and his visitor. Aboneh would have had difficulty controlling one. His master was simultaneously manipulating the content of six. Aboneh was in awe.

Shaeb was not. He spoke without looking up from any of the projections. "You said you have a report. Report, then."

Aboneh realized he could not put it off any longer. "The surviving scrawn from the South Zone warehouse incursion? The three scrim youths?"

Still Shaeb did not look up. "What about them?" The tiniest hint of a humorless smile caused the corners of the thin, almost lipless mouth to tic upward. "I trust they are still in possession of their magnetic personalities?"

Aboneh swallowed. "They're gone, Mr. Shaeb, sir."

The Underhouse master continued studying his half a dozen readouts for another minute or so. Then he drew a hand across his desk, palm facing down, traveling from far left to far right, as if slicing through an imaginary torso. As his fingers passed through the vit projections they vanished, one after another. When the last had disappeared, he carefully placed both palms on the desk—first the left, then the right—and finally looked up to meet the uneasy gaze of his hulking visitor. His voice was very subdued and utterly controlled.

"What do you mean, precisely, when you say they are 'gone'? I am going to assume, and to hope, that in utilizing that verb you are referring in a semi-colloquial fashion to the fact that they have passed on?"

"Uh, no, Mr. Shaeb, sir. I came here in person soon as the word was passed up. They're gone. I mean, they've gone away. Somebody came and broke them out."

"I see. Not a semi-colloquialism, then." Rising slowly and methodically, the left hand ascended, moved to its right, and lowered slowly to come to rest atop the back of the right hand. "Somebody came and broke them out. What does Wu Corsk have to say about this noteworthy but displeasing development?"

Aboneh's words came a little faster. "Wu's dead. So are the Vetris sisters. So is Aradamu-seh, that mercenary from Fluva. You know—the one who liked to stand out in the rain all the time?"

Piegal Shaeb's tone hardened ever so slightly. "I am familiar with the idiosyncratic proclivities of the Sakuntala. All dead, you say? Three good people, and one costly import?"

Aboneh was nodding understandingly. "Holding facility was pretty bad bunged up, too. Fissure in one wall. Holes in—the ceiling."

As if in deliberate slow motion, Shaeb's hands exchanged places; the right one slid to one side and rose, only to descend onto the left with all the grace and technique of an expensive mechanism. "Four employees dead, facility damaged, detainees at liberty. Do we have any information on what assaulting force perpetrated this specific outrage?"

Aboneh nodded again, less enthusiastically this time. "Corsk let them in. Some concealed recording sensors were damaged during the breakout, but there's enough visual information to piece together what happened. This young guy—doesn't look much older than the detained scrims themselves, just taller—arrives with the last uncaught kid in tow, and a girl looks to be about the same age. Tall young guy and Corsk discuss turning the scrug over for the reward. Everything seems to be skying fine. Then there's kind of a pause—hard to figure out from the recordings exactly what's going wrong—then a detonation. Everything goes white for a second, then nothing. Sensors are all flashed, except one. Just functional enough to show the tall guy leaving, along with everybody else. No sign of Corsk, the mercenary, or the sisters. They were found later, when one of our people couldn't get feedback from the place and went over to check on it in person."

He exhaled heavily at the memory, then went on. "The Sakuntala was implanted in a wall in the holding room. Wu and the sisters were—they'd been shoved through the ceiling, headfirst. Took a crew with tools to chop them out. Besides crushing their skulls, the impact compacted every vertebra in their spines. All the nucleus pulposus had been squeezed out from between the bones, like cheap food paste."

Shaeb digested this information. "That's certainly interesting, and bespeaks a line of attack worthy of follow-up, but it remains incidental to the larger picture. The integrity of the Underhouse has been violated. Our reputation has been sullied. This affront to our dignity and standing must be mended. I have a reputation to maintain. If word of this is allowed to propagate and appropriate retribution is not promptly delivered, business will suffer."

Now on top, the right hand rose and tangoed through the air over the desk. A single rectangular vit image appeared. Shaeb's fingers tickled the projection. "We will post a significant bounty. The one for this interfering outsider, evidently a friend or acquaintance of the liberated scrims, will be of such a magnitude that every heavy levy between the poles will drop whatever he or she is doing to focus on finding him. The other scrawn, including the remaining youth to have so far escaped our attention, must also be detained and appropriately dealt with. I did not come into control of the Underhouse by leaving business unfinished."

"No sir, Mr. Shaeb, sir."

"Our own people will of course involve themselves. It would be a positive if we could manage this recovery in-house." This time his smile was wider, and more genuine. "A bounty earned is a bounty saved."

"I'll see to the details myself, Mr. Shaeb, sir." The hulking underling turned to leave.

"One more thing, Aboneh. It is not necessary to use my name every time you address me. A simple 'sir' will suffice."

"Yes, Mr. Shaeb, sir." Aboneh exited the unpretentious office, trying his best not to move too quickly or to show his relief.

Behind him, Piegal Shaeb pondered as he dropped his right hand back onto the desk. Leisurely, he covered it with his left.

One is attended by idiots, he reflected. That thought mulled, he raised both hands in unison and restored the desk's six projections. There was a great deal of business to attend to, disturbing interruptions notwithstanding. The escape of the odious scrawn was annoying, the deaths of four valued subordinates painful. The latter could be absorbed while the former would be dealt with. It was only a matter of time before an inelegant state of affairs was suitably resolved.

One as yet unidentified meddling young man in particular was going to pay rather harshly for his involvement.

Slipping the two battered and abused girls together with the equally beaten-up and mutely grateful Sallow Behdul into his hotel suite had not been difficult. Caring for them, even for a short while, required additional concern and more stealth. Everything from sprayskin to quick-healing medications could have been ordered and sent up, but that would have alerted even an automated supplier to the curious request. The same was true for food, even if it was applied for in-house. Knowing from recent experience on Repler as well as previous encounters just how the types who had mistreated Subar's friends operated, Flinx understood that the less attention they attracted to his room, the better.

The first afternoon's expedition, to procure the minimum necessary medicants, went without difficulty. Though his perception was flashing in and out like a tridee's on–off sensor, he caught no intimation of enmity aimed in his direction. The same was true when he and Subar hazarded an evening jaunt to buy food for everyone.

Even though it was late morning when the two of them went out to purchase a few necessary items they had not been able to find the previous day, the former captives were all still sound asleep. As she had on the previous day, Ashile agreed to remain behind in the room to keep an eye on Subar's slowly recovering friends. Her sentiments as she contemplated the sleeping, beat-up form of Zezula left Flinx wondering if leaving the slender adolescent in charge would find them minus one survivor the next time he and Subar returned. He doubted Ashile would push her hidden feelings to that extreme, though. Despite her rough-hewn exterior, there remained an integrity there he had not encountered elsewhere on Visaria.

He would not be surprised, however, if at some point they returned to find Zezula unexpectedly a bit more banged up than her companions, and healing less swiftly than would otherwise be expected.

Rain had been predicted for the morning hours. That was fine with Flinx. Residents would be utilizing covered transport, with fewer out walking. The life support store he and Subar had shopped the previous day and night was only a few blocks from the hotel. The shop front was typically compact, erected over the much larger supply facility located belowground. As he made his purchases from a tridimensional display in the shop above, fresh food, medicines, clothing, and other selected items would be ordered, inventoried, individually packaged, and shipped upward to arrive in their appropriate take-out containers.

Their charged clothing kept them dry as he and Subar strolled up the main street through the downpour in the direction of the shop. They were halfway there when Flinx perceived a distinctive intensification of inimical intentions. Riding on his shoulder beneath his shirt to stay dry, Pip sensed it, too. Poking her head out, she began searching in several directions for the source of the rising hostility. A jaunty Subar strode along beside them, unaware that their immediate environs had undergone a subtle change perceptible only to Flinx and his pet.

The large private transport that cut them off approached so quickly, not even Flinx had time to change direction. A second vehicle pulled in behind them, cutting off any possible retreat. The few other pedestrians out walking in the rain gaped and hurried to back up or cross over to the other side of the avenue. Because of the shower and the time of day, there weren't many of them. The majority of Malandere's commuters were already at work.

That included the quartet of armed figures who bolted from the first transport to quickly surround the two young men.

"Get in," one snarled threateningly. "There's more cred to be quilted if we bring you in alive—but if you push back, we'll have to eval for the second option."

Standing next to Flinx, an alarmed Subar was whispering urgently, "Do something, Flinx! Do whatever it is that you do. Do it *now!*"

Coming toward them, a woman with an irreparable scar running down her neck jammed a small but lethal pistol in his solar plexus. "Shut up. No talking." As the younger man gasped for breath, she stepped back and gestured toward the lead transport. "Keep your hands where I can see them. Move."

Bewildered, cornered, with no place to run and not knowing what else to do, a stunned Subar followed a complaisant Flinx into the transport. Immediately, the other three figures piled in behind them, settling into the rear seats. A fifth man was seated forward at the manual controls. Looking pleased, he inputted a command. The transport began to move. A glance backward showed that the second vehicle was following close behind.

Seated in the center rear seat, the wiry older man who gave the appearance of being in charge had pulled a communit and was speaking into it. "Yarl, we got him. The stray kid, too. Double cred due." His tone was one of complete satisfaction. "No sign of the others. Not to concern. We'll get the location out of these two faster than post-meal farts." Closing the communit, he leaned forward and grinned unpleasantly.

"You two really think you could just go out for a midday stroll when every scrim and scrug in Malandere is panting for your knobs? Did you think nobody'd be out hunting just because it's raining? You ought to be flattered—you're each singly worth a month's makings."

Showing interest and careful to keep his hands in view, Flinx turned his head slightly so he could see the speaker. "Your paramount must want us very badly."

The speaker frowned. "My crew is independent from Shaeb's. If it wasn't, there'd be no reward coming. We'd be working on salary."

Flinx whisked the name with his lips. "Shaeb."

Next to him, Subar's face went white. "Oh God, no. Piegal Shaeb. That must be who's behind the storage facility we boosted!" All boldness fled; the youth was absolutely terrified. "If Chal had known that, he never would have motioned the scene!"

"You didn't know?" Their inquisitor found this vastly amusing. "What a bunch of dumb scrawn. Soon to be dead scrawn. If you're lucky." He sat back, his tone turning indifferent. "Not my symp. Your fate is my team's cred." Something caught his attention. His expression contorted. "What's that moving under your shirt?"

"My pet," Flinx told him simply.

"Yarl?" The man in charge looked at the scarred woman seated next to him. "Maybe it's a young curlint. I like curlints. I bet Shaeb will let me have it." He leaned forward again. "I can't do bosk for you, scrug. Sooner or later, you're already dead. But if you behave and cooperate in helping us find the others, maybe I can save your darling. Let's see what it looks like."

"Sure," replied Flinx agreeably. Reaching up slowly and deliberately, he unfastened the front of his shirt.

The man's eyes popped as the flying snake launched directly into his face. His yelp of surprise was followed by a grating scream of pain as the minidrag's tiny but potent squirt of venom caught him center on his left eye. Both flanking underlings pulled weapons. One hasty, wild shot blew a hole in the roof of the transport. Shouts and curses filled the interior as the operator swiveled around in the driver's seat.

Covering his head, Subar dropped to the floor. More shots sizzled the internal atmosphere. Several came from the gun Flinx had drawn from its place of concealment in his right boot. It was of a type and manufacture the frightened Subar did not recognize. Gleaming and compact, it looked like something that had been manufactured for use by a nonhuman species. A thranx, for example.

Behind them, the second transport had gone off auto and was pulling up alongside. The opaqued window rolled up to reveal a pair of armed, anxious passengers. As they were considering whether to fire on the lead vehicle and risk the chance of hitting their own colleagues, Flinx chucked something from his duty belt in their direction. It was very small.

The cloud of gas that enveloped the second transport was anything but inconsequential, however. When the vehicle emerged from the dark vapor that had engulfed it there was no sign of its occupants, who had collapsed out of sight within. Its frontward sensors kept it from slamming into the buildings immediately ahead. Swerving to the right, it veered away from the lead craft. Unless internal control was manually or orally re-established, Flinx surmised, it would revert to automatic and to its previous directional programming.

As would the transport in which he and Subar were now the only surviving passengers. Leaning forward, he calmly directed his words toward the control console pickup. Given the character of their would-be abductors, he doubted the instrumentation would be individual-specific. He was right. The vehicle responded promptly to his request to pull over to one side of the avenue and stop. As it did so, he slipped his trim weapon back into its custom, camouflaged boot holster.

Stepping out into the diminishing rain, he started back the way they had come. Not having had time to accelerate onto a high-speed corridor, the two transports had not traveled uncomfortably far from the hotel. Though his mind was working furiously, he still had room to acknowledge Subar's stumbling presence alongside him.

"What . . . ?" The younger man flinched as a brilliantly hued winged shape shot past him to brake to a landing on Flinx's shoulder. It promptly burrowed down beneath the taller youth's open shirt. "You had a gun." He nodded in the direction of the offworlder's service belt. "You had a murk bomb. Why—why didn't you use them *before* they made us get into the transport?"

Flinx's attention was on the avenue, on the pedestrian walkway, on the sky that was visible through the rain and between the tall buildings that surrounded them. One of the reasons he was still alive was because he had learned that no moment is safe, no location secure. But he took the time to answer.

"They were all too tense, too on edge. Expecting us to resist or run, they were ready to shoot if either of us so much as coughed the wrong way. It was necessary to relax them." With a nod he indicated an arm-in-arm couple passing close by, their youthful loving visages lost in each other. "I didn't want any bystanders to get hurt."

Subar stared at him. "Bystanders? What about *me* getting hurt?"

"I was also curious," Flinx continued matter-of-factly, "to know who took your friends and who wanted all of you back."

Subar remembered. "Piegal Shaeb," he moaned. "Why couldn't it have been some small-time smuggling setup? No wonder they found our priv place so fast."

Despite Subar's obvious alarm, Flinx was not intimidated. He had just finished dealing with the likes of Lord Dominic Rose on Repler. If Subar's reaction was to be believed, on Visaria it was apparently this Shaeb individual who floated some weight. It was the way of things. On small worlds, small-time lawbreakers assumed an importance all out of proportion to their actual significance. Though he did not know this Piegal Shaeb personally, he was self-evidently one more smear on the general worth of humanity. One more reason not to sacrifice his own future on its behalf.

Subar knew nothing of what was meandering through his tall friend's mind, however. He knew only that he was still alive and that his continued freedom was due to yet another exhibition of this strange offworlder's unplumbed abilities. Notwithstanding, something continued to puzzle him.

"You used a gun. You used a murk bomb. You used your pet. Why didn't you just—affect them? The way you did Chal and Dirran at the priv place." He did not ask why Flinx didn't repeat the feat he had performed at the building where Zezula and the others had been held captive. Obviously, the release of that kind of energy in such a confined space would be impossible to exploit without risk to the person propagating it.

"There was a humanoid robot among our captors," Flinx explained. "Very expensive, very effective, difficult to identify. Those who picked us up were taking no chances. What I can sometimes do is only effective on sapient organics. Automatons are immune." Reaching down, he stroked the sinuous shape now sequestered beneath his shirt. "They're generally immune to Pip's venom, too."

Now that his breathing was coming more easily, Subar felt comfortable slowing his stride. "At least they sized us out on the street. That means if there are more of them, they don't know where we're staying."

Flinx was less sanguine. "If that ordinary pursue crew could track us to this neighborhood this quickly, there will be others close behind them. We can't stay here any longer." He maintained his constant scan of their immediate surroundings. "We're going to have to move," he added distastefully. That was a pity. He had grown fond of the hotel, if not Malandere itself.

Subar looked up at him, entreating. "You'll help us, won't you? At least till we can replant somewhere else."

There was no reason for him to do so, Flinx knew. He owed nothing to this adolescent and his friends. Nothing at all. He had been planning to forsake Visaria in a day or two. High in orbit, the waiting *Teacher* beckoned. He longed for its familiar surroundings; for the knowledgeable, reassuring voice of ship-mind; for the compliant, accommodating surrounds of the landscaped central lounge. He had come to this outpost world to take the measure of humdrum humankind and had found it wanting. There was no reason for him to remain a day longer, even if his life was not in danger.

Except that he remembered a certain adolescent youth on an even more isolated world called Moth. One who had suffered similar unsought attention and had survived only through perseverance, luck, native intelligence, and his own determination. That and a certain raw, powerful, inexplicable Talent that he would just as soon have been rid of. On more than one occasion, that sorely disadvantaged youth had endured only through the help of others. Other mundane humans.

Looking down at the imploring yet manipulative face staring up at him, he was not at all certain that this Subar deserved such help.

But he felt that at least one other local did. There was no reason to inform Subar of this, of course. The youth would either discover it for himself, or remain the poorer for not doing so.

For all the dangers he had survived and all the obstacles he had overcome, his adolescence on Moth had been one of unending excitement and revelation. It all seemed so long ago.

Maybe, he told himself in a momentary flash of candor, what he really wanted was for at least a day or so to relive that exhilarating time—however irrational and retrograde such a desire might be.

Certainly the ever-prosaic ship-mind of the *Teacher* would think that was the case.

CHAPTER

14

If Piegal Shaeb had been unhappy before, his reaction upon receiving the latest information concerning the small group of youths who had insulted, robbed, and defied him now verged on the apoplectic.

He did not make his feelings visible, of course. There was no screaming, no ranting and raving. It was not his way. Shaeb was a shut Shell, a world unto himself. Only a certain firming around the mouth and at the forehead, a barely perceptible tension in his words, betrayed that anything was out of the ordinary. Even his closest associates would have been hard put to remark any difference.

Inside, however, Shaeb was incensed. More than revenge, more than retribution, a correction was in order. Harmony had to be restored. In order for that to happen, he needed to learn precisely and without possibility of equivocation exactly what the hell was going on.

Street scrawn did not blatantly scrim one of his properties and get away with it. One of their slightly older friends did not penetrate a secure facility, kill all those on duty, and free the perpetrators of the original outrage. It made no sense. For yet another time he called forth the dimensional clarifications based on the sensor recordings that had been taken from the building where the holding cell had been located. They portrayed, in as much detail as possible, an unidentified young man; a much shorter younger one; a slender young woman; and the taller intruder's distinctive winged pet. Not a single weapon was in evidence.

With an irritated wave of a hand he replaced the view floating in the room with the one that showed the aftermath of the trio's intrusion: fleeing captives, holed wall, dead underlings. Separating the two views there was only the mysterious flash and its accompanying concussion. How had the insufferable transposition from view one to view two been accomplished? People he paid to shed light on such things had come up with lame explanations at best. A concealed pulse or sonic weapon could have hurled the Sakuntala through the wall and the human operatives into the ceiling. Neither, however, offered a credible explanation for the mysterious flare.

Identification of the youthful tall intruder had so far proven impossible. There were no records of him in any Shell sybfile anywhere on Visaria. Therefore he was either a genius at identity masking, or possibly a visiting offworlder. Though not yet ready to discard any explanation, Shaeb found himself leaning toward the former. At least it offered some rationale for the stranger's association with the other young scrims. For an offworlder to inexplicably take their side made no sense at all.

But then, he reminded himself for the umpteenth time, nothing about this nasty and hard-to-resolve matter made any sense.

Even if the tall youth was some kind of rogue professional, his taking the side of the imprisoned youngsters was difficult to rationalize. Unless, Shaeb told himself, the other youth had somehow managed to gather together enough cred to hire a pro. Still, it was a bold (or reckless) professional who would take the cause of a bunch of street scrims against the Underhouse of Shaeb. Unless he had been kept in the dark about whose interests he was contesting. That possibility, at least, made a strained if contorted kind of sense.

If it also constituted the actual explanation, Shaeb decided, then it might be possible to make contact with this independent operator and explain to him the unfortunate error he had made. That done, any sensible professional would seek to correct his mistake by turning in, or selling back, his younger employers to the offended Shaeb. Gazing at the projections, such thoughts made him feel better. He had come up with a course of action that could be pursued.

But before the young unknown independent could be inveigled, he first had to be identified and contacted. So far, Shaeb's underlings had been unable to accomplish this. A consequence, he told himself with a resigned sigh, of having to rely on the labored mental exertions of fools.

Time would probably resolve the situation. It usually did. But he was impatient as well as irate. The vile scrawn were not the only ones who had access to superior outside help.

A second wave of his hand banished the projections from the desk. Speaking aloud, he addressed the inner sanctum's omnipresent AI. "I'm going out. If anyone inquires, I am indisposed until tomorrow morning."

"Very good, Piegal," the AI responded. "Will you be requiring transport?"

"Yes. Solo and discreet, please."

"No escort? You are always a target, Piegal."

"I know that," he replied touchily. "I will not go out without being suitably masked."

"As you desire." The AI was programmed to be compliant, not querulous. Unlike some of its cybernetic brethren.

The residence occupied the top floor of a presumptuous twenty-story structure in one of Malandere's best residential neighborhoods:

home to well-to-do merchants, heads of municipal and planetary departments, vit personalities, successful artists, and more. The cream, such as it was, of Malanderean and to a lesser extent Visarian society.

Having been informed of the imminent arrival of his circumspectly anonymous visitor, the owner had instructed his residence's AI accordingly. The apartment AI proceeded to communicate directly with the incoming vehicle. Identification, security arrangements, and arrival protocol thus having being performed without the interpolation of slow-moving organics, Piegal Shaeb's transport was admitted to the subterranean garage without delay or incident.

Ascending the center of the building via one of its multiple lifts, the visitor's personal path proved as smooth and uneventful as that of his vehicle. Once at the top, the lift's door opened into a spacious living area steeped in knowledge and good taste. The internally lit, climate-controlled wall of precious real books was proof enough of the owner's preferences. Holding a softly humming glass of golden, frothy liquid in one hand, he flicked back the oversized sleeve of his richly embroidered silket and advanced to greet his guest.

"Good day, Piegal," he offered courteously.

"I wish it were so, Shyvil." Exiting the lift, Shaeb pushed past the Malandere Municipal Authority's senior situations analyst and into the living area, where he appropriated unbidden a seat on a lounge upholstered with the glossy dark blue skins of several rare Visarian animals.

Bemused and curious in equal measure, Theodakris settled himself into the chair opposite. Below, to his right and to the left of his visitor, green space and mathematically interlaced waterways were visible through the floor-to-ceiling transparent wall. The elegant landscaping formed part of the private parkland that separated one multistory residence building from its equally expensive twin.

"I'm sorry you're not having a good day." Theodakris smiled encouragingly. "My place is secured. You can remove that sprayon if you like." He appreciated his guest's prudence in masking his face and true identity for the purpose of the call. Having the image of a visiting Piegal Shaeb recorded for posterity by the building's multiple security sensors could, at some time in the future, possibly prove counterproductive. Both men were great believers in preventive preemption. It was a caution they had discrete reasons to share.

Impatient as usual, Shaeb waved off the offer. "I am fine, thank you. Quite used to wearing different faces."

"Both in person and in business." Theodakris smiled a second time.

"It is business that brings me here now," Shaeb informed him.

Theodakris gave a slight shrug as he sipped at his drink. The golden froth purred. "I didn't think it was a social call. Not at this time of day. What can I do for you, Piegal?"

The master of the Underhouse of Shaeb reached into a pocket and removed a tiny sphere. Leaning forward over the free-form table hewn from a single crystal of pale green sphene, he handed it to his host. "For a start, identify someone for me."

Theodakris took the sphere. Positioning it over the center of the table, he murmured a coded command. A hole opened in the center of the translucent slab. Irregular in outline, it looked like a melting mouth. Accompanied by a barely audible hum, the sphere sank within.

Settling back in the chic and extremely expensive chair fashioned from plaited metal, Theodakris looked across the table at his guest. "The customary 'consulting fee' will apply."

"Together with the usual concomitant favors; yes, I know." Shaeb neither leaned back nor relaxed. In fact, the usually controlled Underhouse master looked as stressed as Theodakris had ever seen him. Something serious was afoot. The senior analyst went so far as to set his glass aside.

"Since your visit is not social, I presume your need for advanced identification is a matter of some urgency."

Shaeb nodded. There was no need to hide anything from the senior analyst. It was not possible, anyway. "One of my local ventures recently suffered a hostile intrusion. Numerous articles of considerable value were taken. Subsequently, attempts were made to market them."

Theodakris did not try to conceal his surprise. "I'd think your reputation would be enough to protect your interests."

Shaeb offered a diffident wave. "The boosters were almost as youthful as they were clever. In the end, they were undone by a combination of hubris and inexperience. It apparently never occurred to them that any fence on Visaria capable of moving the kind of goods they stole would also have contact with me. It was not difficult to pick them up. Under appropriate questioning, the survivors speedily divulged every detail of their plot." He paused. "One has to admire their audacity, however ultimately fatal it would prove to be.

"Only one member of the group, the youngest, succeeded in escaping incarceration. Everything being under control and the merchandise recovered, I put it out of my mind." Shaeb's immobile expression shifted ever so faintly into a frown. "Then something unexpected happened. I dislike the unexpected. It disrupts routine."

"A kindred sentiment," Theodakris declared.

"The three surviving scrims were freed by the youngest member of their group, acting in concert with a single outsider. I am tending more and more to believe that he is an offworlder, though I as yet have no proof of that."

"The reason being," Theodakris concluded, "that no local professional would go up against you."

A nod, no less languid than the frown that accompanied it. "Common sense aside, there are rogue operators who occasionally are too broke, too indifferent, or too unsane to act rationally. This was no ordinary operative, however. Despite his apparent youth, unmistakable in the sensor recordings"—the Underhouse Master gestured at the hole in the table—"he somehow succeeded in overcoming a quartet of my best people, including one very expensive alien mercenary. So I am doubly plumbed—by the loss of four valued subordinates as well as that of those who committed the original violation." Thin lips tightened perceptibly. To anyone who knew Shaeb, it was the equivalent of a wild-eyed scream.

"I want the at-large scrims back, to face the justice due them, and I most especially want this unknown operative."

Though he could sympathize with his guest's restrained fury, Theodakris still thought him overwrought. "Slacken, Piegal. Anyone as proficient at his art as you depict should be known. If he's not in the city files, he'll be described elsewhere in the planetary Shell."

Voicing a command brought forth a virtual panel in front of his chair. Sitting up straight, the senior analyst leaned forward and began weaving his hands through the glowing, brightly colored configurations. Recognizing him, they responded.

Shaeb looked on with interest. Though he had made ample use of Theodakris's connections in the past, he had never been present when the senior analyst was actually at work.

"It seems foolish to wonder, but I presume this particular search cannot be traced back to you."

Peering at his guest through the hovering virtual as he worked, Theodakris smiled. "I wouldn't enter secure sections of the Visarian Shell unless I could ensure privacy through misdirection." He gestured at the hovering panel he was working with. "I set up this line a long time ago. No one will even be able to tell that the sybfiles in question have been accessed."

Within the table, the information pellet Shaeb had handed over was a rotating blur, spinning at an incredible speed. Precisely focused light extracted information from within. Data was channeled, transshipped, compared. As an adjunct to the search that was being run, a one-third life-sized image of the subject appeared as a separate projection above another part of the supremely functional table.

Plainly compiled from several sensor sources, it was occasionally less than flawless. The portrayed individual was shown standing, speaking, and moving. So was a certain unidentified small flying creature.

Something jarred Theodakris's attention, as if he had been slapped by an invisible hand, hard. His hands stopped working the panel. Hurriedly, he waved it aside, shoving sharply to his right the virtual instrumentation that was partially blocking his view of the projection. Periodically refreshing itself, the hovering image was of a lanky young man with red hair and green eyes. Occasionally the serpentine flying creature darted in and out of the projection.

Though the senior analyst said nothing, his perceptive visitor immediately noticed the change. "Something about this distasteful scrim intrigues you?"

"Intrigues me?" Leaning back, Shaeb slapped both palms down on his thighs. "Oh, this is too wonderful, Piegal! Too marvelous to believe! You see, I have for some days now been debating whether to seek out this very individual myself. And here you have brought him to my notice anew!" His tone turned suddenly, and unexpectedly, solemn. "Why, it's almost as if this individual and I were somehow bound together by a disdainful Fate."

Shaeb felt lost. It was not a feeling with which he was comfortable. "You know the operative?"

Theodakris moderated his glee. "He's not an operative. Not in the sense you're thinking of, that is. I encountered him not long ago while engaged in my normal routine of perusing and analyzing daily police reports. He plucked a kid from the arms of our benevolent authorities by convincing the very thranx visitors who were holding him to let him go. Then he vanished. I've been torn ever since with trying to decide whether to seek him out."

Shaeb folded his arms across his chest. "It is apparent that I lack the information that would allow me to make sense of what you are saying." He gestured at the systematically recycling images. "My interest in him is straightforward. What is yours, that you should take such an interest in an unknown? And if he is not a rogue operative, then what is he?"

"Ah," murmured Theodakris, appearing for the moment as if he were completely alone in the room, "what indeed? There are many things I wish I could tell you, my friend. Much that you would find of interest, and some that would shock you."

Shaeb's gaze narrowed. He had been called many things by many people, friend as well as foe, but never shockable. "Try me."

"I can't." Despite the gravity of the situation, the senior analyst could not keep from chuckling. "I can't tell anyone. To do so would be to invite full mindwipe."

Now the master of the Underhouse Shaeb was intrigued. "Would I be wrong in inferring that others besides myself have an interest in detaining this independent?"

For some reason, this query caused the senior analyst to burst out laughing again. "My dear Piegal, you have no idea!" Wiping first one eye, then the other, Theodakris pointed at the shifting image. "Unless I have utterly misjudged things, and as an analyst of some small skill I believe I have not, the young man is an offworlder named Philip Lynx. He commonly goes by the sobriquet Flinx. That peculiar flying creature you see darting in and out of the projection is from a world called Alaspin. It is commonly known as a minidrag, or 'miniature dragon,' though the name is purely descriptive and not in any way scientific. It has the capability to spit a distance of several meters and with great accuracy a venom that is highly corrosive and inordinately toxic."

Shaeb was nodding, storing the information as effectively as if it were being committed to a subox. "That would partially explain how this person and one adolescent companion were able to overcome those in charge of holding the three incarcerated scrims. But only partially." He eyed the analyst. "Though you say he is no operative, this Flinx person must have comparable abilities."

"You have no idea," Theodakris reiterated. With a surprisingly acerbic snigger he added, "As a matter of fact, if the limited information available on this particular subject is to be believed, no one has any idea."

Shaeb liked straightforward explanations. He wasn't getting any. "That doesn't help me, Shyvil. I am not paying you to be obscure."

"Believe me, I'm not." Smile and accompanying laughter went away with a suddenness that would have shocked anyone but Shaeb. "I've got some advice for you that isn't obscure. Leave this one alone. Swallow your pride, absorb your losses, and forget about him. From what very little I have been able to learn about him over the course of perusing many years of the most intermittent and questionable reports, contact with him is markedly unhealthy.

"There was a time, long ago, when I would have responded differently. But time passes, life progresses, obsessions fade. That's why I decided, after some serious private agonizing, not to follow up on my initial inclinations." He gazed at the recycling images with what could almost have been considered longing. "Believe me, my interest in him far exceeds yours, yet I know without hesitation that it is in my own best interest to ignore him."

Seeking clarification, Shaeb only found himself further bemused. "I do not grasp the fullness of what you are saying, but this I know: I cannot ignore him. He has cost me self-respect and cred. Apparently there are certain unknowns involving this youth that you have decided to let go. I cannot."

Even though it had by now run through the same sequence of enhanced recordings dozens of times, Theodakris found he could not take his gaze off the projection. "Okay. Then instruct your people to shoot him on sight. Don't try to bring him in for questioning or a lingering revenge. Kill him from a distance. As great a distance as possible. Because if my suppositions are correct, you won't get the chance to do so from close up." Now he did take his eyes off the shifting images, long enough to meet his guest's gaze. "I will say it one more time. You have no idea, Piegal, what you're up against."

Shaeb could not be intimidated. Annoyance, however, was something even he was subject to. "Operative or something else, he's just one youth." He waved a hand dismissively. "The flying creature can be contained, or otherwise dealt with." He shifted in his chair as if preparing to leave. His tone was intolerant. "You have no other information for me?"

"I've told you what I know," Theodakris replied, "and that includes information that's not available on any Shell. At least, not on one that's accessible to any but a very few Commonwealth citizens. Consider yourself privileged."

Rising, Shaeb felt otherwise. "You won't help me resolve this matter?"

Theodakris did not stand. "I've done what I can and more than I should. I'm telling you, Shyvil, avoid this young man as you would a drug-resistant plague."

"Why?" Shaeb stared hard at the senior analyst. "Tell me precisely, why?"

Theodakris's gaze fell. "I wish I could, but I don't know the right answer myself. From the tiniest dribs and drabs of information I've been able to acquire over the years—call it a perverse hobby—this Flinx is like a wandering black hole. No one ever sees exactly what he does, or how, but the consequences of his passing are all too evident for those with eyes capable of seeing."

Shaeb hesitated, finally asked, "You called it a 'perverse hobby.' What is your ongoing interest in this offworlder?"

The senior analyst looked up. "I can't tell you that, either, Piegal. Not for all the cred on Visaria. I can't tell anyone."

With a soft grunt, the Underhouse master started for the lift. "Maybe if I bring him before you secured and bound and dump him on the floor at your feet with his lethal pet fried to a crisp and served up on a platter, you'll feel more articulate. That will put an end to it."

"An end to it?" The expression that came over Theodakris's face as he repeated his guest's comment was conflicted. There was much there to see: fear, interest, uncertainty, and, most strangely of all, an almost perceptible yearning, as if for something valued and gone. "I've lived the last fifty years of my life assuming there had already been an end to it." He gestured toward the projected hovering image that was proving persistent in more ways than one. "The universe, my friend, is full of surprises. One just doesn't expect one of this magnitude, on an otherwise fine day in midyear, to be dumped unexpectedly in one's lap." Turning to face his retreating guest, the senior analyst then voiced the most unanticipated comment of the entire visit.

"You know, I've had an interesting life."

Taken aback, Shaeb could only mumble a quick thank-you and good-bye. He left Theodakris still seated in his wonderfully sinuous chair, still staring at the same projection he had already viewed over and over.

The senior analyst, Shaeb decided, was turning senile with unexpected rapidity. All this inane and directionless muttering about unexplained events from long ago. As much as he liked Theodakris personally, the Underhouse master had no room within him for misplaced empathy.

It was clearly time to begin cultivating a new source of information within the Justice Ministry.

Nothing in the hotel suite Flinx and his new acquaintances had been forced to abandon in haste was irreplaceable. Always a light traveler, he had left behind nothing that could not be bought anew elsewhere, on another world if not on Visaria, or reproduced by the engines of profound manipulation that were available to him on the *Teacher*.

Sallow Behdul, of all people, turned out to have a relative outside the city who reluctantly agreed to give them shelter until the tumult surrounding their raid, subsequent capture, and eventual escape died down. Having spent the majority of his life on other worlds and in cities, it was a new experience for Flinx to find himself on an actual farm.

Like all such modern facilities, that of Behdul's cousin was fully mechanized, regulated, and kept in continuous adjustment by a vast array of instrumentation. Food animals received precise amounts of nourishment coupled with the appropriate vitamins, minerals, and supplements. Hundreds of years of genetic fine-tuning had created creatures designed to produce the maximum amount of protein from the least amount of input. The latter took the form of fodder that had been just as proficiently manipulated. There were also extensive fields of food plants, several of which were unknown to Flinx.

All of this was protected and nurtured beneath billowing sheaths of organic polymers whose opacity and thickness was adjusted according to the prescribed seasonal programming. Too much sunshine would burn the crops; too little, starve them. It was the same with the animals. Behdul's cousin reacted with appropriate horror when Flinx wondered aloud why he simply could not do away with the floating polymer swathes. Doing so would mean, Tracken Behdulvlad explained, exposing his precious flocks and crops to the vagaries of the atmosphere. Such a thing was alien to progressive agriculture.

"Kind of pretty."

"What?" Turning from his contemplation of the sunset as viewed through several translucent polymer puffs, Flinx saw that Zezula had come up behind him. Her injuries were healing quickly, though red blotches on her exquisite features still showed where the oppressive metal squares had adhered.

She nodded in the direction of the blurred, setting sun. "Pretty. The scenery out here. But dull. I can't believe that people actually choose to live like this."

He offered up a cordial smile. On his shoulder, Pip dozed deeply. "Fortunately for you and your friends, some do. Somebody has to cultivate the food to feed a planetary population, since not everybody has access to synthesizers."

She nodded. "I've eaten a lot of synthetics, but I never really cared for them. Growing up in Malandere, I never gave much thought to where food came from. I was only ever worried about getting enough of it."

He found himself feeling sorry for the girl. On another world, in other circumstances, she might have had hopes of receiving a better education, or of becoming a vit personality, or perhaps exploring hitherto unsuspected artistic depths. Not only had Visaria's largest city beaten her down, but it threatened to become an inescapable trap. So, for that matter, had Drallar, the difference between them being that he had made it out and, at least so far, she had not.

She moved closer. "I grew up worrying about everything. That's the way it is in the city."

For a moment he wondered if his Talent was functioning. Because while her words and attitude, down to the posture she affected, said one thing, her emotions shouted something else entirely. Presenting herself as winsome and worried, inside she radiated a confidence and self-assurance that bordered on the bold. It began to dawn on him that he was witnessing yet another example of human duplicity. Even though Subar was nowhere to be seen, the present situation was one from which he now sought to disengage himself. Preferably without giving his abilities away.

So instead of coolly informing her, *Your mouth says one thing but your emotions say another,* he replied as distantly as he could without being rude. "Everybody worries about their life. I'm sure you'll make something of yours."

She nodded and edged still closer. On his shoulder, Pip stirred but did not awaken. Her hand rose to grip his upper left arm. It glided downward, past elbow and forearm, and would have grasped his fingers had he not used them to suddenly scratch at the side of his face.

"I'm sure I'll make something," she murmured.

What he sensed within her simultaneously attracted and repelled him. He felt at once sorry for her and disgusted at her behavior. If he referred to it bluntly, she would no doubt deny it, perhaps even mention it to Subar. Though it mattered not at all in the greater scheme of things if she did so, Flinx felt a sort of kinship with the youth. Enough so that he did not want to see him hurt, if it could be avoided.

So instead of pointing out that he could tell she was after power and control and not just the pleasure of his company, he stepped away from her.

"I'm sorry, Zezula. I'm bespoke for, myself."

She smiled and nodded as if she understood, but if emotions were combustible, she would now be a raging spire of flame. No one takes kindly to rejection, he knew, no matter how civilly framed.

"Her name's Clarity," he added in hopes of dampening the furious blaze within her. To change the subject, he raised an arm and pointed. "The sun's almost down."

"*Tshas*," she muttered. Her tone was neutral but her carefully concealed emotions indicated she hoped that the solar furnace in question would land on his head. "A special moment to share." While projecting nothing but loathing for him, she brushed aside his demurral and edged toward him with an eye toward re-establishing their previous proximity.

If only she knew, he thought distastefully as he worked to disentangle himself from her grasping hands, how clearly he saw the truth of her feelings even as she sought to ply him with touches and words. Tomorrow for certain, he told himself, he would leave this place. He had done more for these youngsters, some of whom were clearly more worth helping than others, than he had ever intended to do. As was often the case with those he encountered on other worlds.

Without a doubt his determined resistance to her advances, or for that matter resistance from any member of the opposite sex, was something she was not used to. "Am I so unpleasant to look upon?" she queried him as they struggled gently. "This woman you speak of isn't here now. I am. Even the United Church makes allowances for distance."

He shoved one of her arms down. Another came up, reaching for him with persistence. "We're not as far apart as you think."

"Oh no?" Her eyes, which were as striking as the rest of her, flashed at him. "I bet I can make you forget her. Even if she's on the other side of Visaria. Even if she's on another world, far away and remote." Zezula's moist lips were parted, inviting, her arms extended and open to him. She wanted to possess him, and him to possess her.

But as only he could sense, not in equal degree.

CHAPTER

15

Lal, Dir, and Joh had arranged themselves in a perfect crescent in front of Shaeb's desk. They did not particularly like the man whom they worked for, but they tolerated him. The feeling, they were certain, was mutual. In contrast with their attire, which was loose fitting and baggy, their expressions were taut, and not from stress. In fact, as they stood waiting on the Underhouse master, their facial muscles hardly seemed to move at all. Reaching up, Lal carefully adjusted the lens that covered one eye.

Shaeb looked away from the projection he had been studying. Though they were technically in his employ, he knew it was better for business not to keep these three waiting. That suited him fine. He did not like to waste time on pleasantries.

"We are going hunting." A rare smile creased his narrow visage. "That should appeal to you, I would think."

Dir replied for the three of them. "Normally it would, but we have work to do."

Shaeb was not dissuaded. "This is part of your work." He turned to Joh. "You remember the youths who gassed you and your fellow sentinels at the warehouse?"

Joh gestured broadly. Rather too broadly, but the only one present to witness the peculiar movement was Shaeb, who was already familiar with it.

"I never forget a professional embarrassss—a professional embarrassment."

Resting his elbows on the desk, Shaeb steepled his fingers in front of him. "Would you like not only to rectify it, but to be able to do so in a pleasing manner?"

The operative called Joh looked at his colleagues, then back toward the desk. "Speaking for myself, I would savor the opportunity."

Lal spoke for the first time. "Our activities are circumscribed by care and necessity. We should not get involved in a way that puts our other work here at risk."

"I am aware of your concerns and your individual interests." Shaeb leaned forward slightly. "The location where the hunting expedition is to take place lies well outside the city limits. The risk of encountering problematic bystanders is minimized." He was mildly amused. "At the conclusion of the hunt, you might even have the opportunity to taste the fruits of your labors."

Lal sounded uncertain. "We do not like fruit."

Joh made a strange sound, one that might have caused the unprepared to jump. "It is an expression." His gaze was focused on the placid figure of Shaeb. "I would be allowed to take pleasure in the flavor of those who embarassss—who humiliated me?"

The voice of the Underhouse master was accommodating. "Though such a resolution is hardly to my personal taste, I have no objection to you indulging your own. Should circumstances reach that point, my own objectives will obviously have been achieved."

The three operatives exchanged looks, leaving it to Dir to respond. "You are unusually nonjudgmental, Piegal Shaeb."

A thinner twitch of a smile this time. "I am interested in results. I myself have already been embarrassed three times by these youthful caronis. A fourth embarrassment must not be allowed to eventuate. They have somehow enticed an offworld professional into aiding them."

"Ah," murmured Lal. "That makes it interesting."

"He is young, but manifestly competent." Shaeb brooded for a moment. "He is known to another contact of mine, but that person has been reluctant to lend the full weight of his knowledge to the forthcoming undertaking. That is a conundrum that must also be resolved." He looked up. "Following the successful resolution of this matter, the appropriate bonuses will be distributed, of course."

"Of course," echoed Dir reflectively. "A chance to taste—"

"A chance to resolve humiliation," Joh interrupted his colleague. He exchanged looks with the ones called Lal and Dir. "We will abide." Reaching up, he touched a hand to his cheek. "But to function at our most effective under such challenging circumstances, we will have to do something about *these*."

"And these," added Lal, rubbing his left arm with his right hand.

Shaeb nodded understandingly. "Retribution is often most competently carried out at night. That is when the business will be done. Therefore, feel free to be thee. There will be none to see you except myself and an additional number of those in my employ who are already aware of your unique situation."

Dir sounded surprised. "You are coming also?"

Letting his chair glide back from the desk, Shaeb stood. "Three times offended, I said. The warehouse boost, the freeing of the scrims, and a failed recovery attempt on a city street. Three times fiasco tells me one thing for certain."

"What is that?" Joh asked curiously.

Shaeb was already heading around the desk, leading the way toward the exit. "If you want someone killed right, you've got to do the killing yourself."

Strange how when one is sleeping it is sometimes possible to be awakened merely by a presence. Rarely spending more than half a day at the municipal center, Theodakris had come to look forward to his afternoon nap. It was a cheap pleasure he happily indulged in. As a younger man, he would never have thought of wasting an hour or two of daylight on something as inconsequential as additional rest.

That's what comes of getting old, he thought sleepily as he slowly returned to consciousness. He would have philosophized more if the first thing he had seen upon opening his eyes had not been the business end of a weapon. Half dressed and instantly wide awake, he sat up quickly on the bed.

The only member of the intrusion he recognized was Piegal Shaeb. He did not know the three slightly hunched-forward figures who stood behind the Underhouse master. They were more flagrantly armed. Nor, despite his long years of work with the police section, was he familiar with the specific type of sidearm the Underhouse master was presently pointing at him.

"Get dressed." Shaeb was his usual talkative self.

Dividing his attention between the intruders and their weapons, the senior analyst rose to comply. He moved slowly and deliberately, not wishing to startle any of the trespassers. Before ordering a drawer or closet to open, he was careful to announce beforehand exactly what it was he was going to remove from behind each handle or door. There *were* defensive devices scattered throughout his home, but their services could not be invoked swiftly enough to kill more than one or two of the invaders before he himself was shot. Disliking those odds, he wisely chose not to trigger any of them.

Besides, this was Shaeb. A man he knew well. Malandere's foremost syndicate master was nothing if not reasonable. Whatever had so obviously unsettled him could doubtless be resolved with logic and conversation. The important thing, he reminded himself as he continued to dress, was to ensure that everyone remained calm. He would find out what this was all about soon enough, and then he could deal with it.

"You could have announced yourself." His tone was mildly accusing. "There's no need for this." With a gesture, he indicated his visitor's weapon. "What is that, some kind of sonic projector? I've never seen one like it."

"You be right if you guessed it is of alien manufacture," declared Dir from his position near the bedroom doorway. "The materials of which it is made are not detectible by conventional security sensors."

Which was why no alarms had been tripped when his visitors had entered first the building and then his dwelling, Theodakris reflected. Something very bad must have happened to have so seriously upset his occasional business associate.

He let his shirt seal itself around him as he confronted that individual. "I continue to fail to see the need for this. Are there any circumstances under which I have not made myself available to you, Piegal?"

"There is always a first time, Shyvil." Stepping aside, Shaeb gestured in the direction of the doorway. With a shrug, Theodakris walked. The Underhouse master followed. "I was convinced that if I simply announced my intent, you would balk at accompanying my subordinates and me."

"To what end?"

"Some would say revenge," Shaeb murmured as they entered the outer living area. "I find *resolution* to be a more decorous and civilized description of this evening's proposed undertaking. It involves this disagreeable business of the pod of uncouth youths who stole from me, and whose end I have as yet been unable to bring to a proper resolution."

Theodakris halted abruptly. "The offworlder we discussed is still with them?"

"I do not know that," Shaeb replied honestly. "But until I know otherwise for certain, I have to assume it." He smiled assuredly.

"Following an abortive attempt at recapture, the failure of which has already resulted in the appropriate disciplining of the misbegotten charoni involved, they and the offworlder fled his lodgings in Center District, so the rogue may indeed still be with them. Proper and, if I may say, improper use of government resources makes it a simple matter to trace the friends, acquaintances, and relatives of those individuals one wishes to locate. Process of elimination is swift and efficient. Likely hiding places are quickly checked, those not in use rapidly removed from consideration.

"I am pleased to say that the fugitives have been tracked to a location not far outside the conurb." He indicated his singular trio of companions. "This time I am taking no chances. Every possible resource will be brought to bear so that there is no chance of another failure. With respect to which, this time no attempt will be made to take the offenders alive. This nonsense has gone on long enough." His tone was flat and even as ever. "In the interests of expediency, I will forgo my usual preference for extending the sentences of the blameworthy. They will simply be executed on site."

Theodakris stared back at him. "You know what will happen if I'm seen in your company."

"No one will see you in my private transport. The cleansing itself will be carried out well after dark. None will be left alive to identify you or anyone else." He gestured anew. "The door has not moved, and neither have you. If there is something you will need for more than a two-day, get it quickly."

The senior analyst did not stir. "I told you how I feel about this offworlder. If he's still with your batch of fled scrawn, I'm not coming along."

"If I knew for certain he was not with them, I would not have any need of your presence," Shaeb replied sharply. "My previous visit notwithstanding, I still know all too little of this offworlder. Self-confessedly, you know more than you have told me."

Despite the guns, Theodakris remained unyielding. "Not enough to be of any use to you in dealing with him."

"Any knowledge is more than no knowledge." Shaeb raised the weapon slightly. "Who knows—so to speak. You might remember something useful at a critical moment. Or better yet, beforehand." Letting out a sigh, he lowered himself to ask for the other man's help while trying not to give the appearance of pleading.

"I am not sure if your apparent mind-slippage is due to age, disease, or some other cause. What I do know is that right now I have no time to cultivate a working relationship with someone else in your department. Furthermore, no one else possesses your experience and breadth of knowledge. Tomorrow might be otherwise, but you know of my inclination to impatience. So I must insist that you come with us, please."

No one saw the five of them as they exited the building. Remote sensors would record the departure of the transport from the subterranean parking area. With the vehicle's protective dome opaqued, however, the identity of its passengers would remain anonymous.

"I think you may be making a terrible mistake," Theodakris warned his acquaintance as the vehicle entered a high-speed transport corridor and accelerated sharply.

"I already have." Relaxed and assertive, Shaeb glanced over at his friend, guest, and prisoner. "I had insufficient security measures in place at a building holding millions of cred worth of imported goods. I entrusted the care and interrogation of those who perpetrated an unforgivable crime against myself and my interests to incompetents. Tonight all of this will be appropriately resolved, and none of it will be repeated." He shook his head disbelievingly. "Are you so frightened of one lone rogue operator from offworld?" When the senior analyst did not reply, Shaeb added, "Maybe when you actually confront him, and look on as he expires, your concern will be shown to be as unfounded as it self-evidently is."

Confront him, Theodakris ruminated. It was something he could not imagine. Yet ever since he had caught the first glimpse of the off-worlder on the park surveillance scan and had positively identified him, the perverse fancy had never entirely left his mind. What would he say under such circumstances? What *could* he say? For that matter, if the young man named Philip Lynx knew that a certain senior analyst knew who he truly was, what would the youth himself do? How would the enigma called Flinx respond?

As he contemplated a range of possibilities vaster and more profound than Shaeb could ever imagine, Shyvil Theodakris found himself mulling each and every one of them with an unsettling mix of unabashed terror and unrestrained expectation.

Having nothing to pack except his concerns, and—unusually for him—having difficulty sleeping in a strange place, Flinx found himself wandering alone outside the agricultural facility's main building. Overhead, Pip described lazy circles between himself and the light of Visaria's two moons.

He had managed to snatch a few hours' rest, but had been awakened not long after midnight by the emotional flare-up of someone else's nightmare. When in a city surrounded by thousands upon thousands of projecting inhabitants, the vast sea of emotional ups and downs tended to merge into an emotive blur, as if he were listening to an orchestra with tens of thousands of players. At such times he could only pick out discrete expressions of feeling by consciously focusing his Talent on a single isolated mind, or at most a small group. Without sharpening such focus, the feelings of large numbers of people tended to melt together, creating a kind of emotional white noise in his brain. Seclusion, however, isolated individual sentiments, making them at once easier to identify yet more difficult to disregard. His head hurt.

He wanted to scream at sentience to leave him alone.

The nightmarish emotions had been flecked with feminine overtones—something he had learned to distinguish long ago. Zezula's bad dream, then, or possibly Missi's. At least, he reflected as he moseyed along one of the several quick-poured, hard-surfaced paths that radiated outward from the main building, if it was Zezula's nightmare he could take a walk without fear of being accosted by the girl. He found himself wondering: if she was the one having the bad dream, might he be involved? There was no way of knowing. He could only read the emotions of others. Not their thoughts, and certainly not their dreams.

His present surroundings intrigued him. Despite the considerable extent of his wanderings, he had not spent much time around agricultural facilities. His travels tended to find him exploring vast empty places or large metropolitan complexes. There was a peacefulness to his current environs that appealed to him. It was a prospect he had not previously considered. Who knew? Perhaps one day he, too, would decide to work land somewhere, like Sallow Behdul's helpful cousin Tracken Behdulvlad.

Yes, he would become a farmer. Right after he enlisted a wandering gas-giant-sized Tar-Aiym weapons platform in an attempt to divert the immense, unknown, incomprehensible manifestation of physical evil that was even now rushing headlong and unopposed toward the Milky Way.

Focus on carrotinites, he told himself resolutely. The bright yellow-orange spears that were derived from an ancient Terran edible filled the polymer-protected field before him with puffs of muted green. Kneeling, he used the light of Visaria's nearly full moon and its quarter-bright companion to study the nearest growth. Was it mature and ready to harvest? Could he eat such a thing straight out of the ground?

Light from the two moons showed through Pip's membranous

wings every time she passed between him and one of Visaria's satellites. The minidrag was hunting nocturnal flying things. Though they were native to Visaria and not her homeworld of Alaspin, she didn't care. Proteins were proteins, more or less. He knew from experience that if she consumed something organic that did not agree with her, her highly reactive digestive system would reject it before it could do any damage. He kept alternating his attention between the green-topped carrotinites and the flying snake, not wanting to be beneath her in the event that such a correction to consumption should occur.

A soft hiss filled the air around him as the automatic hydro system sprang to life. Condensing out of the air, water appeared beneath his boots. Straightening, he turned to go back the way he had come. The farm's single-story living quarters were a sprawl of interconnected buildings behind him. Tracken Behdulvlad had a fetish for constantly upgrading his facility. As Visaria grew and Malandere boomed, the market for his soil-ground produce expanded steadily.

First thing in the morning, Flinx decided, he would make his way back to the city, to its main shuttleport, and to the compact craft that would carry him skyward back to the waiting *Teacher*. He had done all he could here. Good deeds for the benefit of some disadvantaged youths. A better outcome than he had managed on recently visited Arrawd, where he had found himself the cause of a local war, but less so than on Repler, which he had helped to save from an alien life-form the likes of which he hoped never to encounter again. Life balanced out. He was reasonably pleased with himself.

Sadly, his visit to this mushrooming outpost world had only served to validate his developing opinion that his own future would be better served by seeking some sort of personal happiness while leaving civilization to its own devices. Nothing he had seen, heard, or experienced during his time in Malandere had convinced him that humankind was worth the sacrifice of the years ahead.

The thranx, now—they were another matter. Whether their future was his responsibility constituted an ethical quandary from which he had yet to extricate himself. Exhaling resignedly, he turned and started back toward the darkened complex. He was tired. It was both too late and too early to leave. If he was lucky, and if the lurid dreams of another that had startled him out of an uneasy slumber had abated, he might be able to sneak another hour or two of sleep before it was time to leave.

He was almost back to the buildings when a rush of entirely novel emotion flooded his perception. At this late hour, that in itself would have been enough to bring him up short. The nature and diversity of the feelings he was perceiving, however, caused him to tense and turn. That Pip also sensed them was confirmed by the speed with which she abandoned her nocturnal hunting and raced back to her perch on his shoulder.

Scanning the silent, almost windless expanse of polymer-shielded fields, he saw nothing—with his eyes. His erratic but distinctive Talent, however, made known the presence of a number of approaching sentients by detecting and conveying what they were feeling directly to his empathetic mind.

All but one of them were fraught with expectation, controlled ferocity, and homicidal intent. The emotive emanations of the sole exception among them were—confused. Furthermore, the emotional projections of the three most bloodthirsty intruders were more than passing strange. At once passing strange and—strangely familiar.

At the moment none was dangerously near, but all were coming steadily closer. With a last scan of the still deserted, bucolic fields, he whirled and sprinted for the entrance to the nearest edifice.

Identifying him as an approved visitor, the portal opened to admit him. Struggling to remember the layout of the complex in the dark, he hesitated. Since Tracken was not dreaming and therefore not projecting, Flinx had to find him physically, by searching the rooms off first one, then a second accessway. When he finally did locate the agricultural engineer's sleeping quarters, he burst in without waiting for the door to announce him.

Like all those whose professions require that they be ready on short notice to tackle an emergency, Tracken was awake and alert in seconds. Flinx filled him in as quickly as he could.

"Intruders? But how did they find . . . ?"

"It doesn't matter how they found this place. Or who they are, though I can guess. They're coming with killing in mind." Clutching Flinx's shoulder, Pip could hardly keep still. "First thing is to wake the others."

Tracken started to say something, then ended up just nodding. Slipping out of his bed, he was fully dressed in less than a minute.

Though unmarried and unpartnered, he was accustomed to entertaining guests, both friends and travelers on agricultural business. The room that was designed to accommodate one or two visiting couples had been enhanced with the addition of several instant beds for the use of Sallow Behdul's friends. While Tracken activated the walls, flooding the room with light, Flinx shook and prodded its five occupants to life.

Irritated at the outset at being roughly awakened, their lingering drowsiness fled as Flinx told them what he had sensed coming toward them. Missi started crying, which did no one any good, while a grim-faced Ashile moved closer to Subar. He did not step away from her, but neither did he take her hand or offer any comforting words. Zezula looked resigned, while Sallow Behdul's attention was concentrated on his older relative.

"We can't fight them," Subar muttered. "If they're Piegal Shaeb's people, every one of them will be a trained slayer." He indicated his distraught companions. "We can hold our own on the street, but not against professionals." He looked, unsurprisingly, at Flinx. "We have to run. Again."

"Can't this time." If the younger man was hoping for greater encouragement from the tall offworlder, it was not forthcoming. "They're approaching from all sides. We're surrounded here." *Surrounded,* he decided, sounded better than *trapped.*

Tracken was eyeing him curiously. "How do you know we're surrounded? For that matter, how do you know we're under attack? How many did you see?"

Subar took a step forward, away from Ashile and toward the agrigeneer. "If he says he knows, he knows." His gaze returned to the offworlder. "I don't know how he knows, but he has—I don't know how to describe it. A nose for things."

If only that were the pertinent organ, Flinx mused. His head was pounding, but medication would have to wait. "We have to fight them. Somehow." He looked hopefully at Tracken.

The agrigeneer wiped at his forehead. "There are some defenses. To dissuade produce thieves. Nothing that will deter professional killers, but we'll try. I also have a gun. One."

Flinx nodded understandingly. It would have been unreasonable to expect an agricultural specialist, even on an outpost world such as Visaria, to be outfitted with an arsenal.

"Get it." He turned back to the huddle of anxious youths. "The rest of you might as well arm yourselves as best you can with whatever Tracken can find for you. Knives, farm instruments, any kind of cutting tool. Split up. Find hiding places." He nodded in the general direction of outside. "They'll have tracking gear to hunt you down. Infrared seekers, carbon dioxide analyzers, whisper sensors. Don't wait for them to corner you. If you hear approaching noise, come out fighting. Use what surprise you have." He turned to go. On his shoulder, Pip was alert and ready.

"You talk like you've had to do some serious fighting yourself," Ashile called after him.

He looked back at her. She was deceptively calm on the outside, but like the rest of her companions her emotions were churning. In response to her comment, rambling memories of a lifetime of running, hiding, and striking back flashed through his mind. He offered what he hoped was an encouraging smile.

"Now and then," he told her. Then he was out the door and sprinting back up the hallway.

He did not want to get caught inside the building. Ill-equipped as they were in the way of armament, Subar and his friends still had their street-smarts. They might not have adequate weaponry, but they knew how to conceal themselves, how to hide while on the move. If they could just avoid the attackers long enough . . .

Long enough for what? he asked himself as he burst out the main entrance and raced around toward the back of the complex. For him to pick off the bevy of skilled attackers one at a time? Even if he could do something, why should he bother? Why not just steal through the contracting line of oncoming assailants and make for the city and the shuttleport? These Malandere street kids were nothing to him. Hardscrabble urban urchins with little to recommend them, dubious futures, and questionable morals.

Just like another hard-up youth he had once known well. Just like the underprivileged kid he had once been. He thought he had Subar and his friends pegged, but who was he to say for certain? Maybe there was another Flinx among them.

No, that wasn't possible. There was only one of him, provided one discounted his roving, raving half sister. Then why was he identifying with them so strongly? Why was he identifying with them at all? Why couldn't he mind his own business and just let them all die?

Maybe, he thought, because there *was* only one of him, and whatever else he was, whatever horrors and wonders and contradictions the man that was him contained, stark cold indifference was not among them.

He halted. A dark outline was approaching—from behind. He did not panic; nor did he draw any of the devices that were attached to his belt. He knew the fast-moving figure posed no danger to him because by this time he was more familiar with its emotional output than he wanted to be.

Gulping air, Subar slowed as he drew alongside the taller youth. His tight smile was easy to discern in the subdued illumination. Moonglow flashed off the body of the industrial cutter he held in one hand.

"Tracken says this beam'll cut right through bone." Thumbing a control, he triggered the portable implement to emit a short, narrow shaft of intense green light.

"What are you doing here?" Flinx muttered while keeping his eyes and attention focused elsewhere.

The smile became a challenging grin. "You told us to split up, didn't you? Look for safe places to hide? I figure the safest place right now is in your butt's umbra."

Flinx started to snap a rejoinder, found himself breaking out into a grin of his own. Subar might not be another him, but there were similarities to his younger self that could not be denied. Much as he might wish to.

"All right. Stay close, keep quiet, and be careful where you point that thing."

Slightly wide-eyed, Subar nodded. "What are you going to do?" he whispered expectantly.

Seeing rather than sensing movement out among the billowing moonstruck waves of protective polymer, Flinx suddenly dropped into a crouch.

"Empathize," he murmured forcefully.

CHAPTER

16

A moment or two elapsed before the sharp-eyed Subar also detected the methodically advancing figures. There were several of them spread out across the back field, advancing down different rows among the polymer-protected vegetation. Something about the way they moved reminded him of a previous encounter. It took a few seconds before realization stabbed him like a stiff finger to the gut.

"The ones there," he whispered to Flinx as both of them crouched low against the side of the building, "they walk funny."

"I know," Flinx told him. He had drawn the compact, alien pistol from its boot holster and was holding it easily in his right hand.

"I've seen movement like that before. One of the guards at the storage facility we scrimmed walked like that."

Flinx spared a quick glance for the youth huddled close to him. "Is that so?" His gaze returned to the warily approaching shapes. "That's very interesting."

Subar frowned up at the offworlder. "You talk like you know why they move like that."

"I do." This time, Flinx did not look back at the younger man. "I could explain it, but you'll see for yourself soon enough. Just remember to keep quiet no matter what you see."

A perplexed Subar complied. Another couple of minutes passed, during which time he was able to identify four, maybe five approaching figures. Those who walked strangely began to exhibit other peculiarities. He strained to see better. The nearest one, for example. Its head didn't look quite right. Moonlight glinted off a long weapon, a rifle of some kind. That much was familiar. But the arms that were holding the rifle looked awfully thin, while the figure's legs looked too big. Something brushed moonbeams aside. It could have been the arm of another infiltrator, waving from behind. Now Subar's eyes grew truly wide as the truth of what he was seeing struck home. Even in the reduced light, he could not deny the evidence of his eyes. What he had seen waving was not another arm.

It was a tail.

He stared for a long moment before it occurred to him to query the seemingly all-knowing offworlder. "Is that . . . ?" Fascination with the approaching, slightly bent-forward figures caused him to pause midquestion. He had seen plenty of images of the type of oncoming being, and viewed a number of spellbinding vits, but had never expected to see one in the flesh. He certainly had never expected to encounter one on, of all places, Visaria.

Flinx nodded tersely in response to the youth's awed whisper. "Yes, they're AAnn. There are a trio of them, together with a pair of humans flanking them farther to the east." He gestured sharply. "There are the only these three, I think. As near as I can perceive, those closing on the other sides of the complex are all human. That's why I chose to come back here. These three pose the greatest danger, and need to be dealt with first." He hesitated briefly. "Also, I was curious." A ghost of his previous grin returned. "It's always getting me into trouble."

"But AAnn, here—why?" Subar could only mumble.

Keeping his eyes and Talent fixed on the figures coming closer through the moonlit field, Flinx shrugged. It was not an expression of indifference, but a physical command. Lifting into the night sky, Pip began to circle, gaining altitude.

"Could be any of several reasons," the tall offworlder hypothesized softly. "You said you remembered something similar from the warehouse you and your friends boosted. Now here we have three of them. It would seem that at least that many are in the employ of, or at least have a mutually advantageous arrangement with, this Piegal Shaeb person who wants all of you dead."

"But," a disbelieving Subar protested, "they're *AAnn*. They're the enemies of the Commonwealth."

"Even more than humans, the AAnn are driven by the need for individual advancement. While they cooperate among their different clans and extended families to expand the Empire, personal ambition is what motivates them in their everyday lives." He nodded in the direction of the approaching assassins. Close now to the first outlying structure, they had slowed their advance. Clearly visible were the muzzles of weapons held upraised and at the ready.

"Remember when we freed your friends? There was another alien there, representative of a species I'm not familiar with, working alongside the other human operatives. Plainly, this Shaeb is no simian chauvinist. Making use of offworld contacts, he not only deals with but in fact employs help without regard to species." He let his Talent rove, pinpointing the location of each individual approaching threat. "An admirable trait in an otherwise unpleasant person."

Subar pondered his friend's analysis. "I didn't think humans could cooperate with AAnn, or that AAnn would work with humans."

Remembering a recent sojourn on Jast, Flinx peered down at the youngster. "It always amazes me how altered circumstances and a convergence of goals can change different sentients' perceptions of one another. Everywhere I've been, I've seen that even when governments can't get along, individuals can. Even individuals of different, supposedly mutually hostile species." He gestured in the direction of the moonlit fields. "If they run true to type, these AAnn probably hold their human employer in outright contempt. That doesn't prevent them from working for him in order to advance themselves. Accepting such employment means these are probably very low-ranking AAnn." He considered. "Unless they've done so at the behest of an Imperial department, and their work for Piegal Shaeb is subsidiary to their real reasons for wanting to be on Visaria."

Subar's eyes grew wide. "Spies?"

Flinx was not smiling now. "Maybe we'll get the chance to ask them."

Why was it, he thought resentfully as he hunkered down behind a pile of empty storage casements, that every time he set down on a new world with only the simplest of intentions in mind, he invariably found himself caught up in situations whose significance far exceeded his aims?

On the other side of the complex, Tracken Behdulvlad was monitoring the infiltration of more than a dozen assailants. He was able to do so not because he had exceptional night vision, but because his property was equipped with a fitting complement of commercially available sensors and scanners. Installed to watch out for produce thieves and marauding animals, the hidden instrumentation showed the precise location of each of the approaching trespassers.

When the shadowy figures were positioned for optimal results, the agrigeneer addressed several commands one after the other to his master control console. Once he was certain these were being processed, he picked up his gun and headed for the furniture-reinforced position he had hastily thrown together in the vicinity of the front door. Ordinarily, not more than one such command would be issued in a week. Submitted in rapid sequence, they caused the property to erupt.

Surprise was complete. Having been assured their quarry would not be expecting them, Shaeb's professionals were caught completely off guard as every light mounted on the residential complex, storage facilities, border fence, outlying structures, and cultivated fields sprang to life concurrently. Intense illumination flooded every corner of the property. Hidden speakers blasted sound effects that, at more modest volume, were designed to frighten away the native fauna that periodically tried to steal Behdulvlad's hard-earned crops.

Dashing forward and concentrating their attention on the main residential building, two of Shaeb's minions failed to notice the camouflaged trap that was designed to ensnare marauding ferezal grazers. Both men went down hard, their weapons flying out of their hands. One cursed loudly, his leg broken. Half blinded by the lights, half deafened by the amped-up sound effects, his partner struggled to help the injured man retreat in the direction of the fence line.

Approaching rapidly from the east side of the complex, a trio of would-be attackers suddenly found themselves running through heavy precipitation. Only it wasn't rain. Frowning and looking up, one hired gun blinked, then began to wheeze heavily. Flanking him, his fellow killers began to rub frantically at their eyes as automated sprayguns sent a dense shower of powerful aerated pesticide raining down on them. Choking and gasping for air, they ran, stumbled, and finally crawled back the way they had come.

Charging from the west side, three of their colleagues found themselves splashing, then wading, through a bowl-shaped field of rising liquid. Thick and glutinous, it stuck to their boots and pants, slowing them down. What stopped them, however, was not the knee-high flood itself, but its chemical makeup. First one of the would-be attackers began to gag. Then her neighbor started to retch. All of a sudden the residential complex they had been ordered to penetrate seemed very far away, and reachable only by struggling through the rest of the fallow field that was being completely inundated with liquid manure.

Beset by a deluge of stinks, sounds, rotating lights, and the occasional blast from Behdulvlad's rifle, the carefully planned assault dissolved into chaos. Straying from their preassigned routes as they sought safer, less manic approaches to the complex, several of Shaeb's less gifted hirelings panicked and began shooting at one another, thereby adding another layer of pleasant confusion to the rapidly mounting mayhem that had enveloped the property. In frustration at the absence of live targets, some of them began shooting at lights, sound generators, any piece of equipment they could pick out. One of them fired into what turned out to be a storage tank for pressurized gas. The resulting explosion lit up the sky, producing a shower of bits of metal, plastic, and human body parts that served to further demoralize the surviving attackers.

Only those approaching the back of the complex retained their composure. Natural carnivores, trained from birth for combat, the approaching AAnn maintained their positions as they continued to advance steadily. Shaken by the raucous upheaval but buoyed by the steadiness of their reptilian counterparts, the two humans who accompanied them likewise continued to press forward.

Subar could see all of them clearly now. "They're still coming," he whispered apprehensively.

"I know," Flinx murmured. "Look to the beam cutter you're holding, and be ready." His head tilted back as he glanced skyward. In the collision of lights and the darkness of night, something small and superfast was descending.

Despite the low-light sensors built into the face shield he was wearing, the underling who raised his pulse rifle and aimed it in the direction of the residential complex had not yet espied Flinx or Subar. His purpose was plain enough to the diving minidrag, however. Plunging almost vertically, she spat once, pulled out of the dive, and soared off into the night. The man never saw her, but he felt something wet starting to drip down his forehead. It started to burn his skin almost immediately. Reaching up, he rubbed frantically at the tiny trickle of mysterious fluid, with the result that the corrosive liquid began to eat into his fingers. Recklessly brushing them on his pants, he stared in horrified fascination as the fluid began to eat several holes through the fabric. Concentrating as he was on his legs and fingers, he neglected to wipe away the last droplet of fiery fluid on his forehead.

It dripped down into his right eye.

His screams brought his colleagues, human and AAnn alike, to an immediate halt as all four sharply turned in his direction. Dir and the other human raced toward the horrifying sounds. By the time they reached the man he was dead, his prone body madly contorted from the effects of the toxin. One eye had been melted away, and there were ugly burns on his forehead and right leg.

"Facronash!" the woman cursed. She turned furiously on the phlegmatic AAnn standing nearby. "You were the closest to Gerul. Why didn't you do something?"

"Sseeing nothing," the AAnn replied, no longer having to disguise its voice, "I could do nothing." A clawed hand holding a pistol gestured in the corpse's direction. "I ssorrow politely for your loss."

"'Sorrow politely'?" Stomping back and forth, hands trembling, the woman sought for a suitable response. She and the now gruesomely demised Gerul had worked together many times. "I swear on my insides, I don't understand why Shaeb has anything to do with you lizards! You don't care, you have no professional ethics, you breathe funny, you stinking, slimy, stand-up snakes who think you can—!"

Her tirade was terminated, not because she ran out of breath or insults, but because a thoroughly annoyed Dir shot her through the head point-blank. A shocked expression frozen forever on her face, the female mercenary fell over backward to land with a muted *thump* not far from the man who had preceded her in death.

When voiced, the AAnn's observation was as subdued as it was scornful. "Ignorant human, knowing nothing even of your own homeworld. Terran ssnakess are cool and ssmooth to the touch. Not ssoft and flaccid like yoursselvess." Turning, she loped back to rejoin her waiting companions.

Lal and Joh regarded her out of bright, vertically pupiled, no-longer-masked eyes.

"Difficulty?" Lal inquired.

"One dead by meanss unknown and dissturbing. The other I wass compelled to terminate to halt a foolissh flowing of thoughtless inssultss." Free now to communicate normally, she added a forceful second-degree gesture of disapproval.

"Our number with whom to sstrike hass been reduced by two," Joh reflected contemplatively. "Converssely, in the abssence of dawdling humanss, we gain the advantage of now being able to proceed more quietly." Slipping through the polymer-clad field on broad-soled sandals, tails swishing from side to side and weapons held at the ready, the three AAnn made little noise as they resumed their advance on the residential complex.

Two approaching emotional streams had been abruptly terminated: one male, one female, both human. Flinx was not surprised. One termination had been carried out by Pip. He knew this because he had been with the minidrag emotionally when she had carried it out. The source of the other was not known to him; he had caught only the moment of actualization.

That left the three AAnn slayers still advancing on the complex. He was all too aware of the threat they posed, both to him and to those who were relying on him. It was possible to project onto them, though manipulating alien emotions was far more difficult than working those of his fellow humans, and if he lost control there might not an opportunity to recover in time to make use of the tools he carried. There was also one other option.

On several previous occasions the offworlder had surprised and even startled Subar. Yet none of these emotions approached the shock he felt on seeing his tall friend suddenly holster his weapon, rise, and walk out into the moonlight.

"Stay here," Flinx told him brusquely. "Don't do *anything*."

"'Stay here'? *Tney*, Flinx, what are you . . . ?"

Calm and composed, the older youth looked back and made a calming gesture. Alarmed and bewildered but not knowing what else to do, Subar held tightly to the beam cutter as he crouched back down behind the protective pile of storage containers. True, Flinx's deadly flying snake was still out there, circling somewhere in the dark, but still . . . He could not imagine what the offworlder had in mind, exposing himself like this.

He was about to find out.

Seeing the tall bipedal figure materialize from the shadows, Dir immediately raised the sidearm she carried and aimed it directly at the human's forehead. As she did so, the softskin turned slightly to look directly at her. Without knowing exactly why, she held off depressing the trigger. Flanking her on either side, Lal and Joh rose from their stalking crouches and closed in. Like her, both had their weapons raised and aimed.

Catching sight of their lightly clad, undisguised scaly forms outlined clearly in the moonglow, the human stopped. Turning his head to one side, he deliberately exposed his jugular. Being beyond arm's length, he could not reach for Dir's neck. In lieu of sheathing the claws he did not have, he curled his fingers inward. The ritual tail swipe that should have concluded the greeting was, self-evidently, out of the question.

"*Tssrinssat ne vasse nye,*" he hissed sibilantly into the semi-darkness. "Flinx LLVVRXX of the Tier of Ssaiinn extends a closed hand across the sand."

It was difficult to tell who was the more stunned by this greeting: an openmouthed Subar looking on from concealment, or the three hired AAnn assassins who formed a line at the edge of the field. Weapons were lowered slightly while Lal's voice rose.

"How comess a ssoftsskin by a truthful name?"

"And ssuch fluency in the right tongue?" an astounded Joh added.

Flinx took another couple of steps forward. "I have commanded the right tongue for some time. As to the naming, it was bestowed on me by the Ssemilionn of the bespoken Tier, on the neutral planet Jast. Artisans of the first water they are, whose works you would find pleasing to eye, mind, and tail."

Even Dir, who of the trio always knew best how to interact with humans, was forced by her astonishment to pause a moment in her search for wordings. "Never have I heard of a human being given a truthful name. Yet your knowing burrowss too deep to be the invention of a facile ssanderling."

On her left, Lal was clearly troubled. "Thiss iss no *nye*, but rather a clever sspeaker-after-water." He started to raise his pistol. Above him, unseen, Pip circled a little lower.

Dir made a gesture of second-degree prohibition. "Not a *nye*, truly—but perhapss more than ssimply ssoftsskin, alsso." She looked back at the human, who was taller than any of them but unlike many of his kind appealingly slender. Graft on a tail, she mused, sharpen the eyes, engineer some suitable claws instead of the ridiculous and useless keratinous nubs softskins possessed, swathe that disgustingly slick flesh with proper scales, and . . .

She scratched herself, grateful for the cultured pain. This was neither the time, the place, nor the circumstances for indulging in fanciful perversions.

"Knowledge of a modesst sstanding iss not enough to ssave you. We are honor-bound by the sstricturess of our employ to sshoot you, and to kill or bring out alive all thosse hiding within the buildingss you sshield."

"By the-sand-that-shelters-life," Flinx responded, curling the fingers of both hands into his palms to illustrate even more vigorously that he intended no harm, "I remind you that no matter what you may have set claw to on this world, your honor binds you only to the laws of your own kind. Would not the opportunity to profit more both individually and as a group release you ethically from any agreement you may have made with a worthless human? Truly, would it not almost require you to do so?"

The three heavily armed AAnn exchanged glances. After a pause of ritual significance, Dir looked back at the slim shadow standing before them.

"Our ssureptitiouss employment on thiss world demanded that for much of the time we appear only in awkward and uncomfortable camouflage dessigned to give uss the appearance of ssoftsskinss." Her head inclined slightly forward on its flexible yet powerful neck, she strained with sharper eyes than those of any human. "Are you certain you are not *nye* dissguissed as human?"

"What opportunity do you flourissh?" the thoroughly pragmatic Joh hissed. The muzzle of his weapon had sunk even lower.

Though showing no outward change of expression and knowing he was far from successfully resolving the confrontation, Flinx allowed himself an internal smile. "A number of extremely valuable items were taken from the one who employs you."

"Thiss iss known," Joh responded immediately. "They are the sspark of our pressence here."

Further amazing the trio, Flinx executed a perfectly timed gesture of third-degree concurrence. "What care *nye* such as you for the spark of a softskin? You owe him no allegiance. Who among you would not be better off taking these objects, which are valuable to my kind but meaningless to you, and profiting from them many four-times over and above the comparable pittance you are being paid?"

Another tripartite exchange of glances was followed by Dir inquiring directly, "We are on thiss dissmally damp world charged with following other interesstss, but . . . Joh hass sspoken sseveral timess of thesse objectss. You know their pressent location?"

"Truly," Flinx assured her.

"You would reveal thiss to uss? Here, now?"

"I sswear by the ssacred sshalowss of Blassussar."

Dir did not sheath her pistol—but with her free four-fingered hand she did perform a first-degree gesture of concordance. The tip of her whip-like tail touched the ground in a sign that was as deliberate as it was unprecedented. Turning her head sharply to one side, she drew in her claws, looked back at him, and voiced what was, at least at that moment, the most consummate compliment she could think of.

"I have been sstranded on this wretched globe for longer than I care to think, longing for the warm ssandss of home, and in all that time you are the firsst ssoftsskin I have met whom I have not felt an insstant and insstinctive urge to desstroy."

A hand came down on Subar's shoulder, and he nearly jumped out of his skin. It was an appropriate simile. Watching from the shadows as the offworlder chatted easily and fluently with the three lizards, Subar had found himself thinking about skin in ways he had never previously contemplated.

"Ashile!" He untensed and lowered the beam cutter he had raised. Not that there was any need to do so. He had been so startled he had forgotten to activate it. "Don't *do* that!"

She was crouching slightly to one side and behind him, raising and lowering her head to obtain the best view while still keeping out of sight. "What's going on? Are those *AAnn*?"

Subar nodded tersely. "Flinx is talking to them." He heard the astonishment in his own voice. "In their *own* language." Turning away from her, he stared back out at the impossible moonlit scene. "I never heard a human talk AAnn before. Not even in propaganda vits."

She rose slightly, risking exposure for a better look. "Where are Shaeb's other people?"

"Out front, I guess," he murmured. "Or somewhere else on the property. If there were any more back here, they'd be gathered together with the AAnn."

She didn't hesitate. "If Flinx can keep them occupied, it means we have a chance to slip away! Once beyond the fields, we can hide until morning, then walk to the nearest corridor and hail a transport!"

He looked back at her, uncertain. It was a tempting thought. "What about the others?"

Even in the dark he could make out her indignant expression. "You mean Zezula." Before he could respond, she rushed on. "Everyone else has the same chance as us. They can make their own decisions without you. Haven't they always?" Keeping low, she started to back away from him. "I'm going, Subar. We might not get another chance."

Torn, he found himself looking from her back out to where Flinx was still conversing with the three AAnn. What the result of that conversation might be he did not know. Would they let Flinx go, or would they shoot him down where he stood despite anything he and his flying snake said or did? And if they let him go, what would they do subsequently? Was Flinx, perhaps, tiring of trying to help Subar and his friends and quietly arranging his own escape? Doubt crept into Subar's mind. In its presence, Ashile's insistence was a powerful lure. And for insurance, he had the beam cutter.

"Are you *coming*?" She was already halfway around the nearest corner.

Staying in a low crouch, he backed away from the shielding mound of containers and worked his way around to where she was waiting for him. Together they surveyed their immediate surroundings, finally settling on a route that would take them far to the right of the implausible hissing conversation. Sprinting across the first moonlit gap, they headed for the property's main storage building. No shots were fired in their direction, and no shouts remarked on their passage.

The final speak was formal and respectful. Flinx lingered for a moment, watching as the three AAnn melted away into the night. Returning to the city, they would redon their human disguises and, following his instructions, set about vastly improving their financial status at a shaken Piegal Shaeb's expense. They would regard it as fitting recompense for having to spend so much time on a soggy, human-settled world. Unlike the youngsters in the residential complex, the trio of mature *nye* were not afraid of retribution from their former human employer. Skilled agents, they could well look after themselves.

His satisfaction ebbed as he made his way back to the complex. A distinctive and unexpected shift had taken place in the emotional resonance of one particular individual he had been closely monitoring. As Pip descended toward him, he worriedly increased his pace.

"Subar? Subar!"

Disregarding the instructions to stay put, the youth had vanished. Reaching out, Flinx passed lightly over various emotive identities, some frightened, some determined, some homicidal, until he located the one he sought. It was accompanied by a second whose powerful emotings he also recognized. While Subar's feelings were muddied and confused, those of Ashile were clear-cut and unambiguous. And powerfully linked to his. Having experienced such sentiments himself in relation to another, Flinx identified them immediately. Identified *with* them. His unease deepened.

Even at the most copacetic of times, such emotions were both dangerous and distracting.

CHAPTER

17

Moonglow lit their way as they raced around the side of the storage building. Reaching the far side, they paused. Across one of the farm's smaller fields, a glistening horizon seemed to beckon. Panting hard, struggling to control his breathing, a cautious Subar leaned out around the pebbly side of the structure in an attempt to search as much of the field as possible. Occasional shouts, curses, and the sporadic burst of weapons fire from other parts of the property continued to pierce the nocturnal silence.

Ashile crowded close behind him. "I don't see anything."

"Doesn't mean there's nothing there," he told her.

She started to push past him. "The longer we wait here, the more likely there will be."

Reaching out, he grabbed her left arm and held her back. "Don't rush it. Haven't you ever watched migrin?" he asked, referring to the small native black-bristled arthropod that was the Visarian equivalent of omnipresent urban vermin. "They don't just scurry out across open spaces they want to cross. They dart from one corner to another, pause, look around, then run, pause, look around, and repeat, until they reach their destination."

The moonglow turned her perspiration to pearls as she looked back the way they had come. "*Tkay,* we've paused. Now it's time to dart." Pulling free from his grasp, she turned away and sprinted for the cover of the half-grown field.

He started to follow. A reflection caught his eye. It should not have been where it was, because there was nothing for the moonlight to reflect from. It took him only a second for knowledge to reconcile with memory.

Slantsuit.

"Ashile, no!"

Too late. In a flurry of glints and glimmers, the two slantsuit-wearing operatives rose from the polymer-shrouded field and closed on the oncoming young woman. Catching sight of them at last, she slid to a halt, whirled, and tried to race back the way she had come. Weapons appeared from beneath the concealment of the military-grade camo gear. Slantsuits bent light around them, virtually rendering the wearers invisible unless they moved. Now they were in pursuit of a desperate, frightened Ashile. They could easily have shot her down, but were unmistakably making an attempt to take her alive.

Anguish is a lens that often brings otherwise obscured realities into sharp focus. Seeing Ashile running toward him, her hard-nosed pursuers gaining ground with each relentless stride, he remembered in a sudden rush who his true friend was. Who had always been there to listen to him prattle on, often vaingloriously. Who had taken him in and given him shelter when the screeching and infighting of his insufferable family had grown intolerable. Who had shared food with him and, when he was broke, loaned him cred for whose return he had never been pressed. Who had stared at him in a certain distinctive, inimitable way when she thought he didn't notice. Who had laughed with him and walked with him and sometimes cried with him. The person whose attention he had so often shrugged off, frequently with a disdainful laugh. Not Zezula, she of the flawless face and unobtainable body and overarching ego.

Ashile. Always Ashile. And now that he had finally managed to substitute understanding for folly, perception for obliviousness, it was too late.

Or not. Activating the meat cutter and raising it high, he waved it in front of him in as active and threatening a manner as he could muster and charged out from behind the side of building, screaming at the top of his lungs the most bloodthirsty curses in his developing streetwise repertoire.

She might have stopped, or at least slowed, but she was running full-out. He shot past before it registered on her what he was doing. Though in stature he was far from threatening, in the reduced light the nature of his "weapon" was sufficiently ill-defined to bring both of the oncoming attackers to an abrupt halt. Raising their weapons, they fired almost simultaneously.

Instead of just a foot or finger, every muscle in Subar's body seemed to go to sleep at once. The beam cutter fell from his spasming fingers, bounced across the ground, and automatically shut down. Sprawling forward, he gritted his teeth against the paralyzing tingling that had assumed control of his nervous system. Whatever the nature of the weapon that had brought him down, it had been set to stun, not kill. Whether that would prove the more benign alternative remained to be seen.

Approaching guardedly, his slantsuit-clad assailants eyed him with caution. One nudged the youthful form none too gently, then looked toward the shadowed structural complex.

"The girl's gone."

"We'll get her soon enough." His half-visible partner scanned the conjoined buildings through special night-vision lenses. "We'll get them all. Give me a hand with this one."

Shouldering his rifle, he bent over the uncontrollably quivering body. It was not heavy, and he was able to carry it easily by himself while his companion, rifle at the ready and held parallel to the ground, defended their retreat.

Flinx had sensed the shock and confusion in Subar's mind the instant the younger man was struck by the pulse from the infiltrator's weapon. With Pip flying cover, he hurried around one small structure, ducked beneath a brace of strapped-together conduits, and rounded another building. As he did so, he nearly ran over Ashile. A quick change of emotional focus laid bare the panic and distress that were raging within her.

So out of breath was she that she could barely stand, stumbling against him as he reached down to grab her shoulders and keep her upright. "Subar—they've—they got Subar!" She was gasping and crying at the same time. "I was running and—I didn't see the men, and Subar, he—he came running past me, running right toward them, and . . ." She gulped air. "You've got to—you have to . . ." She started to choke on her own desperate sobs. "Please . . . !"

"Easy, easy." Still holding on to her, Flinx peered into the night, his eyes half closed, reaching out until he found what he was searching for. "He's still alive. His feelings are—that's odd." He frowned.

Slowly regaining her wind, she stared up at him. "What? What!"

He blinked, turned his gaze back to hers. "As near as I can tell, emotionally he seems at ease."

"That doesn't make any sense."

Flinx was not old—and as he would have been the first to admit, he was far from wise. But he was older, and a little wiser, than the young woman struggling to collect herself in front of him.

"Maybe it does."

Still breathing hard, but easier now, she was able to step back and stand by herself. "I don't underst—" She broke off, looking at him, then turned to stare out into the moon-illuminated night. "Oh," she mumbled softly.

Flinx moved to stand next to her and join her in peering out into the darkness. He had detoured to Visaria out of a sense of despondency, a feeling that he might be embarked on the sacrifice of his life for something not worth saving. In his brief time exploring a small bit of the planet he had seen little to change that opinion. The scales remained weighted heavily against sentience that all too often seemed selfish, self-centered, and indifferent to the fate of others. If individual humans and the representatives of the other intelligent species were first and foremost inclined to pursue their own personal interests at the expense of everyone else's, why should he forfeit his future on their behalf?

Street-bred Subar, the least likely of avatars, had shown him why. Out of love and on behalf of another, the otherwise wholly self-centered youth had performed that most remarkable of deeds: an utterly unselfish act. Contemplating an action that was as righteous as it was unexpected, Flinx knew that had Clarity Held been in Ashile's place, he would have done exactly the same thing.

Recognizing this did not make him feel any better about himself, but it did make him feel a lot better about the species to which he belonged. Maybe even hopeful enough to think it worth saving.

He did not have to search for the captured youth, either visually or empathetically. Once he had escorted Ashile back inside the complex, Piegal Shaeb saved him the trouble. Boosted by a thumb-sized amplifier, the Underhouse master's voice reverberated throughout the buildings. Flinx was able to understand the carefully enunciated ultimatum without straining. So was a shaky Ashile, and Tracken Behdulvlad from his position near the front door, and the rest of the frightened but resolute youths who continued to take shelter within the facility.

"Listen to me, Philip Lynx!"

Amazement at hearing his real name was such a shock to Flinx that Tracken, who was standing next to him at the time, wondered if the younger man was about to pass out. The emotional jolt her master suffered caused Pip to flutter her wings in alarm.

Shaeb gave him no time to wonder how the Underhouse master had learned his identity. "I don't know what you are doing on Visaria, where you come from, or what your interest is in this miserable pod of street scrawn who have robbed and insulted me, but if you will pause a moment to take an objective look at your present situation, I think you will find your commitment misplaced. Despite your unjustified, unwarranted, and I must say inexplicable intervention on their behalf, I hold no animus against you. I am prepared to guarantee you safe passage away from this agricultural facility. All you have to do is step out and walk away. No one will shoot at you." A pause, following which the Underhouse master's words were embellished by a note of sardonic humor. "Do not mistake that I make this offer purely out of altruism. It is as much for the protection of my people as for yourself."

Ashile was eyeing him apprehensively. To varying degrees, so were Zezula, Sallow Behdul, and Missi. Tracken Behdulvlad simply clutched his rifle and waited expectantly.

Flinx walked to a window. Like all its counterparts within the facility, it had been darkened by Tracken. A touch of an embedded control rendered the material porous. Designed to allow the entry of fresh air while keeping out pests, it now permitted his voice to carry.

"I have no quarrel with you, either, Piegal Shaeb! Let the pod come with me and I promise I'll work to settle both your insult and your financial loss!"

There was no mistaking the incredulity in Shaeb's reply. "From what I have seen and heard, you do not strike me as someone with access to the resources necessary to impart the necessary degree of compensation I seek."

Darkened or not, Flinx kept clear of the window as he responded. "You would be surprised."

"I have already been surprised by you, Philip Lynx. Or Flinx, whichever you prefer. That is why I am reluctant to trust anything you say. I am weighed down by the need to suffer no further surprises. Therefore, I make this proposal. All of you set aside whatever weapons you may possess and come out. I promise to discuss a variety of possible resolutions to this discomfiture, but only when I can sit face-to-face with those with whom I am in disagreement. In return, I promise not to vivisect millimeter by millimeter the polluted member of your precious pod whom my people are presently holding. If you doubt my resolve in this matter, I will be happy to send you a small portion of some significant portion of his anatomy, chosen at random." Another pause, then, "You have five minutes to respond."

Flinx turned back to the anxious faces waiting on him. Missi spoke up timidly. "Maybe we can talk our way out of this." She stared hopefully at Flinx. "Did you really mean what you told him? That you could cover his financial losses from our boost?"

Expression glum, he nodded. "Yes, but it doesn't matter. If we do as he asks, he's going to kill all of us."

Tracken frowned at his offworld visitor. "How do you know that?"

Flinx replied without hesitation. "I can perceive it. His speaking voice is unruffled and controlled, but his emotions are feral. There's no safety to be found in complying with his demand."

Zezula swallowed. She had been crying a lot and her face was badly swollen. "Then how do we respond?"

Flinx peered over at Tracken. "I'm afraid our praiseworthy host doesn't have any more surprises in his agricultural bag of tricks. That shock has worn off." Slowly he slipped his lustrous, stubby pistol back into its boot holster. "We have only two guns. Shaeb's AAnn recruits have taken their leave and gone their own way, and some of his human subordinates have been put down, but I sense that he still has a dozen or so dedicated supporters with him." His expression knotted. "Along with one other whose sentiments I can't quite sort out."

He nodded toward the agrigeneer. "Mr. Behdulvlad and I might be able to negotiate with them, and we might not. If we try and fail,

Subar is become meat." To her credit Ashile somehow maintained her composure, though he could sense that emotionally she was on the verge of a total breakdown.

He sighed heavily. Subar had given himself up to save Ashile—a gesture of profound nobility that would mean nothing if they threw themselves on Shaeb's sham mercy. "I'm going to try something," he told them, "but for it to have the best chance of success I have to go out there and confront him." He looked at Tracken. "Stay here and do what you can. Don't try to run. Shaeb's no fool. Half a dozen of his people are spread out around the main residence, just waiting for someone to try to bolt. The rest are with Shaeb himself." He turned away. "If I can deal with him in the manner I hope, I don't think the others will see a vested interest in hanging around." He started for a hallway that led to a side doorway.

Ashile took a step toward him, halted. "What are you going to do, Flinx?"

Sallow Behdul chose that moment to speak up. "I know what he's going to do." He was looking straight at Flinx, with a gaze that was not as simple as those who spent time in his company liked to think. "He's going to make them fall down and cry, like he did to Chaloni and Dirran and me. Aren't you?"

Flinx managed a slight smile. "Maybe not cry. But fiddle with feelings so that they don't feel like shooting us, either."

Ashile stared at him. "Subar told me about that. He said you could—could make people feel a certain way. Can you really do that to somebody like Piegal Shaeb?"

Shrugging, he turned away from her and started for the hall. "We're about to find out."

In response to his declared announcement that he was coming out, Shaeb responded favorably, but added a demand that the off-worlder at all times keep his pet in view and on his person or she would be shot. Flinx complied, having to reach up once or twice to physically restrain the increasingly nervous Pip from taking flight.

"Relax." Murmuring soothingly, he added something in the indigenous language of Alaspin as he reached up to stroke the back of her head. "Just relax. It'll be all right. Everything is under control." While he could manipulate his words, it was considerably harder to mask his true emotions. The resulting discrepancy between her master's words and his feelings left her feeling edgy and ill at ease even while riding comfortably on his shoulder.

Appearing in the shadows, a tiny point of blue light rocked up and down, beckoning him to a spot around the side of the main storage building. Turning the corner, he found himself confronted by a clutch of armed men and women. Their presence was no surprise: he had sensed their location and number before he had exited the residence, just as he had detected the emotional resonance of those who had formed a perimeter around it to prevent any possible escape.

A figure that was innocuous in appearance yet commanding in attitude stepped forward into the moonlight. Piegal Shaeb looked Flinx up and down, reserving particular attention for the jittery flying creature curled around his left shoulder. Behind him, an older man pushed forward for a better look. Both his expression and his feelings were an agitated mix of awe, fear, and expectation. They simultaneously drew and puzzled Flinx, but he had no time to probe either them or the man who was projecting them.

The Underhouse master shook his head sadly. "All this trouble, so much intercession, on behalf of such unworthy scrims."

"Unworthiness is a distinction founded on shifting perceptions." Though Flinx sensed Subar's presence, he could not see him. "Where's the other one?"

"Such a waste of commitment." Glancing back, Shaeb murmured a command.

A large, slantsuited figure ambled out of the shadows. In one hand he held the glistening, tapered shape of a neuronic pistol. The other clutched a still-stunned Subar by the collar, dragging the listless form forward. Indifferently, the operative released his grasp, letting the numbed captive crumple to the ground. Flinx studied the limp form for a moment, then returned his attention to Shaeb.

"You're a very unpleasant person."

The Underhouse Master pursed his lips. "I did not achieve my present prominence on account of a predilection to conviviality."

Flinx's expression stiffened. On his shoulder, Pip grew tense. Gradually, almost imperceptibly, he let his caressing fingers slip away from her scales. "You need, I think, to be nicer." Deliberately, he reached forth with his Talent.

Nothing happened.

Staring at him, Shaeb's head tilted to one side. "Interesting. I sense that you're trying to do something. I know that is how you freed the other scrims from receiving the balance of the reprimand due them, though the nature of the method involved continues to elude me." Turning, he spoke to the older man who continued to hover behind him. "You see? He is only a resourceful if peculiar young man. Not nearly so dangerous as you proposed."

Flinx strained to engage his damnably erratic abilities and to project strongly onto the now confident individual standing before him. It was all to no apparent effect. His Talent had chosen that moment, as it sometimes did, to slip from his mental grasp. As if that were not enough, the worst headache he had experienced since touching down on Visaria threatened to split the back of his head.

The Underhouse master turned back to him. "Despite your apparent inability to affect this meeting, I have no intention of waiting until something *does* happen."

While possessing only a fraction of her master's potential, Pip's perceptiveness had the advantage of being consistent. Sensing the lethal intent that was escalating in the speaker's mind, she unfurled her wings preparatory to rising. A bolt from a carefully aimed and downtuned neuronic pistol caught her before she could rise from Flinx's shoulder. Stunned, she fluttered to the ground. A traumatized Flinx immediately knelt beside her. His relief as he found that she was only paralyzed was overwhelming. Incensed beyond speaking, he turned to glare fiercely up at Shaeb.

The Underhouse master immediately put a hand to his forehead and took a step backward. Whatever the offworlder had sent forth and despite his earlier avowal, it had not made Shaeb feel "nicer." Like a wave that had receded with the tide and was now flowing back inland, Flinx could feel his Talent returning. He readied himself to project forcefully.

Without waiting for orders, the same alert subordinate who had grounded Pip put a neuronic charge into the flying snake's master.

Flinx felt himself crumpling. A second charge from another pistol struck him in the stomach before he hit the ground, further numbing him. Other underlings were on the verge of firing their own weapons, some of which were set to do considerably more than stun.

Shaken but still in control of himself, Shaeb threw up a hand. "Don't kill him!" His voice returning to its more moderate, controlled level, he added, "Not yet." Leaning forward, he frowned thoughtfully at the motionless young man now sprawled on the ground in front of him. His right hand was still rubbing at the front of his head.

"That was interesting, what you just did. I'd like to know how you did it." Behind him, Theodakris was crowding cautiously close, striving for a better look at the paralyzed offworlder. Though unable to move, Flinx sensed that the older man was torn between desires: to approach even nearer or to turn and run away as fast as his legs would carry him.

"But interested as I am," Shaeb was saying, "I don't think I want to risk a repetition, or chance something even worse. My curiosity has its limits."

I wish mine did, Flinx found himself thinking.

Stepping back, the Underhouse master addressed a man and a woman who were holding rifles that were designed to annihilate rather than stun. "You may kill him now."

Unable to move a muscle, his entire body tingling from the dual neuronic charges his nervous system had absorbed, Flinx strove one last time to project. Though his Talent was returning, he could sense he was not quite there yet. Another ten or twenty seconds of recovery was all he needed. Or perhaps the unknown faculty that had saved him previously, most recently in the holding chamber in Malandere and prior to that on Arrawd, would bring about yet another inexplicable last-second miracle.

Something fiery tore into his right arm. The pain was excruciating, overpowering; worst of all, it overwhelmed any attempt on his part to concentrate. Dimly he heard a male voice mutter, "Damn—missed. Won't this time, Mr. Shaeb, sir."

Flinx tried to raise his head, and could not. Tried to focus his mind, and could not. Struggled desperately to rouse his Talent, and could . . .

A perfect circle of solid blackness appeared off to his right. Astoundingly, a figure stepped out of it. Then another, and another, and finally a third. Two of them appeared to be arguing even as they tumbled out, to the point that they were exchanging heavy, clawed, seven-digited blows with each other. While neither of the cantankerous combatants appeared to be suffering any damage from this contest, it was evident to any bystander that the slightest of their thunderous thumpings could easily take off a man's head.

The muzzles of assorted weapons swung away from Flinx to aim in the direction of the three newcomers as Shaeb's startled minions hastened to transfer their attention. As well as his suddenly unsettled emotional state, the expression on the face of the Underhouse master showed that for the first time since arriving at the agricultural complex, he was completely taken aback. As well he ought. Not only was their means of arrival utterly and completely alien, so were the three beings.

While two of them continued to wrestle and argue between themselves without doing any actual damage, the third hulking, black-and-white-splotched, brown-furred figure leaned over to peer down at the still-paralyzed Flinx out of amber-hued, black-pupiled eyes that were the size of dinner plates. A voice sounded inside his head. One with idiosyncratically clear, bell-like overtones.

"Hello, Flinx teacher," resonated the simultaneously joyful, child-like, wise, and uniquely telepathic greeting.

Fighting the effects of the twin neuronic bursts, Flinx fought hard to make his lungs, his lips, and his larynx cooperate. His mouth moved. A feeble gasp emerged. He tried again. Words formed. Words he had not spoken in a long, long time.

"Hello, Fluff."

Since he was eight years old, Piegal Shaeb had never lacked for an appropriate response to even the most difficult and unforeseen situation. Now all he could do was stand and gawk. Those of his minions who were not doing likewise kept glancing nervously at him for orders. None was forthcoming.

Keeping a watchful eye on the three enormous ursinoids, all of whom continued to ignore their surroundings, several of Shaeb's subordinates tentatively approached the black disc. It hovered a couple of centimeters off the ground, absolutely motionless. One of the more enterprising armed underlings walked behind it, noting that it was no more than a few millimeters thick. Pulling his monitor, he aimed it in the direction of the disc's back and played the sensor across the eldritch apparition from top to bottom. No information appeared on the readout. No measurement of sound, no indication of photonic activity, no ambient radiation: nothing. This was patently impossible. As impossible as the three outrageous creatures to which it had given birth.

Taking note of the presence of other humans, Fluff took delight in switching to the mode of communication that involved intricate oral modulation of ambient air pressure.

"Sensed Flinx in trouble, we did. Trouble even Flinx teacher could not play out of. So we dug a quick tunnel and came to help with current game. If Flinx dies, a part of the game comes to a stop."

Being able to connect a voice to a body helped a stunned Shaeb out of his daze. "Tunnel? Game? What is this? What are *these*?" Whirling, he glowered at the openmouthed figure of Theodakris. "You never said anything about this offworlder having oversized, furry, contentious alien allies!"

"I don't—that is, I didn't . . ." Words simply failed the senior analyst. He could only stand, and stare.

"You should have," Shaeb said quietly before he pulled the trigger on the pistol he was holding. Theodakris dropped to his knees. Looking down at himself, he marveled at the tiny, smoking hole that had appeared in his chest. He could not, of course, see the corresponding one that had appeared in his back. Not even when he fell over sideways.

With Fluff helping him, an unsteady Flinx was able to stand. Painfully and slowly, the effects of the neuronic bursts were wearing off. Nearby, Pip was struggling to get airborne. On the ground, Subar had recovered control over much of his nervous system, though not from the effects of the casual beating he had received. Wisely, he stayed where he was and made no attempt to rise.

"Your digging has gotten faster," Flinx mumbled as his brain regained control of the mechanics involved in forming recognizable speech.

Fluff straightened proudly. "We've had a lot of practice since we saw you last." Turning, he rumbled an admonition. "Moam, Bluebright! Stop fighting and come say hello to teacher."

Immediately, the other two aliens ceased their rough-and-tumble discussion to crowd close around Flinx. He remembered each of them as if it were yesterday, and why not? When folk make one a present of a starship, not to mention a ship unlike any other in the known cosmos, one retains fond memories of the givers.

Something about the reunion steadied Piegal Shaeb's nerves. Despite their size, there was nothing especially intimidating about the trio of unexpected arrivals. Perhaps he was reassured by a chronic cuddliness that seemed at variance with their still-unexplained method of arrival. Whatever the reason, in all his long and difficult life he had never gained anything by giving in to hesitation. Also, in his business he was nothing if not thorough.

"All right," he barked decisively. "Kill them all!"

Rifles and pistols were steadied. As aim was taken, Bluebright and Moam jumped back into the coin-thick disc from which they had emerged. In the instant of astonishment that ensued, Shaeb's subordinates neglected to open fire. One finally did so, but her shot went wild as she fell into a second disc. An exact duplicate of its predecessor, it had materialized beneath her feet. And those of the fighter standing next to her, and the one alongside him. It was wide enough to swallow every one of them, including a disbelieving Piegal Shaeb, who could not countenance that the natural laws of physics had been convinced to conspire against him.

A hesitant Flinx staggered over to the edge of the second disc. It lay on the ground like a circle of dull black plastic. Leaning over carefully, he peered down and in. Shrieks and screams and wails drifted up to him. They arose from figures that were growing smaller and smaller with every passing instant. In a few seconds the sight of them had faded from view and the sounds of them from earshot.

Turning, he looked back at Fluff as Moam and Bluebright crawled out of the vertical disc into which they had jumped. "How long will they fall?"

"Awhile," the easygoing Ulru-Ujurrian assured him.

"Forever?" Flinx asked uncertainly.

"Oh no!" Clambering back out onto the surface of Visaria, Moam laughed both audibly and telepathically. "A tunnel goes from place to place. Forever is not a place."

"Tunnel starts on Ulru-Ujurr," Bluebright elaborated, "so bad people come out at end of tunnel there." Sharp white teeth showed in powerful jaws. "Maybe Maybeso will be waiting for them."

That, Flinx reflected, remembering what was essentially a wild and undeveloped world lying under strict Commonwealth edict, should give Piegal Shaeb and his cronies something to think about. Especially if the nebulous and unfathomable Maybeso was waiting to greet them at the other end of their terrifying plunge. He walked over to one figure, now sitting up, that had not been caught within the consuming circumference of the second disc.

"Subar, are you all right?" Reaching down, he gave the younger man a hand up.

"My body feels like I've ingested three weeks' worth of customi depressants in one sitting." He nodded in the direction of the three ursinoids. "The fact that those things are still here doesn't help."

Smiling, Flinx turned to join him in facing the Ulru-Ujurrians. All three of them had fallen to loud arguing. Being the only known true telepaths, they did not have to vocalize their wrangling. But they liked the noises that came out of their mouths.

"They're friends of mine," Flinx explained. "Old friends. Good friends."

"Really weird friends." Subar eyed the two black discs, one hovering perpendicular to the ground as if it had been pinned to the air, the other lying flat and unfathomable upon it. "I like their timing, though."

Flinx nodded. "We have between us—a kind of connection, I guess you'd say. That, and some history." He considered the quarreling Ulru-Ujurrians fondly. "I guess, when they're not 'digging,' they occasionally keep an eye on me. Ursinoidus ex machina."

"Keep an eye on you?" Still dazed, Subar could only shake his head in disbelief. "Keep an eye on you how?"

Flinx's tone was somber. "If I knew that, I think I'd have the answer to one or two questions that would keep Commonwealth physicists busy for a hundred years or so."

Careful to keep his distance from the edge, the younger man indicated the inscrutable black disc lying at their feet. "And this is?"

His tall friend made a face. "Children like to play with toys. You and your friends like to play with more grown-up things, like guns and thievery." He indicated the chattering ursinoids. "The Ulru-Ujurrians are kind of like children, except they like to play games with the fabric of space–time. Think of it as crocheting with superstrings."

"I'd rather not think of it at all." Looking past the inscrutable off-worlder, past the pushing, shoving, big-eyed aliens, Subar gazed longingly in the direction of the residential complex. He was remembering something, or rather someone, more important.

"Ashile?"

Flinx allowed himself the first unadulterated smile of the night. "She's fine. They're all fine. Why don't you go and reassure them as to the future of their respective fineness?"

Nodding briskly, the younger man started toward the building. After a few steps, he broke into a run. Flinx could sense his elation. Belatedly, his Talent had returned.

Nor were he and Subar the only ones to recover from the shock they had absorbed from the neuronic weapons. Landing on his shoulder, a still woozy Pip slithered forward and nearly slid off before catching her tail around the back of his neck. One pink-and-blue wing kept hitting him in the face. Reaching up, he steadied her and was preparing to rejoin the three Ulru-Ujurrians when a voice made him look back. The words were barely audible. Peering into the darkness, which would soon give way to the blurry Visarian dawn, he saw that one other figure had escaped plummeting into the gaping mouth of the Ujurrian tunnel.

Though he was physically fading fast, the man's emotions were still strong and focused. Focused on him, the approaching Flinx noted. Kneeling beside the prone figure that had rolled over onto its back, Flinx took careful note of the hole in the chest, the faltering respiration, the glaze that was spreading like milk over the wide-open eyes.

"I can't help you," he murmured. "You need full healing. I have that capability on my ship, but not with me." He looked around. "Tracken has a haulage skimmer. We can try getting you to a facility in Malandere, but I don't think there's time." He added, almost as an afterthought. "I know a fatal wound when I see one."

Theodakris's lips fluttered. "Philip Lynx." Reaching up, a trembling hand touched the younger man's chest. The fingers traveled sideways and downward, stroking Flinx's arm, his wrist, the back of his right hand. "You shouldn't be here."

Flinx did not know how to respond. "Where should I be?"

The barest suggestion of a smile creased the dying senior analyst's lips. "You're an Adept. You shouldn't be anywhere. You shouldn't—be."

Suddenly Flinx found himself leaning closer. "What are you babbling about? Who are you, that you know my name?" A sudden thought, too terrifying to contemplate, nearly overcame him. "You're not—are you my *father*?" While it was not the response Flinx feared, the man's reaction was also completely unexpected.

He laughed.

It wasn't much of a laugh. More of a choking cough. The senior analyst did not have much strength left in him. But a laugh it was. Thoughts flying from every mental direction, Flinx wanted to lift the man up by his shirtfront and shake him.

"What's going on here? Who *are* you? Why are you laughing?"

"I am—not your father, no, Philip Lynx. Philip Lynx—Number Twelve-A. But I know who your father *is*."

Fighting to restrain himself, starting to shiver, Flinx put his face as close to that of the dying man as he could. "You know my father? How—how do I know you're not lying?"

Eyes from which the life force was fast fading met his own. There was in them a wonderment and desperation—and also, oddly, a contrary kind of contentment.

"You are not the product of a natural union. Your birth mother was a woman named Ruud Anasage. Your place of birth is listed as Sarnath, on Terra. You had one full and one half sister, both of whom are presumed dead."

"Not so," Flinx told him, remembering the one of the two who was, in all probability, still alive.

A surge of interest momentarily rejuvenated the rapidly weakening senior analyst. "Is that so? Fascinating! It only further confirms the potential of the twelve line." He began to choke on his own blood.

No longer able to help himself, Flinx clutched at the front of the man's bloody shirt with both hands. Alarmed by the strength of the emotions she felt surging uncontrollably through her master, a frightened Pip took to the air, searching for a threat that did not exist. In the distance, the sky was beginning to lighten. *"My father,"* he husked. "The male donor responsible for the genes that Ruud Anasage carried to term. *Who are you?"*

"My name—my name is Shvyil Theodakris. Né Theon al-bar Cocarol. I am a proud member of the Meliorare Society. The *last* member of the Meliorare Society." He choked again, blood trickling from a corner of his mouth. "The last un-mindwiped member, anyway. The experiments—experiments are not supposed to have knowledge of their biological progenitors." Suddenly and quite unexpectedly, in one of those astonishing and unpredictable but not unprecedented occurrences that immediately precede death, Theodakris–al-bar Cocarol reached up, grabbed Flinx's shirt, and pulled himself into a half-sitting position.

"Gestalt," he rasped, wide-eyed—and died.

Prying loose the dead man's clutching fingers, Flinx let Shyvil

Theodakris–Theon al-bar Cocarol, senior situations analyst for the city of Malandere and last surviving sensate member of the outlawed Meliorare Society, fall gently back to the ground. Rising, he beckoned Pip back to his shoulder. Doing so meant looking upward, and looking upward meant involuntarily contemplating the stars whose brightness was being slowly overcome by the approaching dawn.

Gestalt, the old man had gasped. Searching his excellent memory, Flinx found the definition quickly enough. "A physical, biological, psychological, or symbolic configuration or pattern of elements so unified as a whole that its properties cannot be derived from a simple summation of its parts." Searching elsewhere, he recalled something of even more significance. Gestalt was also an H Class VIII colony world with a single moon. Located on the other side of the Commonwealth, it was about the same relative distance from Earth as the important thranx system of Amropolous.

The inescapable inference of Theodakris–al-bar Cocarol's last word was that he should look for his father on Gestalt. How appropriate.

A world was bigger than a book, or a sybfile. But Gestalt was not Terra, or New Riviera, or the Centaurus system. He would be searching among millions, not billions. A hand came down on the shoulder not occupied by Pip. No, not a hand. A paw. Dexterous beyond imagining, but a paw nonetheless. Turning, he found himself gazing up into the wide, flat face of Fluff.

"Great game goes on, Flinx. We keep playing our side, you keep playing yours. Always new elements are being introduced." Teeth flashed in an enormous—and to anyone else intimidating—smile. "Keeps the game interesting."

Moam and Bluebright joined him, surrounding Flinx. "Changes brewing and bubbling and festering, Flinx teacher. Big changes. Sinister changes. Time is tick-tick-ticking away. Like the clocks you described to us, the universe is winding down."

"Don't want it to stop too soon," Bluebright added somberly.

"At least, not until the game is finished," Moam added encouragingly.

Falling once more to arguing between themselves, the two of them turned and, without hesitation, hopped into the ominous black disc that was lying flat and round upon the ground. As soon as the last suggestion of brown fur had vanished within, so did the mouth of a kind of tunnel the most advanced contemporary physics did not possess a mathematical means of accurately describing.

Retreating to the hovering, vertical disc, Fluff stuck one foot in. As it disappeared, the massive Ulru-Ujurrian hesitated.

"Make sure you make the right moves, Flinx teacher. We can move our world, but we can't move you. Only you can move you and—maybe other things."

The significance of the advice was not lost on Flinx.

Fluff stepped the rest of the way into the tunnel. In his wake it proceeded to *poof* out of existence. Walking over to where it had hovered suspended in space, time, and who knew what other dimensions, Flinx passed his hands through empty air where a moment earlier there had hung a scandalous distortion of reality. A faint and rapidly fading warmth was the only indication that this corner of existence had just been occupied by something immeasurable and inexplicable.

A voice called out to him. Several voices. In the strengthening light of morning he could see several figures making their way toward him. Their faces, and their emotions, were full of jubilation. His rifle now hanging at his side, the affable agrigeneer Tracken Behdulvlad brought up the rear. Walking in front of him were Missi, Zezula, and Sallow Behdul. To Flinx's satisfaction, and not a little to his surprise, the soft-spoken Sallow Behdul had his arm around Zezula's faultless shoulders. She was not shaking him off.

Ahead of them, Subar and Ashile walked hand in hand. They

were all of them exhausted both physically and emotionally, worn and battered but alive. Unless the Underhouse master Piegal Shaeb was far more adept at a certain remarkable kind of tunnel-digging than Flinx suspected, none of them had anything further to fear from either him or his murderous minions.

As for himself and Pip, the dubious search for a wandering planet-sized weapons platform of the long extinct Tar-Aiym would have to wait just a bit longer. After more than a decade of intensive searching for the merest clue to his father's identity, he had unexpectedly been given a specific locality to search. Irrespective of anyone else's priorities, be they ex-stingship pilot, Eint, Counselor of the United Church, or Commonwealth representative, he had no intention of neglecting that suggestion. The Commonwealth, the cosmos itself, would have to wait on him awhile longer.

Setting that momentous decision aside for the moment, he let himself reach out to the primarily youthful oncoming group, let their feelings of joy and relief wash over him. Those of Subar and Ashile were especially cleansing and refreshing. He luxuriated in them because he had experienced them so fully himself, in the company of a woman named Clarity.

Clarity. She would wait awhile longer, too, he knew. He wondered what wonders Bran Tse-Mallory and Truzenzuzex were showing her even as he stood lost in thought.

Then his new Malanderean friends were clustering around him, the men clapping him on the back—careful to avoid contact with the minidrag dozing lightly there—and congratulating him, while the young women praised him with thankful smiles and the occasional virtuous kiss. In response, he smiled and laughed and joked back with them as together they started toward the residential complex. Safe now and for at least the foreseeable future, every one of them including Flinx discovered that they were absolutely starving.

The galaxy might be in imminent danger, he knew, and its future survival might rest ultimately on his shoulders, but at least these kids who reminded him so much and not always flatteringly of his younger self—these kids who were among the current representatives of his often objectionable species—they were all right.

And maybe, just maybe, worth saving.

About the Author

ALAN DEAN FOSTER has written in a variety of genres, including hard science fiction, fantasy, horror, detective, western, historical, and contemporary fiction. He is the author of the *New York Times* bestseller *Star Wars: The Approaching Storm* and the popular Pip & Flinx novels, as well as novelizations of several films including *Star Wars,* the first three *Alien* films, and *Alien Nation.* His novel *Cyber Way* won the Southwest Book Award for Fiction in 1990, the first science fiction work ever to do so. Foster and his wife, JoAnn Oxley, live in Prescott, Arizona, in a house built of brick that was salvaged from an early-twentieth-century miners' brothel. He is currently at work on several new novels and media projects.

About the Type

This book was set in Times Roman, designed by Stanley Morrison specifically for *The Times* of London. The typeface was introduced in the newspaper in 1932. Times Roman had its greatest success in the United States as a book and commercial typeface, rather than one used in newspapers.